MK

03767031

CW00516629

767031   F.

Steed, N.

Dead cold

This book is due for return on or before the last date indicated on label or transaction card. Renewals may be obtained on application. Loss of transaction cards will be charged at 10p. each.

Loss of Reader's tickets will be charged at 25p. for Plastic Type. 10p. for Manilla Type.

PERTH AND KINROSS DISTRICT LIBRARY

DEAD COLD

DEAD COLD

A Peter Marklin Mystery

Neville Steed

CENTURY

LONDON SYDNEY AUCKLAND JOHANNESBURG

767031

© Neville Steed 1992

The right of Neville Steed to be identified as the author of this
work has been asserted by him in accordance with the
Copyright, Designs and Patents Act 1988

First published in Great Britain in 1992 by
Random Century Group
20 Vauxhall Bridge Road, London SW1V 2SA

Random Century South Africa (Pty) Ltd
PO Box 337, Bergvlei 2012, South Africa

Random Century Australia Pty Ltd
20 Alfred Street, Milsons Point, Sydney, NSW 2061
Australia

Random Century New Zealand Ltd
PO Box 40–086, Glenfield, Auckland 10
New Zealand

British Library Cataloguing in Publication Data

Steed, Neville
Dead cold.
I. Title
823[F]

ISBN 0–7126–3980–2

Printed and bound in Great Britain by
Mackays of Chatham PLC, Chatham, Kent

For the Warmth of My Family

1

'Well, how's it going, then?'

I had been waiting for Gus to pop the question, so to speak, ever since the grizzly old mate of mine had clod-hoppered into my shop. For I knew darn well that Gus had not just 'happened' by. Dear old Gus doesn't happen by anywhere. There's normally method in his madness (and vice versa), even if it takes time to rear its shaggy and, by no stretch of anyone's imagination, clear-cut head.

I looked at his face, forged into craggy wrinkles by his myriads of years at sea, fishing for a buck. My own was as po as I could make it.

'How's what going, Gus?'

He sniffed a giant sniff, a regular overture to greyer than grey cells being dusted down.

I waited, elbows on counter. Gus avoided my gaze and his thick digits played over a thirties tin-plate Gnom sports car that I had all ready to pack up and send off to one of my mail-order customers. It was what I had been about to do when I saw, or rather heard, his old upright Ford Popular bang and squeal to a stop outside my Toy Emporium.

'Well, you know . . .' he mumbled.

'Do I?' I persisted, without a shred of guilt for my feigned obtuseness. It was a fairly rare case of the old biter being bit as far as I was concerned. For Gus must be one of the greatest 'haver-onners', even in today's tricky world, and has had me going more often than I've had hot dinners, or hot anything else, I shouldn't wonder.

'Well, you know . . .' he repeated, his gruff old voice now betraying an edge.

I blinked. He put the toy down with as much loving care as a cat gives a canary and rubbed his fingers across the grey-white stubble of his chin.

'I wish I did, Gus,' I sighed. Gus glanced across at me. Once more I waited with baited breath.

'Well,' he came out at long last, 'I wouldn't worry about it, old lad.'

I frowned. 'Worry about what?'

He shuffled his bottom off the stool and unfurled his great frame. 'Never mind. Wasn't important.' He sniffed again. 'Least said, soonest mended. What the eye doesn't see . . .'

I threw my eyes to the heavens. Hell, Gus is full of more clichés than a sports commentator.

'So that's it, is it, Gus?' My voice now borrowed an edge from his.

He clapped his old hands together. 'Yep. Guess so.'

I came out from behind the counter. 'You came around here just to tell me you've got some question or other that you now think is better left unasked?' I threw up my hands. 'Gus, the ruddy Sphinx couldn't do better than that.'

He made a move towards the door. Sod him. He'd got me beat all hands down and he knew it.

'All right, Gus, you win.'

His head turned and I saw the Fisherman Friend smile. 'Well then?'

I held up two crossed fingers.

'Going that well, eh?'

I uncrossed the fingers and made a so-so wave with my hand.

He turned back towards me. 'So what's the trouble, then?'

I sighed. 'I wish it were only one.'

Gus pointed towards the counter. 'Like to talk about it, then, old lad?'

I didn't need to give him an answer. The bugger had known I'd been longing to find some excuse to share my worries from the very moment he'd darkened my threshold.

Gus took the can of Heineken from me, pulled the tab and started to drain it before I could even settle into my chair. He must be the Ayrton Senna of the Dorset drinking circuit. As he braked for the first time he said, entirely without malice, 'So you reckon she thinks her daughter might have lighted on someone a mite . . . younger?'

I held up my hand. 'I didn't exactly say that, Gus.'

He grinned. 'Near 'nough, old love. I mean, that's what you reckon all her references to 'Arold Macmillan, that Khrushchev fella and that greasy berk, Presley, are all about, don't you? Little digs to her daughter that you're nearer her bleedin' generation than Arabella's.'

He downed another draught, then, wiping the froth from his mouth with his hand, he went on: 'Still, don't you fret, old son. All the digs in the world her bloomin' mother could make in a month of Sundays will bounce off your Arabella. She's got her head screwed on the right way, she has.' (The way one's head is attached is very important in Gus's great book of reckoning.) Then his old face broke into a broad smile. 'But on second ruddy thoughts, maybe she hasn't, falling for a whatsit like you.'

'Thanks, Gus. That's just what I need right this second, when I'm suffering from a bad attack of the would-be in-laws.'

'That your second little problem? They want you and yer Arabella to get hitched? Though really, I suppose she's their Arabella, not yours yet.'

I snorted. 'Yes and no.'

'What yer mean?'

I sat back in my chair and took a draught of my own beer.

'Well, as I've said, I'm not too sure they want their little girl to be mine at all. But I get a strong feeling that they think, if she will persist in ignoring our . . . age gap . . . then we should do something a little more acceptable to them than just live together. I think Mother Trench might just about tolerate me then, if I came gift-wrapped with a gold band, a date in church and a dandy wedding reception to which they could invite all their well-heeled friends in Shropshire.'

Gus looked at me. 'She might have a point, old love. The thought had struck me once or twice. After all, you and Arabella have been together for quite an old time now.'

9

I frowned at him. Lot of good it did. He ploughed on.

'If I'd ever met the right woman – ' (Over his close-on seventy years, Gus must have met, and was still meeting, thousands of women, and if ever there was a case of the pot calling the kettle black . . .) ' – and had had a ruddy daughter, I wouldn't want her . . . well . . .'

'Living in sin?' I smiled.

'Yeah, well, I'm not religious, mind, but you must see, old love, they may think you're just treating their beloved daughter as some kind of . . .'

He hunted for a word. And, as ever, got the wrong one.

'. . . toy girl.'

I laughed. He took umbrage.

'No, I'm serious, old mate.'

'I'm not laughing at your thought, Gus. Just your word, toy girl. There are toy boys, yes, but – '

He suddenly stopped me. ''Ere, there's a thought.'

I did an Eric Morecombe and looked behind me.

'Where?'

He waved his hand and spilt a dribble of beer down his hairy sweater, which already had enough stains to give a forensic scientist a field day.

'No, shut up. I mean, it just occurred to me, you're a toy boy, aren't you?'

'Me?' I laughed, then suddenly got his drift. 'Oh, you mean because I make a living out of dealing in old toys. I'm far too old to be – '

'Go to the bloody top of the class,' he mumbled, then his eyes brightened again. ''Ere, that's it. You're an old toy boy.' He leaned forward in his chair. 'Get it? Old toys. Old toy . . . boy.'

'The only one in the whole wide world,' I sighed, dodging his prodding finger.

'So what yer going to do about it? Please Mum and Dad or please yourself?'

'Gus, it's not "myself". It's "ourselves". Don't think Arabella and I haven't discussed it from time to time. But right now Arabella is happy just the way it is. In a way, she says, she feels more committed without legal bits of paper

10

or church blessings and gold bands to remind her not to be a naughty girl.'

'And what about you?' Gus rightly queried.

'I made a mistake once,' I pointed out quietly, 'when I was only a year or so older than she is now. I'd rather she took her time.'

Gus got the point and, bless him, changed tack.

'When d'they go back, then?'

'They're down for three weeks. Two more weeks or so to go. That is if they can stand the weather. Trust Dorset to pull the coldest January temperatures for years whilst their dear Shropshire, I gather, is unseasonably mild. Almost ten degrees up on us here. It's like they brought their weather with them.'

'Perhaps that's why they're being a bit frigid with you,' Gus grinned. Would that it were that. 'Still, could have been a sight worse, old lad,' he went on. 'At least they're staying in a hotel and not shacked up here with you two over the shop.'

I placed my hands in praying mode. 'Thanks be. Though Arabella tells me they're none too happy with the place. Seems it has changed quite a bit since they last stayed there some years ago. I gather the owner died a year or two back and the widow is running it now.'

'Their grumbles might be just a hint, old love,' Gus winked.

I put down my Heineken. 'Hint they'd rather be living here with Arabella and me?' I laughed. 'You're kidding, Gus. In our poky guest bedroom? If you'd seen their place up in Shropshire . . . why, give it a couple more rooms and pop some stone lions on top of the gateposts and it could be a stately home. It's set in a thousand acres, to boot. No, I don't think *chez moi* is quite their kettle of caviar. Any more, I suppose, than I am. Think of all the chinless wonders up to their green wellies in filthy lucre that they must have earmarked for their darling daughter. And what does she go and do – '

Gus cut in with the answer. Well, *an* answer.

'She gives the V sign to that old lot and says leave me

11

alone to make my own . . .' He paused, just as I thought he was going to say 'life', but then, with a grin, finished with the word, 'mistakes.' I almost threw my beer at him. But, luckily, the phone rang and brought our homely homilies to an end.

I did not recognise the voice. Indeed, I could hardly hear it at times, it seemed so hesitant. But at last I did make out that the lady, who had a strong Dorset accent that hardly helped matters, was someone with an old toy to sell and would I be interested? This, at least, helped explain the hesitancy, as, in my experience, would-be sellers are often very coy about – clear throat twice – coming to the real point. And in a way I don't blame them. The old-toy game has its unfair share of sharks, even if it doesn't yet approach the level of other forms of antiques trading.

To make my caller feel a little more relaxed before we talked actual turkey I asked her how she had got hold of my name and number. She cleared her throat and replied that a friend had mentioned seeing my shop when passing through Studland on his way back to Bournemouth. 'Okay,' I said sweetly, 'so what exactly are you thinking of selling?'

Another pause and then she came out with, 'A pedal car.'

Now it was my turn for hesitation. I have dealt with almost every type of old transport toy – cars, lorries, aircraft, boats, ships, dolls' furniture, you play with it, I sell it – but as yet something as large, bulky and specialised as pedal cars had never passed into or out of the Toy Emporium portals. For one thing, my shop is a mite small for such objects and for another, the ride-in toy market, whilst definitely extant, is hardly one of impulse purchase or mail-order suitability, unless the postman is the Incredible Hulk and the letter-box as big as Mick Jagger's mouth.

However, there was nothing to be lost in probing further, so I asked her whether she knew the age and make of said machine. For who knew, she might just have a real gem on offer that I knew I could shift fairly easily. Like those splendid pre-war Vauxhalls by Triang, complete with electric lights and oil cans on the running board. Or maybe a

Daimler by the same firm. Or – I hardly dared think on't – a baby Bugatti made, would you believe, by the great Bugatti itself in the early thirties.

But such extravagant hopes were immediately dashed by her replying that it was an Austin. She could tell that, she said, because there was a 'Flying A' mascot on the bonnet.

I knew the type instantly. It was a 'J40', made between 1949 and 1971 in a factory in Wales to give employment to disabled miners. Desirable enough, but hardly thin on the ground. Fairgrounds still employ a lot of them on their carousels and even mint ones at auction rarely reach four figures. However, if she was not too extravagant in her asking price there might just be a bob or two for me in the deal. I asked its condition. 'Very good,' she said. 'Not repainted or anything. And the electric lights still go on.' But when I got round to pricing it, she was far less forthcoming. Why didn't I pop over and look at it? After that we could talk money.

And that's the way I had to leave it. Luckily, she did not live too far away. In a cottage just off the Studland-Corfe road. I arranged to inspect her J40 at three sharp that afternoon.

Gus had sidled past me with a wave of the hand whilst I'd been on the telephone and a moment later I'd heard his Popular churn into what passed for life and rattle off down Sea Lane.

So, I was left alone to get on with my mail-order packing. Correction. I have a Siamese cat called Bing, who decided that brown paper, Sellotape and string were more interesting right then than pushing 'Z's on his favourite chair or daring the frigid elements to trace the unfriendly neighbourhood rodents. As a result, packing up the diminutive Gnom tourer took about as long as that crazy sculptor would take to wrap the Empire State building. To put the final kibosh on the operation, the telephone rang again before I'd time to put an address on the parcel.

It was another female. But this time one I recognised, and as the legitimate government of my love life. She was

13

ringing from the local TV station where she is head researcher for a crime-busting programme. You know the kind of thing. 'Have you seen this photo-fit man? If so, ring us.' 'Here's a selection of recently recovered property. Is any of it yours? If so, ring us.' Plus the odd, cheaply (it has to be on a local station) produced reconstructions of more serious local crimes, such as muggings, rape, bank and building society robberies and, once in a while, murder. For don't let all the cosy cottages, cream teas, winding lanes and Thomas Hardy countryside blind you. Dorset's current character list is no more free of villains and vagabonds than Hardy's Wessex novels.

After the usual love-happy badinage, I asked Arabella why she'd really phoned.

'Dinner,' she replied in a word.

'Dinner?' I queried. 'You mean you'd like me to pop into Swanage to get something for tonight?'

'Nope. Bit better than that,' her voice smiled.

'You mean there really is something better than dragging around supermarkets?'

'Shut up and listen,' she observed summa cum tact, then asked, 'Do you feel strong enough to face my forebears again?'

Whilst I was checking out my condition, she went on, 'Because if you do, they have just rung me to invite us both over tonight for dinner at their hotel.'

'Bit sudden, isn't it? I mean do you think there's any –'

'Ulterior motive?' she cut in. 'Yes, I do. Because they admitted there is.'

'Your father hasn't brought his shotgun down with him by any chance?'

Arabella laughed. 'Not as far as I'm aware. No, the motive has nothing to do with my parents. Or me.'

I didn't like the sound of the limited nature of the exclusion clauses.

'I didn't hear you add, "Or you".'

'For one good reason, my darling. You're the motive.'

'I'm the motive? What have I done?'

'Made a bit of a name for solving the odd crime, that's all.'

My heart sank. 'Your whiter than white parents involved in some crime?' I asked incredulously.

'Course they aren't. But there's an old lady at their hotel who seems to have heard of your sleuthing around. Directly my mother told her a bit about you – the Toy Emporium and so on – she asked whether you were the same vintage-toy man whose "criminal activities", as she put it, she'd read about in the paper in the last year or two.'

'Oh God,' I sighed. 'And your mother said Yes, right? Now this little old lady wants me to find her long-lost grandson or is worried that another guest is putting arsenic in her tea, tarantulas in her bed or piranhas in the mug of her false teeth.'

'You finished?'

'Probably. Depends what your mother's said.'

'She's said nothing, I promise.'

'Doesn't sound like your mother,' I said unkindly, then added quickly, 'So tell me, what did the old lady want?'

'Nothing for herself. But it seems she's got this great friend – '

'Male or female?'

'Female. Another little old lady. And her house in Bournemouth has just been broken into and it's really upset her. The first old lady, the one in the hotel, just said she'd love to meet you. So that – '

'She can embroil me in solving her friend's burglary. Well, you should have told your mother to tell her that the police are there for solving break-ins and burglaries and, no doubt, will have the culprit under lock and key in next to no time.'

There was an ominous pause before Arabella replied, 'Appears she doesn't want the police involved.'

'Why on earth not?'

'I don't know, darling. All my mother said was that the first lady I mentioned is so very sweet with everyone in the hotel, she didn't like to say a flat No to an introduction to you. She thought if we both came to dinner tonight, you

15

could just give her a quick word or two of advice to pass on to her friend before we leave.'

'Sure that's all?' I queried, pointedly. 'I'm not going to find myself up to my neck in the fertiliser that flicks off fans in no time flat?'

'If it looks as if it might head that way, you can always say No, you know,' she reminded me.

'But not to a dinner invitation from Mum and Dad?'

'Up to you. But I think we might win the odd Brownie point if we humoured them this time.'

'Odd is the word,' I grimaced. 'Okay. What time do we have to be there?'

'Seven-thirty, eightish.'

Remembering how stuffy British hotels can still be, especially outside the big cities, I asked, 'Will I have to wear a tie?'

'Stick one in your pocket, in case. You'd lose your Brownie point if the maître d' frogmarched you out of the dining-room.'

She wasn't wrong, my beloved. But it just might be worth risking simply to see the look on her parents' faces.

There was one tiny problem in that J40 pedal car being a few miles from *chez nous*. I froze to death on my way over that afternoon. Despite sheepskin coat. Ditto gloves. Woolly scarf. And ditto knitted hat with Lake Placid lettering blazoned across it. (No, I've never been there. But an American lady I once helped* brought it back for me last year.) Volkswagen, when they designed the Beetle, obviously ran out of inspiration by the time they came to the heater, which takes ages to warm up. And that's in the saloon. I've got an old, unrestored convertible version whose vinyl roof has now given up all pretence of keeping out rain and draughts.

The cottage I was after turned out to be a little more difficult to find than I had been expecting. It lay some way back from the Corfe road, up what was obviously a farm track which led on past it to a larger house whose chimneys I could just see over the next ridge. From this I assumed

Die-cast (1987)

the cottage, as is common in rural districts, was part of a farm estate and was probably tenanted by one of the farmworkers. Certainly, from the outside neither cottage nor small garden had that spruce and cared-for look that goes with owner-occupiership.

As I pulled up outside I spotted a face at the window. This instantly disappeared to become a face and a figure at the front door. She was slightly younger than I had imagined from her voice on the phone. Just the right side of forty, I guessed. (I'm just the wrong side, more's the pity. Next year I'll be celebrating the third anniversary of my thirty-ninth birthday.) Fair hair done up in a plait around her head suited her roundish face, and her big blue eyes needed no mascara to grab attention.

It was not until I'd walked up the overgrown path that I realised how tall she was. Not far off my own height. And from what I could judge of her figure under the fisherman's knit sweater, she had kept herself in pretty good shape.

'You come about the pedal car?' she said, in lieu of greeting.

I nodded.

'Round the back,' she announced, looking me up and down. 'Thought you'd like to see it in daylight.'

'Yes, thanks,' I smiled. 'Good idea.' She pursed her shiny red lips and her big blue eyes seemed to scan the horizon behind me. I looked round. There was nothing but Dorset there. By the time I looked at her again, she was halfway round the side of the house. I fell in behind her undulating jeans.

Round the back we reached what appeared to be an outside privy, joined to the cottage by a bridge of rafters and covered with corrugated iron sheets. Under this roof was the J40, its red paint glinting back at me, even in the dull winter light.

'Well, there 'tis,' she pointed.

I took a walk around it. She hadn't been lying. It was in surprisingly good nick. Beige upholstery untorn, fascia unscratched. Flying A emblem unbroken and the chrome of radiator grille and even hubcaps almost as good as new.

17

The only real signs of wear were on the steering wheel rim and the pedals, which was only to be expected.

'Well, what yer think?'

I looked up. She stood, hand on hip and again her eyes seemed to want to focus rather more on Dorset than on me.

'It's very nice,' I replied truthfully.

'Well then, are you going to make an offer or not? I've got things to do and I can't just – '

'What kind of money were you thinking of?' I cut in, not wishing to waste her time (or mine) further.

'No, don't try that,' she said gruffly, lids shuttering down her eyes. 'Make me an offer. Decent one, mind. I wasn't born yesterday. I've seen on telly what old toys fetch, you know.'

Oh dear, I wonder if the producers of *Antiques Roadshow* know how they've complicated us dealers' lives?

I took a flyer.

'Two hundred. And if it would help you, I could give it to you in cash.'

Without a second's hesitation or as much as a blink, 'Three,' she said.

So she was one of those. Okay. As I reckoned I could pass the car on for anything from four hundred and fifty pounds to six hundred and fifty, I played her game.

'Two thirty.'

'Two ninety.'

Drat.

'Two fifty. Pedal cars aren't the easiest – '

'Two eight five.'

Double drat

'Two sixty. Cash. Now that's my – '

'Two eight.'

I pretended to weigh it up, hand on chin.

'Now hurry up. I told you, I can't hang around.'

I reached into my coat pocket and withdrew my wallet. Holding it away from her, so she could not see how many notes it contained *in toto*, I shelled out five fifties and placed them in a stack on the pedal car seat. Then, watching her now acquisitive eyes, I very slowly added a tenner and a fiver. Then I repocketed my wallet.

'Two six five, Mrs . . . er . . .' I'd forgotten her name.

'Mrs Sandle,' she reminded me with a frown.

'Now I'm going back to my car,' I said firmly, 'to give you a moment to think. If you want to accept, just wheel the car round to the front and I'll pick it up from there. If you don't, just come round to hand the notes back to me.'

I moved off, then, as I reached the corner, added, 'I'll wait five minutes, then I'll be back for the money.'

It's amazing how difficult handing back crisp or crinkly cash is to most people. Cheques don't excite the taste buds in nearly the same way. And I wasn't taking any risks. She couldn't scarper with the money without me seeing her go. So I wasn't surprised to see the J40's bonnet peep around the front of the cottage in under half the time I'd allowed.

I got out of the car and went up the garden to save her pushing it any further. But of the seller, there was no sign. To be polite, I went round to the rear of the house to say goodbye. Again there was no one. I was half tempted to knock on the back door, as I'd really have liked to ask her a little of the history of the car and how it had survived all those years in such good condition. However, remembering her rather blunt and nervous attitude, I opted to leave her in peace, since that's what it appeared she wanted.

Unfortunately, loading the bulky pedal car meant I had to lower the Beetle's roof. It was far too big to go under the bonnet that served as a boot and so would have to ride on the rear seat all the way home, top still down. Which hardly thrilled my brass monkeys, I can tell you.

It was whilst I was furling and folding that I had a weird feeling of being watched. I looked back towards the cottage, but there was no one at the windows. I finished collapsing the roof, then bent down to get sufficient grip on the heavy J40 to lug it up and over onto the rear seat. Again I sensed, somehow, that I wasn't alone. I shivered and not just because of the arctic temperature. I looked around warily. There seemed to be no one, but I could only see the farm

19

track immediately in front of me, owing to the unkempt and therefore high hedge that bordered it on the cottage side.

I quickly finished humping the car in and was only too glad when I was back on the road and leaving the whole shebang behind me. Maybe it had been the woman. Maybe the rather sorry state of the cottage. Maybe the grey and forbidding weather. Maybe the whole scene had just been all too Wuthering for me. All I knew for a fact was that, by the end, I had an almost childlike attack of the creeps.

2

I did need to wear a tie. Not for the bar beforehand, but as a passport to the dining-room. I felt as if I was being throttled throughout the meal, so long has my neck been free since trading the rat race of advertising for the joys of old toys.

The stiff apparel worn by the guests in the Dendron Park Hotel dining-room made it look like a film set for a Poirot series, only the ersatz Versailles decor giving the game away. That and the fact, I suppose, that no Agatha Christie cast list has gathered together quite so many geriatrics in one place. British seaside hotels must need built-in doctors and a clutch of pacemakers at the ready throughout the winter season.

However, to my relief, that evening Arabella's parents proved to be anything but starchy and formal. From the moment we met them in the bar they were both warm and welcoming. Later, when Arabella and I talked about it on the way home that night, she reckoned they were trying to make up for what they realised had been a rather shaky start to their visit.

'They're playing away,' she said, 'for the first time. The only other occasion they've seen you was that time up in Shropshire, when everything was familiar – except you – and under their control. What's more, Dad really hates being away anywhere, at any time. Creature of habit, only thrives in one environment.'

'Like a panda,' I observed, then went on quickly, ducking her hand. 'I think there's another "what's more", though. Although we've told them about my shop and how we live over and around it in the house my old aunt, bless her, left me, I think the reality must have come as a bit of a shock.'

'Nothing wrong with Studland's pride and joy,' she reassured me. 'Stop running it down.'

'It's hardly stately, though, is it?'

'You open part of it to the public,' she grinned. 'How many homes can say that?'

Anyway, I digress. I was saying how affable the Trenchs were that evening. By the time the waiter had cleared away the debris of our second course (lobster, supposedly local), I was starting to forget my strangulating tie and relax a little. Enough, indeed, even to introduce the subject of the little old lady myself. After waving a hand vaguely towards the other guests, I asked, 'Which one of the hearing aids wants me to say a few words into it?'

Mrs Trench – Julia to me, she'd instructed, maybe as another hint as to how much nearer my age was to hers than to her daughter's – actually laughed. Timing was off, though. She was drinking her wine at the time. I think by the time she could answer, almost everyone in the room must have patted her on the back. Her long face vermilion, she stammered, 'She's not back yet.'

'Back?'

Mr Trench – Clement, as he insists. Bit of a misnomer, but there you are – twitched his close-cropped moustache and came to his wife's rescue.

'Went out. Late afternoon. To her friend's. Supper. Back before ten. Promised. See you.'

I forgot to mention that Clement's conversation is staccato obligato. I think his mother must have married a machine-gun.

'Same friend who was burgled?' I queried.

He nodded into his serviette. 'Believe so. Often together. Lives near. Chappie took her over. In her Daimler.'

I raised my eyebrows. 'Chauffeur? Daimler? Winter holidays? Some old lady.'

By now, Julia had recovered enough to string out a few longer sentences in reply.

'No, she's not on holiday, Peter. Mrs Meade actually lives here in the hotel. Has done for ages. We remember her from our previous visit years ago.'

'Better and better,' I smiled.

She held up an elegant hand. The clear varnish on her nails glinted its immaculate perfection.

'I think what Clement said may be misleading you. You see, the Daimler's not an XJ or anything. It's ages old – '

'Conquest,' Clement crisply inserted. 'Lanchester thing they made. Early to mid-fifties.'

I knew the model. Rounded and homely and more middle class even than the granny Rovers. Betjeman would not have been averse to driving one. When the trains weren't running, of course.

'Well, anyway,' Julia went on, 'it's certainly seen far better days.' (Did she give me a sly glance at that point, or was it my imagination?) 'And she has no chauffeur. She just gets whoever is free or willing at the time to get behind the wheel and take her places. The chef normally does it, apparently. But he's on duty tonight, so . . .' she raised her pen-cilled-thin eyebrows, 'it's TB.'

I saw Arabella's frown copy mine. Then Clement's rather bluff forehead caught the infection.

'Julia,' he admonished.

'TB?' Arabella queried. 'Who's TB?'

Her father cleared his throat. 'Your mother is referring to a Mr Brand. A . . .' he hesitated before bringing himself to say the words, '. . . Jason Brand.'

'I don't believe it,' Arabella laughed. 'No one is called Jason Brand outside bad movies.'

'Well, darling, I don't believe it's his real name,' her mother explained. 'Mrs Meade says she believes it's some-thing like Fern really and he changed it to Jason Brand when he became a male model a few years back.'

'A male model staying here?' I couldn't stop myself saying.

The observation seemed to make Julia blush, which Arab-ella noticed instantly.

'Yes, Peter's right. Dendron Park is hardly the in scene around these parts. So, come on, Mother, out with it. What's this Brand fellow doing here and, what's more, taking old ladies for rides in ancient Daimlers?'

'Really, Bella,' Julia fluttered, 'you do ask the most awk-

23

ward questions.' She played with the emerald, as big as a Buick, on her finger.

Arabella looked at me. 'So it's like that, is it?'

Her father cleared his throat and said quietly, quietly that is, for him, 'Wish your mother. Not brought the thing up. Mrs Robbins. Pays a visit. Dining-room this time of evening.'

At least, I'd heard her parents speak of Mrs Robbins. She was the widow who now owned and ran the hotel, following her husband's death.

Arabella's eyebrows shot up and she whispered to her mother, 'So this Jason fellow has something to do with Mrs Robbins, does he?'

Julia's face verged on the vermilion once more and looked towards her husband for help. But he had obviously decided to opt out of the fine mess his Stanley had got him into and was staring out of the window at a Granada that was making a bugger's muddle of parking.

In lieu of any direct response, Arabella read her mother's face. 'So Mrs Robbins has got over her bereavement, has she?'

Julia held up a finger that had never indexed in its life. 'Now, darling, please. Clement's right. We shouldn't be talking about it at all. It's none of our business what Mrs Robbins does with her life. None at all.'

I loved it. A disavowal and a moral condemnation all in one sentence. I couldn't but run with it.

I leant forward and said confidentially, 'Their secret's safe with us, Julia. We won't breathe a word.'

'Er . . . thank you,' she smiled and frowned in one.

Arabella nudged her mother. 'How old is this JB?'

Now I frowned too and asked, whilst her mother was still playing with the mega asset weighing down her finger, 'Wait a minute. I thought he was called TB just now. The "B" is right but Jason doesn't make a "T".'

Julia put her hand to her head. 'Oh dear, oh dear. I can see I'll have to explain.' She looked round the room to see that no one had an ear cupped in our direction. Then, in a whisper, went on, 'TB is what Clement and I call him,

24

you see. They're not his initials. They stand for . . . toy boy.'

Arabella sat back from the table and grinned. 'So that's his age, is it? Good old Mrs R.'

'Ssshhh,' her mother glowered. 'Please, Bella. Now that's enough. Your father and I didn't invite you two here to . . .'

Her daughter was not to be frustrated. 'Is TB the fly in the ointment, then?'

'What ointment?' Julia asked, but I could see from her eyes that she really knew the answer.

'You two not enjoying your stay here so much this time.'

Her mother refolded her serviette by her side-plate. 'Well, I'm not sure I would go as far as saying that. Just let's leave it that we think the place misses the late Mr Robbins' quiet dignity and certain touch, shall we say?'

'We shall,' Arabella and I said in unison, as we eyeballed each other and winked.

It was at that moment that the sweet trolley squeaked its way across the carpet to chloresterol us all.

'There she is.'

I looked up from my coffee and saw Julia's hand indicate the window.

'Getting out of the car, see?'

I saw. Both the cosy old shape of the Daimler Conquest and the even cosier shape of its owner, muffled up to and above the eyeballs in woolly coat, scarf, gloves and a hairy angora hat, what my mother would have termed a tammy. The last mentioned gave her an almost childlike appearance, which impression was only heightened (or should it be 'lowered'?) by her extraordinary lack of height. She couldn't have been more than four feet nine or so and made Kylie Minogue look like Sigourney Weaver.

But just as I was hoping to get a good view of the old lady's face, a long dark form materialised from the other side of the car and came between me and her.

I looked at Julia. 'That you-know-who?' I breathed.

She nodded.

I glanced back. He was tall, dark and, I suppose, handsome. That is, if you like tailor's dummy-style looks.

25

Straight out of the plaster cast. Not a ragged edge. Not a millimetre off factory spec. Don't try to knock it. You'd get an echo.

I had to admit he was putting on quite an act for the little old lady, though. Supporting her arm, whispering sweet everythings in her ear, smiling wider than a Colgate advert and helping her up each step of the hotel with little pauses after each one, more, I guessed, to make play of his concern then for her recovery of breath or strength. Indeed, by the time they had both disappeared from our sight, the old lady's sweet face looked a trifle miffed by it all.

'She *must* be loaded,' Arabella observed to me.

Her father looked across at her, anything now but clement.

'Really, Bella. Not right, saying things like that. Money. Not everything, you know.'

Funny how often that comment is made by people who have the everything that money is not.

'Well,' my beloved went on, 'don't tell me, Father, that TB there was putting on that show all for charity. Because I don't believe it. What's more, nor do you.'

'I . . . er . . . er,' Clement started, but his wife bailed him out.

'We know next to nothing about this young man, Bella. So don't let's start being uncharitable.'

Arabella looked at me and ran her fingers through the brush of her short hair.

'You started it, Mother, with your TB remark.'

Julia's coffee cup shook in her hand, so she carefully lowered it back to its saucer.

'I shouldn't have mentioned it. It was just a private joke between me and your father. Now can we let the whole matter drop?'

And dropped it was. Which I guess was just as well. A minute later, Mrs Robbins, the main object of TB's attentions, entered the dining-room to do her round of the tables.

Arabella had met her before. But I hadn't. So I gave her the surreptitious once-over from behind the brim of my

26

coffee cup. At a distance, I'd have put her age in the later thirties. She was slimly elegant and held herself in a way that clearly displayed her self-confidence in her physical attractions. It was not until she was close to our table that I saw that she was probably older. Say early forties. And it wasn't just the footmarks those damned crows will insist on leaving around the eyes. Or the slight slackness around the neck that she was attempting to hide with a jauntily tied silk square. Those extra years were *in* her eyes, not around them. The shine had gone. And in its place a matt weariness that spoke more of the past and the present than of the future. I told myself, perhaps I should have seen her before her husband died.

'Good evening, Mr and Mrs Trench. All well?'

Clement, with a nod, barked a 'Fine' and Julia added the 'Thank you'.

The proprietress's dark eyes turned to me and Arabella.

'I hope the menu was to your liking too.'

A second later I had been introduced and was standing shaking hands with her. The strength of her grip somewhat surprised me.

'So you're the Peter Marklin,' she observed, looking me straight in the eye.

'One of them,' I smiled back, anxious not to probe into the motive of her remark.

'One of them?' She tossed her dark hair back from her face.

'Well,' I explained, 'I can't be the only idiot going by that combination of names in the world.'

'Oh . . . I see.' But I didn't escape by that stupid sally, for she licked her generous lips and went on, 'But I bet you're the only one that sells old toys.'

I breathed a sigh of relief. For a moment I'd thought she was going to refer to my amateur sleuthing. A subject I keep as under my hat as possible. Though even so, little old ladies seem to get wind of it.

'Could be,' I conceded. 'But old-toy collecting is growing so fast, I wouldn't bet your bottom dollar on it.'

27

She laughed. But not really. Politeness was its sole pro-
mpter.

'Well, nice to meet you, Mr Marklin. I must let you all
finish your coffee in peace.'

With that and a big smile she moved off to an aged couple
across the room who looked frail enough to be on borrowed
time.

'Nice woman,' Julia observed, when she was out of earshot. 'Such a – ' she stopped abruptly, as she realised what
she was about to say.

' – pity her toys take human form,' Arabella took up the
lead with a grin.

'Enough, Bella,' her father fired off and then suddenly
cleared his throat and, looking pointedly at me, inclined his
head towards the door.

I took the hint and looked round. The reason for my
meal ticket had just entered. Looking even more minute
without all her woolly winter doll's clothes.

'Like a sherry, Mr Marklin, or something stronger?'

I waved my hand. 'I'm driving, so I'll pass, if you don't
mind.'

We were in her room, or rather suite, I suppose it could
be called, as the sitting area was divided from the bedroom
and bathroom by a three-quarter wall. But it was not like
being in a hotel at all. Especially that hotel. For Mrs Meade
– Bessy she asked me to call her – had certainly stamped
her quarters with her own identity. There was not a hint of
glitz or plastic Versailles. It had the warmth and cosiness
of a home, which, of course, it was and had been for many
years for Bessy Meade. The wallpaper, a William Morris-
style design, was somewhat faded (she told me later she
fought off many attempts by the hotel's owner to redecorate
as 'too disturbing for words'), but it didn't really matter, as
the walls were festooned with pictures of every kind, from
delicate Victorian watercolours to miniatures, from darken-
ing oils of what I took to be ancient ancestors to sepia
photographs of formal family groups that made the figures
in Madame Tussaud's look full of life. The clutter on the

walls was matched by ditto on every possible surface. You could be forgiven for imagining you had walked into some Sunday get-together by the local antique-market mob. God help her if any of those Lovejoys were to catch sight of her little hoard.

'Do sit down, Mr Marklin.' She extended a veined and liver-spotted hand towards two chairs by the window. I took one. She the other. Anxious to get our private parlé over as quickly as was polite, I kicked off immediately.

'Well, Bessy, why exactly did you wish to see me?'

Her eyelids fluttered. 'Oh . . . didn't Mrs Trench tell you, then?'

'Not very much. Just that you had a friend who was a bit worried about a break-in at her house.'

She patted her tiny knee. 'That's it, Mr Marklin. That's why I wanted to see you. Poor Muriel – that's Muriel Purkiss, my friend. Known her ever since . . . oh . . . well before I even met my poor late husband – yes, she's very worried. I must say, I don't blame her. Burglaries are such nasty things.'

'But nothing was stolen, is that right?'

'Nothing. Nothing at all.' She fiddled with the lace-edged arm cover of her chair. 'Window smashed. Drawers and cupboards opened. Dear Muriel's stuff strewn everywhere, I'm afraid. I had to go over to her house – she has a bungalow in Sandbanks – and help her clear everything up. But, unless Muriel has made a mistake and forgotten something – she *is* getting rather forgetful these days, I'm afraid. But aren't we all?' She suddenly stopped and looked at me. 'Oh, I'm so sorry, Mr Marklin, I didn't mean to include someone so obviously young and hale and hearty as yourself in our memory-losing little lot. Oh dear, oh dear, please forgive me.'

I loved her. I loved her. From the word 'young' onwards.

'Nothing to forgive,' I smiled.

She continued. 'As I was saying, unless she's missed something, nothing seems to have been stolen. Muriel's possessions may be a little on the modest side – she's never had much money, you see – but you'd think if someone's

29

gone to all the bother of breaking in, something would be taken, wouldn't you? So you can see, Mr Marklin, it's all a bit of a puzzle, now isn't it?'

'But it's just the kind of puzzle that we pay our taxes to have solved,' I pointed out.

'You mean the police?' she asked, as if they were something from outer space.

'May the Force be with you at times like these,' I smiled.

Her eyes lit up, like marbles in a spotlight.

'*Star Wars*,' she said instantly. 'Alec Guiness, wasn't it?'

I nodded. This was no run-of-the-hearing-aids old lady.

'Your friend should have called them. And left everything where it was until they arrived. There might have been clues – '

She cut me off. 'You don't know Muriel. The break-in had upset her enough, without then having to go through all the palaver that dealing with the police would entail for maybe weeks and weeks afterwards.'

I sighed and leant forward in my chair. 'It may be nothing to the palaver of another break-in, Bessy.'

She put her hands up to her face in horror. 'Oh, no, Mr Marklin. You don't mean you think poor Muriel might be burgled again?'

I shrugged. 'I have no idea. But it's obvious that whoever broke into your friend's house must have had a reason. People don't just open drawers and cupboards and throw things around just to have some kind of fling, you know.'

'No, I don't suppose they do,' she admitted quietly, and then asked, 'So you think that . . . they might have been, perhaps, looking for something?'

'Could be, couldn't it?'

She frowned. 'But what on earth could that something be? And who could it be? I mean, Muriel has no enemies, I'm sure. And no relations, really. You see, unlike me, she never married and all her generation are now dead and their children and grandchildren don't seem to bother about her at all. Except to send the odd Christmas card, when they remember it.'

'I don't know. But if I'm right and those person or persons were searching for something, they could return to give the bungalow another going over. That's why I think it's important that your friend calls in the police. It's not too late. They might even keep a watch on the house for a bit, just in case there's another attempt.'

Poor Bessy Meade looked as if I'd knocked her crest to the ground. She cleared her throat and then said softly, 'Oh . . . we had been thinking that perhaps you might have been able to, you know, help a little bit. I've read about you in the paper once or twice, you see. That's why when Mrs Trench mentioned she knew you . . .' Her voice faded away and she looked down into her lap.

I felt very embarrassed about what I had to say next.

'Bessy, I'd love to help your friend if I were a professional investigator. But I'm not, I'm afraid . . .'

'If it's a question of money,' she began, but I held up my hand.

'No, it's not. It's a question of, well, accident, I suppose. I didn't really choose to get involved with the cases you may have read something about. It just happened that way. I knew someone or they knew me. Or, as on the last occasion, I actually found the body.'

She put a hand to her mouth. 'Oh, yes, I remember. How very, very distressing.'

'What I'm saying, Bessy, is that I didn't put up a billboard saying "Murders, Burglaries and Break-ins solved. Fees moderate. Money back if suitable solution not found in thirty days". I am an old-toy buff and happy just to idle away my time discovering them, owning them and dealing in them.' I grinned. 'The nearest I've ever got to being in the murder and mayhem business professionally was when I worked in an advertising agency. And I chose to abandon that back-stabbing little con game some years ago now.'

She looked across at me with eyes that reduced my height to below even her own.

'I understand, Mr Marklin. I've never been able to understand myself why anybody should ever wish to be a – what do they call it now, in America – rubber shoe? No, that's not it. It's gumshoe, isn't it? That's it.'

31

'I'm sorry,' I said and I really, really was. But I just can't get involved in every bit of chicanery dreamt up in dear old Dorset. Even when it involves the sucker punches of all time. Sweet little old ladies.

I rose from my chair. 'Look, Bessy, if it would be of any help to you, there is one thing I would be very happy to do.'

She got up and stood next to me. Again she reminded me of *Star Wars*. Remember the little people? Well, I admit she wasn't wearing a cloak, but you know what I mean.

'Oh, how kind, Mr Marklin. Any little advice you could give.'

'It's not much,' I conceded, 'but if after you've had a word with your friend and told her that I think she should call the police, even at this late stage . . . well, if she's still worried, then I'd be willing to meet her. To explain how the law would go about it and to show that there's nothing complicated or intimidating about the whole process or about the Dorset CID.'

God, I hoped that if she followed my advice the response would not be the flabby frame of one Inspector Digby Whetstone weighing down her doorstep. Then I could see two little old ladies stuffing those last few words right back down my throat.

'Would you, Mr Marklin? That would be most kind. I'm sure if you met Muriel and she met you, why, who knows, she might even agree that . . .' she stopped and every wrinkle in her face suddenly turned upwards and smiled '. . . the Force really is with us.'

I laughed. And it was on that happy note that we parted.

Downstairs, the Trench gang had 'repaired' to the hotel lounge and were wading knee-deep in family reminiscences when I found them again. Arabella looked up as I came over. I could see her gorgeous eyes trying to read my expression.

'Not in the press-gang yet, by the looks of it,' she smiled.

I sat down in the chair next to her.

'Not yet,' I agreed. But all the same, I had a quirky feeling that I might have already set sail into dangerous waters, without even ruddy knowing I had slipped anchor.

3

Now, Arabella isn't quite into old toys the way I am. Don't get me wrong. She likes them all right. Otherwise she'd have shied away from sharing part of her life with them. And it's not just a case of 'Love me, love my Dinky', either. The affection stands up on its own, without me as a prop. She's always eager to inspect my latest buys or discoveries and I often catch her in the shop giving the stock a twice-over. Especially if the recent buy-in has been big on tin-plate. That's her scene, really. Not die-cast.

I guess it's because realism in a model isn't important to her. So what, a Wells tin-plate Rolls-Royce doesn't represent any actual pre-war Rolls type. Nor a Schuco 'Command Car' any vehicle outside the futuristic imaginings of a thirties graphic artist. It's the feel and spirit of the whole shebang that matters. The dreams it conjures up in every sweep and fold of its metal. Longings, often unspoken, delicately expressed in miniature. Even the very fragility of tin-plate has its own message. You can bang life around just so much before the scrapes begin showing and the dents become deep and permanent. It's no accident that Arabella's favourite item amongst my current stock is a 'dream' car. A tin-plate 'Phantom' automobile by Tipp, a sleek and rounded projectile that looks as if it drove straight out of the pages of some Dan Dare-style comic of the fifties. Its curves are so wildly sensual, it makes even an E-type seem boxy as hell.

'I don't know how you can bear to sell it,' Arabella observed after I had just brought it home as part of a lucky find at a house clearance auction. We were seated at the kitchen table at the time and I just pointed a digit towards the bread bin.

'Oh that,' she had smirked. Whereupon I had instantly offered to give the Phantom to her as a present. But she

33

wasn't having any. I didn't press it, not because I really did need to make the seventy-odd oncers on its resale, but because ... well, I have always insisted, from the first moment Arabella moved in with me, that money shouldn't come between us. Her money, that is. Or rather, her parents' money. And the allowance I know they still insist on paying into her bank, though she'd rather they didn't. But they won't really believe that her job at our local TV station can possibly raise enough to keep a true-blue fly buzzing about. And I'm sure they'd rather not think of what yours truly might make out of his hobby-cum-job. But facts are facts. Arabella and I survive okay on what we earn with our bare brains and, I dare say, a little ditto-faced effrontery. No king's or queen's ransom, admittedly. But then we've not been asked to get a royal out of trouble recently, so we're the odd quid in. Enough to cover our overheads, inmouths and odd outings, anyway. Arabella, I know, makes a real point of never touching the parental divvy. Not to build nest eggs, but self-esteem. Good on 'er, I say. Out of earshot, of course.

But back to the point. My beloved and my other love toys. After we'd breezed home from the Dendron Park do (yes, 'breeze' is a good description for our mood on that drive. I tell you, even the ice-dagger draughts in my Beetle are a welcome breath of fresh air after the centrally heated, blue-rinsed claustrophobia of that place), she accompanied me on my pre-bed check-up of the old shop and its locks, bolts and chain. And almost came a cropper over the pedal car, whose bonnet, I had omitted to warn her, jutted out into the main walk way between the counter and the door.

When she recovered her balance, she looked at me, wide-eyed, and said, 'Hell, did you know one of your toys has developed elephantiasis?'

I nodded. 'Bad case,' I said. 'No cure, I'm afraid. Always this size now.'

'Poor little – sorry, big – thing,' she went along, patting its shiny red bonnet. Then she swung a long, slim, black, woolly stockinged leg over the side of the car (boy, David Bailey should have been around to capture it for *Vogue*) and

34

tried to squat down on the Rexine-covered seat. But model girl as her figure is, it was a J40 (J for Junior) and not an A40, the bigger brother it was modelled after.

'Ouch,' she grinned and extricated herself with the help of my hand. 'Where on earth did you get it? I didn't think you – '

'Pedalled pedal cars?' I smiled back. 'Thought I'd give one a try. I got it from a weird woman who rang me about it this morning. She lives just off the Corfe road. In a cottage that looks as if it hasn't had a lick of anything since licking was invented.'

Arabella walked around its gleaming shape. 'But this looks as if it's been very carefully licked and looked after over the years.'

'Yeah,' I muttered. 'Does, doesn't it? Thought the score was a bit funny when I was there. Toy: ten. House: zero. But there you are. Didn't stay to enquire too much; the lady seemed to have her mind on anything but me.'

Arabella put hand on hip and slit-eyed at me, femme fatale style, 'Just the kind of woman I like you to meet, Marklin. And just you remember that.'

I grabbed her wrist and swung her to me. 'You and who else?' I rapped and the non sequitur made us both corpse. Into each other's arms, praise be. And that's the way we stayed, give or take a yawn, most of the wee small and growing hours.

I suppose it must have been around two hours or so after she had left for the TV station the next morning that she rang me with the news. I was in the middle of revising my mail-order list of customers, deleting those who had been over eighteen months without ordering a dicky-bird and adding those I'd met or heard from or about too recently to have been on the old list. Every month I mail every customer an updated stock catalogue but paper and postage cost far too much to waste on those who leave too long gaps between orders.

I could tell immediately, from her voice, that something was up. Or rather, down. So I lied and said she hadn't interrupted anything and what on earth had happened. Her reply took me aback, to put it mildly.

'You know your great-aunt's grave?'

I swallowed. 'Er, yes, of course. But what on earth makes you bring her up?'

It was this aunt who had bequeathed me the Toy Emporium house and premises in the first place. Only it was a sweet shop-cum-tobacconist-cum-paper-shop-cum-everything in her day. She sold buckets and spades, kites, bats and balls (some of the latter were attached to a ping-pong bat by a length of elastic that was guaranteed to perish long before your next holiday, if it didn't break on the very first day. As a kid, my balls were rarely attached to my bats for long), blow-up swimming rings and lilos, and seashore goodies of every kind. When she died, quite a few years back now, I got me a house and store and she a place of rest in St Mary's churchyard with a headstone I'd had carved in as near a lollipop shape as I reckoned the vicar would sanction on consecrated ground.

Arabella's embarrassment came down the line in a great big lump.

'Well . . . you see . . . we've just heard a police report that . . . er . . . something's happened to . . . er . . .'

Now, in my shock and confusion, I interpreted the non-word 'er' as the on-word 'her'. I should have waited. It would have saved my adrenalin dinging the bell.

'God, come on, Arabella. Stop all this ruddy nonsense. Who the hell round here would think of necro-wotsitting with my poor old aunt. The whole idea is – '

'No, please. Hang on, Peter. Your aunt is fine. No, I mean, she isn't exactly fine, but you know what I mean. No one's disturbed her or anything.'

I was tempted to put a finger in my mouth to push my heart back down.

'So what are you talking about? What's all this about her grave, then, and the police and God knows what?'

She hesitated, then said quietly, 'They've found something lying on it.'

'Oh,' I started to relax a little, then almost instantly

reversed the process with a second, 'OH?' in big caps, followed by an even bigger 'WHAT?'

Bigger hesitation, then, barely audible, 'A body.'

'A bo . . . bo . . . bo . . . ?' I was starting to sound like Ronnie Barker's Arkwright in *Open All Hours*, so I pulled myself together and added, '. . . ody?'

'Yes, darling. 'Fraid so. I'm so very sorry to have to bring the news, but I wanted you to know right away, in case the police come round to you or ring or something.'

I tried to get a few thoughts glimmering through the fog.

'Er . . . this body. Don't tell me that you and I might even know who it belongs . . . belonged to?'

'No. The body hasn't been identified yet, apparently. All we've heard is that it's a man. We don't know how he died or even how long he's been dead. Or how he got there, for that matter. I'm going round to the church as soon as I put the phone down.'

My brain was beginning to function again. Only one cylinder. But it was a start.

'This man . . . could be one of those tramps, couldn't he? You know they've had trouble with them at St Mary's before. Doss in the church daytimes, then, if they're turfed out, pull up a tombstone and make themselves comfortable.'

'Could be. Maybe, then, he could have died of hypothermia. It was minus eight last night, according to our weatherman.'

So that's more or less how we left it. Arabella signed off by saying she hoped I wasn't too upset by his choice of a last resting place and I lied and said I wasn't and then tried to get back to the editing of my customer listing. But it proved mighty hard going. For my mind was very much elsewhere. Not so much in my old aunt's graveyard, as you might imagine. But in one Digby Whetstone's office over in the glass monstrosity the police had built for themselves in Bournemouth in the sixties. 'Marklin . . . Marklin,' I could hear him repeating, before his fat features fractured into the biggest smile seen on a peeler's face since the invention of the truncheon.

From then on, that day, I had half an ear cocked towards the phone. I'd even prepared a saucy comeback for Whetstone's first words. Something along the lines of his 'making a grave mistake etcetera etcetera' but no call came. From him, that is.

I had a couple of calls about toys, each one giving me the willies before I found out who was ringing. One was a regular who rang each and every month to see whether, by chance, I'd yet discovered any of the hand made wooden prototypes Dinky had made of their models before committing themselves to full-scale die-cast production. (Some, made in the thirties, have miraculously survived, but all are jealously guarded in private collections.) The answer is always the negative same and I'm sure will be for ever, but you can't knock the guy for dreaming. As far as I can gather, he's got almost every model in every colour variation that Dinky ever made, so where else can he go but prototypes?

The second call was from a stranger. I instantly added him to my listing, for he was a peach amongst peaches for the likes of me. A rarin' to spend newcomer to the toy-collecting scene. In total contrast to the previous caller, he still had everywhere to go. And would I advise him how and where to start? What an opener! What's more, after a little probing, I discovered his interest had been sparked by a book he'd taken out of his local library – David Pressland's *Art of the Tin Toy*. Now, tin-plate may be thin, but it demands mega-thick wads of money to indulge in, if you're after the better stuff. And he seemed to be. I sold him eight pieces, there and then, sight unseen. A Tipp double-decker bus. A couple of pre-war Schucos. A Meccano car No. 3. Two small Minics – a Ford 8 van and a refuse truck. And ditto number of fifties American cars, so beloved of Japanese manufacturers – a Nomura Edsel and Beetle convertible. (Yes, like my Volks, only in maroon, not yellow.) All in all, a tidy one thousand, nine hundred and fifty pounds' worth. Cheque to be in the post pronto. I couldn't believe my good luck. And wouldn't until said cheque had been passed kosher by my boys and girls at Barclays.

Now, in normal non-tombstone times, I would feel pretty

chipper for the rest of such a trading day. But Arabella's news took quite a bit of the gilt off that particular gingerbread, for I was pretty positive that I hadn't heard the last of my poor aunt and her latest (late) lodger.

However, no more calls were to come that afternoon. Down the Telecom line, that is. Punters weren't exactly beating a path to my now tin-plate depleted stock either, but the store had to be minded, just in case. A task Bing insisted on sharing with me that day, a decision he must have regretted since every time the phone had rung, my lap had disappeared from under him as I trotted back into the hall to answer it. In the end, however, I made it up to him by bringing forward his Whiskas time by an hour, to five. And it was as I went back into the shop, leaving him noshing away, that I saw the walnut-and-leather-ridden Range Rover pull up outside.

Oh, goody, goody, gumdrops. I'd have almost preferred a Whetstone-ridden squad Rover in ghostly white.

I waited by the counter until they finished climbing out of their covered wagon. Not to be deliberately unwelcoming but to give myself time to work out why on earth my common-law in-laws might be popping over, unannounced, at an hour they more or less knew their Bella would not yet be home. Thinks: They've decided to appeal to me direct to let their daughter go. 'Consider, Peter, when you are a hundred and seven, she'll still be only a slip of a thing of eighty-nine, with all her dotage still ahead of her.'

(True.)

'She's too young to know her own mind. Do you really want to be around when she suddenly wakes up?'

(Answer: 'Yes' to the last part.)

'You're holding her back. If it weren't for you, she could probably earn a fortune on some big national TV programme and not stick in the sticks.'

(She's a sticks insect. But not because of me. Big, buzzing big city bluebottles make her fly a mile.)

'We had such plans for her. With her education, natural talent and rare beauty, why . . .'

(. . . she could marry any green wellie in the land, open her legs, if she hasn't fallen asleep already that is, and produce a line of little green wellies who'll grow up to throw themselves about at Hooray Henry thrashes.)

'You didn't admire that toy boy much at our hotel last night. Well, my husband and I have no wish for our daughter to be just your plaything.'

By this time they had actually entered the shop, so, pulling myself together to squeeze out the teeming suspicions, I strode out from my counter with the nearest I could muster to 'what a wizzo surprise' old smile.

After the usual pleasantries, I tried to shepherd them through into the house. I didn't feel in the mood for naive or barbed comments about my toys or my interest in them. I had endured both some days before on their first visit to the Toy Emporium and I felt that I'd more than had my quota for the year.

Julia was quite willing to pass on through, but Clement, no doubt recalling his National Service days as a lieutenant in the artillery, would insist on inspecting a small display of German Hausser-Elastolin models and figures that I had recently bought from a retired colonel, who had acquired them whilst serving in the British army of occupation in 1945. I must say in Clemmie's defence, they were worth an official inspection. Hausser army vehicles are amongst the best ever made and highly covetable.

I watched as he picked up a Horch staff car, complete with driver, map reader, adjutant and general with a movable 'Heil Hitler' arm. But as the price tag of two hundred and twenty-five pounds met his eye, he instantly replaced it, and in his hurry, knocked over a group of standing figures. These, made of a composite mixture of sawdust, casein glue and kaolin, were the German equivalent of Britain's lead soldiers, and if you can bear the inclusion of the Nazi hierarchy, have an odd charm over and above their historical significance.

I sped to his aid. 'Don't worry, Clement. No harm done. They're only made of a German kind of porridge.'

He frowned at me, as I set Mussolini, Goebbels and two *Wehrmacht* infantry figures back on their jackbooted feet.

'Porridge?' he queried. 'Thought they'd be lead.'

I touched his elbow. 'Why don't you come on through? I was just about to lock up shop anyway.'

He dithered for a second, then nodded, smiling. 'Before I cause. More confusion. Eh?'

I went to the door, snapped the lock and slid the bolts across.

'No, not at all.' I came back to him and smiled. 'It's not every day I have such a good excuse for a beer at this hour.'

His eyes flickered. 'Oh, I see . . .'

I'm not sure he did. But anyway, he took Julia's arm and escorted her in the direction my arm was indicating.

It was Julia who chose to explain their unheralded appearance on the Studland stage.

'You must be wondering, Peter, why we've suddenly landed on your doorstep like this.'

I waved my hand. I couldn't really say no, now could I? I braced myself for Trench warfare.

'Well, Clement and I stood it for a bit, you see, and then decided it would be better, or anyway more pleasant, if we spent the evening elsewhere.'

She beamed at me, as if I knew what she was talking about, then said quickly, 'Oh, don't worry, Peter, we have no intention of imposing on you for the whole time. No, we thought we'd just go into Swanage and eat somewhere there tonight. But as we came on the Sandbanks ferry and had to pass your place, anyway, en route, we felt we couldn't not pop in and say hello.'

'Hello,' I couldn't stop myself saying, with a foolish grin. Didn't win Brownie points. I could see that from the concrete set of Clement's mouth.

I went on hurriedly, at least somewhat relieved that their visit had seemingly been sparked by something other than an overaged, daughter-wasting, impoverished, puerile toy

41

fanatic like you-know-who. 'But I don't quite follow. Do I take it you've had some altercation or something at the hotel?'

Julia looked at Clement. Clement looked at Julia. Both cleared their throats, but only Clement made use of the clearance.

'Julia. Should have been plainer. At the start. Police, you see. All over the place. Hardly get out of the drive. No consideration. Should park their cars. Properly. Like they expect us to.'

My spirits having risen slightly, now sank again, stone style.

'Police?'

Julia nodded. 'Oh dear, somehow I knew from the very first day that we shouldn't have gone back to Dendron Park. It's changed so. I suppose we didn't realise how much Mrs Robbins' late husband contributed to the place. He must be turning in his grave to see his beloved hotel swarming with police. It would never have happened in his day.' She paused for breath. 'I tell you, Peter, the other guests don't like it either. You remember Bessy Meade? Well, she's quite horrified and says if it wasn't her home, she'd be moving out by the end of the week.'

At last, she seemed to have finished and I leapt in with the question she still had not answered.

'The police – what are they doing there? I mean, has there been a robbery or has a guest gone haywire or . . . ?'

Clement held up a hand like a traffic cop. 'No. 'Fraid might be. Worse than that.'

Julia looked worried. 'We don't *know*, Clem . . .'

'All right, my dear. Don't know. Can guess, though. Bet bottom dollar. Got something to do. With that Brand.'

'TB?' I queried, but knowing the answer.

'Heard this morning. Mrs Robbins asking round. If anyone had seen him. Gone, apparently. No word. Nothing. Very upset. Don't blame her. Be counting the silver. If I were her.'

'Poor Mrs Robbins,' Julia sympathised. 'But in a way, it could be a blessing. I'm sure he's been mainly responsible for the change in the place. That's what some others are saying. They're hoping he never comes back. You know. Good riddance.'

'But how have the police got involved?' I frowned. 'Did Mrs Robbins send for them? If she did, I would have thought it was a trifle early yet for a missing person hunt.'

'No idea, old chap. After lunch. Reading the paper. Look up. There they were. Blue lights. In the drive.'

'We haven't seen Mrs Robbins since they came,' Julia commented. 'We gather an Inspector Somebody-or-other asked for her, and when we left they were still closeted in her rooms on the first floor.'

'Bobbies. Everywhere in the grounds. Give place a bad name. Decided to leave. Case we got roped in.'

'Even so,' Julia chipped in, 'Clement and I were asked, as we were leaving, what time we were likely to be back, as they might want to ask us some questions.'

'Damn cheek. Tempted tell 'em. Mind their own business. Didn't come to Dorset . . .'

Julia patted her husband's hand. (She didn't have to stretch far. They were sitting together on the settee.) 'Now, now, Clement, I'm sure Peter doesn't want to hear what you didn't come to Dorset for, but what you *did*. Anyway, that's enough of our little problems.' She looked back at me. 'I expect by the time we get back tonight, they'll all be gone. Let's hope so.'

'If they're not. Good mind move out. Dare say, Royal Bath. High Cliff. Got some rooms. This time of year.'

I rose from the arm of my chair. (Yes, arm. I'd been on my way to get drinks and had only perched there to hear the excuse for their visit.)

'After all that, I bet you could do with a drink.'

Now if I'd said that to the likes of Gus, the applause would have been deafening. But from them? A flicker of a smile. Amazing. There's a certain class of Englishman-stroke-woman who are taught (I assume) only to allow themselves to explode with one emotion. Rage. Never pleasure. Do they ever realise what they are missing? What they've traded in for a stiff upper lip and a bucketful of phlegm?

43

Anyway, I took their orders – straight Scotch (no ice, of course) for the straight man and 'just a glass of white wine, if you've got a bottle open', which I hadn't, but I would have by the time I'd brought the drinks back.

I took a little longer than their decanting and pouring really necessitated. I needed time to digest the news they'd brought from their hotel. Why? Because something inside me was digging at my ribs and saying 'Watch out, Marklin. It's all getting a bit hairy.' First Bessy Meade wants me to investigate her friend's break-in. Okay. Maybe fine on its own. But then my poor old aunt goes and gets an overnight lodger who's dead on his feet. Okay, twice. Could be pure coincidence he chose the name Marklin, but then again . . . And now, only a few hours later, the police flood the hotel I'd supped at only the previous evening. Maybe on its own, that, too, was kosher. After all, if it was the toy boy they were after, what possible connection could anyone say I had with him? Whether he'd decided he'd had all he could get out of Mrs Robbins and had just scarpered to new hunting grounds, or had stolen the Robbins' family silver, or had been up to something shady elsewhere in Bournemouth or wherever, there was no way I could see that any of that could involve me.

Even so, the little fella inside my ribcage still gave the occasional dig, blast his eyes. I decided to try drowning him. And joined straight man in a stiff (of course) Scotch.

When we'd all said 'Cheers' (correction, Clemmie actually fired off 'Better times' – I preferred not to think to what he might be referring) and were seated, drinks in hand, staring into limbo in case any eyes met, Julia suddenly broke the ice with, 'Bella looks very well, I must say.'

I was about to take this as an oblique compliment to me, via, say, her happiness showing in her face or whatever, when she added, 'The Dorset air must suit her.'

I hid my disappointment by crossing my legs.

'It's not usually this frigid.' I smiled thinly. 'It's the coldest winter I can remember.'

Out of the corner of my eye, I saw Bing sidle into the

room, take one look at the funny strangers blocking access to his favourite corner of the settee, then snootily sidle out again. I wondered if he returned the sympathy I felt for his predicament.

I inclined my head towards the door. 'Bing hates it,' I went on. 'Only goes out long enough for you-know-what and then is back in to snuggle radiators.'

I noted Clement's uneasy look. I guess he never goes to the loo. In conversation, that is. Yet I would have thought that in his public school days half his chat would have been lavatorial and the other half equally below the waist.

Anyway, there followed a resounding silence. All sipped drinks to try to hide the hiatus. Then, to my utter astonishment, Clement suddenly looked me in the eye and said, 'Sorry, old chap. 'Bout last night.'

'Sorry?' I mumbled.

'That Bessy Meade. Bella's told us. Your feelings. Incognito. All that.' He downed a little Scotch, as if speaking about emotions really took it out of him. Probably did.

'Quite understand. Shouldn't have mentioned you. Sorry. But must say.' He cleared his throat. 'Admire what you've done. In the past. Bella told us. Just a bit. Helping people. In trouble. You know. Justice done. All that. Good show.'

Wow! Did this mean I was a little bit forgiven for having lived so long and indulged in juvenile pastimes like toys and a more adult interest in their daughter? I attacked my own dram to let the burn in my throat reassure me I wasn't dreaming.

Julia ran a shiny-tipped feather of a finger round the rim of her wineglass. 'That's right, Peter. Clement and I were talking about it in the car coming over. I suppose all those policemen at the hotel really set our minds thinking. About how much crime there seems to be around these days. Wherever you look, I'm afraid. More and more people seem to be getting away with it.' She sighed. 'And sometimes even when they do make arrests and convict people, you find, years later, they have to release them because the evidence was faulty or rigged or something.'

She looked up at me. 'So that's when Clement said

45

"Lucky there are a few people like you around to set things straight".'

Whilst naturally chuffed that Arabella's father didn't think me a complete wash-out, I doubted her description of his exact words, which I suspected were more akin to a 'Marklin fella. Not all bad. Suppose. Crime. Helps out. Kind of thing' kind of thing.

'No need to apologise for Bessy Meade. Really,' I offered in return. 'I can see why some people, like her friend, are a bit wary of calling in the coppers. I expect she imagines a scene like the one you've just left at Dendron Park.'

Julia shot me a 'Don't mention it' look, then changed tack.

'What time, Peter, do you expect Bella?'

I looked at my watch.

'Usually around six. Six-thirty. In just over an hour, I guess.'

But I guessed wrong. For at that very second the telephone tinkled. I excused myself and went out to answer it.

'Peter, are you alone?' the voice asked instantly. I knew it had to be Arabella. Or a very upfront burglar.

'Why do you ask?' was my helpful reply.

Arabella saw through it.

'They're with you, aren't they?'

'How did you know?' I was all questions.

'Well, they're not here at Dendron Park. And that Mrs Meade says they mentioned to her something about spending the evening in Swanage and maybe calling in on you on the way.'

'Mrs Meade speak without forked tongue. Heap big parents here,' I whispered. 'Came just before closing time of trading post.'

'No, be serious, Peter,' Arabella chided (sounds as if it should be 'chid', past tense of chide), 'and tell me what they've told you about – '

'The police?' I cut in. 'Only that they were swarming around the place. They reckon it's probably got something to do with Mrs Robbins' TB. They say he's run off or something.'

46

'It's now not a matter of "probably", Peter. It's "definitely".'

'What's he done? Vamoosed with the hotel safe?'

'It's not a case of what he's done. But what someone's done to him.'

Hell, the devil in my ribcage started up his antics again.

'Don't tell me – ' I began, but Arabella stopped me.

'Be careful what you say, Peter. I don't want my parents going loco about it all, before I have a chance to get home. Can you keep them there?'

Not a scintillating prospect, but what could I say?

'Of course, don't worry. Just tell me what happened. I'll keep my responses bland and uninformative, in case they overhear anything.'

'Thanks, darling. Well, as I'm sure you've guessed already, TB is no more.'

'Right.' Bland enough? The boy's working well.

'His car has been found burnt out in a lay-by. But the police aren't divulging where exactly, yet. You know how cagey they are. Well . . . *he* is.'

I closed my eyes. 'Digby?'

'Very same. Sorry.'

Hello, hello, hello. Or, rather, in his case, a trio of good-byes. My pet hate of the Bournemouth boys in blue. Inspector 'Get-off-my-patch-Marklin' Digby Whetstone.

'Not your fault.' Course it wasn't. Only people to blame were Whetstone's parents, if he had any and wasn't found under a stone.

'But TB's body . . .' she hesitated, so I supplied the innocuous word.

'Ashes?'

'No, he wasn't in the car. He . . . er . . . was found . . . er . . .' Again she hesitated, which isn't like her. Arabella's about as direct as an arrow as a rule. The only time she isn't is when she doesn't want to wound . . . Oh my God, suddenly the cause of the er-ing hit me like . . . well, a tombstone.

'Don't tell me,' I began.

'Don't say it,' she warned.

47

I looked back towards the sitting-room. I could just see a hand reaching out for a glass.

'Aunty?' I croaked.

' Aunty,' she confirmed. 'Male Caucasian identified. It was TB.'

Shit and derision hit the fan of my mind. My mouth made do with, 'Nasty disease for Aunty to have got.'

'Real name, so the police say, is Fern. Would you believe Jacob Fern?'

'I guess I'll have to.' The bland follows the bland.

'You're doing well, my darling. Only you may get a question or two from them about this Aunty.'

I cupped my hand round the mouthpiece and whispered, 'With any luck they're too busy talking about me to have overheard a thing.'

'They're not that bad,' she said, but then asked, 'are they?'

'Back to Jacob,' I sidestepped. 'Is there any more? You know.'

'Not much. Turns out he was a local lad. Father's a farmer over our way somewhere. Ted Fern. Apparently he's shattered by the news and the police have warned all the media to keep off him for a while. Only other bit of news they've released so far is the cause of death.'

'Which was?'

'Blow to the back of the head. Usual unidentified blunt instrument. Gets around, doesn't it?'

'That it?'

'It.'

'When will you be home?'

'Soon as.'

'As what, do you think? The boys in the fort want to know.'

'Tell the boys the cavalry will try to whip their nags into bringing relief seven-thirty, eightish.'

'We'll do our best to hold out, General.'

'Peter . . .'

'Yes?'

'Don't worry.' Her voice now was super-serious.

48

'It's okay.' I cupped my hands again. 'So far it's going well. Even got a compliment, just before you called.'

'I didn't mean my parents. I meant about Fern. And his being found . . . where he was.'

''Sall right. Aunty was always broad-minded.'

'I meant . . . you know . . . the possible complications.'

'You mean the family name being a red rag to the likes of Digby?' I didn't need a reply, so I went on, 'You haven't come face to face with him today yet, by any chance?'

'No, thank God. But I gather he's probably going to hold a press conference first thing in the morning.'

'Sufficient unto the day.'

'Amen. Meanwhile, be sure to open the gates, directly you hear the bugle.'

I would have saluted, only I was holding the receiver.

But the shoot-out never occurred. Right from the time I returned to them from the phone, the Indians proved heap big friendly. Maybe being left alone in the Marklin camp for a few moments had made them feel more at ease. Lord knows. But holding the fort certainly held no really perilous moments. Mind you, I was careful not to let the conversation wander too far into dangerous territory. Clement had me rattled for a second, when he seemed to be about to blame half the Western world's troubles on the divorce rate, but a determined look from Julia obviously reminded him, just in time, that I had been through those particular courts not so very long ago. His machine-gun abruptly stopped firing, then readjusted aim and fired off against violence on films and television instead. A subject that more or less took us through until the bugle sounded and their beloved Bella breezed in.

I had to admire her. The way she kept the temperature down when she broke the news to them about the toy boy. You'd almost have thought she was talking about the frigid weather or the price of fresh veg in the supermarket, so determined was she that her parents' enjoyment of their time in Dorset should not die a death, so to speak. However,

49

as you might imagine, even with the control at regulo nought, her parents could not exactly remain totally unmoved by the tidings. But no real outbursts ensued. Just a sort of stunned silence. At first, that is.

Clement was the first to get his act together.

'Well.' Clear throat. 'Shouldn't say it. Suppose. But place better off. Without him.'

Julia fluttered a hand. 'Poor Mrs Robbins. First a widow. Now a . . .' She was stuck for a word. Not surprising. I don't think there is one yet for those left behind by toy boys.

Thereafter the conversation became mainly conjecture. As to why anyone should want to have done away with said TB or Brand or Fern. (By the way, bless her, Arabella had refrained from telling them about Aunty's role in all this. Just mentioned that his body had been found in a church-yard – a location Clement found singularly inappropriate for the dislikes of TB.)

I myself purposely did not get too involved in this guess-ing game. And not just because I had nothing to lead me to any conclusions. (No one in the room had, of course.) But I kept having visions of Digby Whetstone staring at the name Marklin on the grave and then discovering the name Trench in the Dendron Park's guest-book and putting one and one together and snapping his lead making a note in his diary: 'Toy Emporium. Soonest.' And when that 'soonest' moment came would be the time for me to start guessing. Not before.

By the time her parents left at around ten-thirty – they had been persuaded to stay to dinner, their daughter having wisely bought four chicken Kievs from a late-closing super-market on the way home – Clemmie and Julia had come to the conclusion that TB had died because the likes of him, by definition, must have 'unsavoury' friends. And that there-fore he could have fallen out with or double-crossed one of them and paid the penalty.

Arabella did not discount such a theory, but, on tiptoes so as not to shock her parents overmuch, hinted that per-haps the motive for his murder might have been more 'personal and emotional'. Julia instantly took this to mean that Arabella was getting at Mrs Robbins and dismissed the suggestion out of hand. Clement rat-tatted total agreement with his wife. In fact, as Arabella told me afterwards, she had not been thinking of anyone in particular. For who knew how many women TB had loved and left before Mrs Robbins. Or how many marriages he had fouled up or husbands he had incensed. Any of his previous indulgences could have fired enough emotion, jealousy or anger to lead to reaching for the nearest blunt instrument.

It was not until we were safely tucked up in bed that night and I was lying on my back trying to get sheep to jump over Digby Whetstone, that Arabella, curving her lithe body over mine, whispered, 'There's something I haven't told you. I ran into him as I was leaving the hotel.'

If she hadn't been lying on me, I'd have sat bolt upright.

'With your car, I hope,' I muttered. 'If not, give me the worst.'

She reached up and kissed me lightly on the lips. Now for the bad news.

'He was in the car park. I couldn't avoid him when I went to get my Golf.'

I put my hands around her delicious waist. They almost met.

'Has he made the connections?'

'He remarked on the grave having the same name as yours. But I doubt if he's made the aunty jump yet. After all, your particular family aren't the only ones bearing that moniker. And I didn't let on.'

'He will. He will,' I muttered. 'Anything else?'

''Fraid so. He asked whether the Trenches registered in the hotel guest-book were anything to do with me.' She sighed. 'I had to tell the truth, now didn't I?'

'And he said?'

'That he would be interviewing all the guests and that he'd no doubt be meeting them in the morning. I didn't dare tell them that tonight. Father would have had kittens.'

'Correction. Beagles or Dobermans, I suspect.'

51

She smiled. 'Well, at least you didn't say Rottweilers. Your view of Dad must be improving.'

'Know something?' I shifted her weight slightly and moved one of my hands to cup a breast. 'I do believe it is. Holding the fort alone tonight might have brought dividends. At least, we all know each other a little more now.'

'Know when you went out to the loo?'

'I normally do, yes.'

She kissed me quiet. Silence really can be golden. Then she went on, 'Both Dad and Mother said more or less the same thing. That they were glad of the opportunity to get to know you more.'

'And . . . ?'

'*And*, they both said they liked what they saw.'

I sniggered. 'And what did you say? Anything?'

'That I did too. And the reverse.'

I frowned. 'The reverse?'

'Saw what I liked. The first moment we met.'

My other hand deserted her waist, but this time, travelled south. And arrived around the arc of her derrière. (The 'Arc de Triomphe', as I dub it.) She, in turn, nuzzled her mouth around the lobe of my lug.

'So, so far, so good. Boy's working well.'

'Maybe,' I conceded, 'But it's tomorrow that's fertiliser/fan time. For all of us, I wouldn't wonder.'

'But tonight's tonight,' she whispered into my now damp orifice.

There was no answer to that. So I kept quiet. And let my hands start a whole new conversation.

4

Next morning, after Arabella has Golfed off TV-wards, I dealt with the post, and then decided that if the day was going to turn out the way I dreaded, I needed a breath of fresh air before the fan started to revolve. Besides, Bing wasn't likely to venture out into the icicles unless I took him. So on went the lead and out we went. Down sea lane. God, it was frigid. Our breath looked like a steamy scene from a Turkish bath.

We hadn't got further than the first cottage in the wee, winding road when we saw it. Or rather, heard it. Sound travels a mite faster than even a fit Ford Popular. Now, despite the bangs, roars, squeals and rattles of its progress, Bing has no fear of that black, perpendicular peril. Indeed, I think he actually likes it. (Only being in Britain who does.) For, inside he knows there's a bundle of rags whose every stich holds a memory of a meal gone by. And he doesn't have to sniff that hard, either, to have a nasal orgasm. Gus, you see, tends only to wash his vestments when they can walk to his old copper and climb in all on their own.

The basket case slithered to a stop alongside us. An arm reached out of the window for mine.

'Snap,' he grunted.

'You mean the weather? Snap as in "cold snap"?' I jauntily offered, removing my woolly-wonder scarf from around my mouth so that speech could issue.

'No, you prize berk,' he snapped back. 'Bet I'm coming up for the same ruddy reason you're coming down.'

'You're going for a walk,' I annoyed. 'In a car.'

He blinked his great eyes, then tumbled. 'Oh, get off. Don't try and tell me you aren't coming down to chew the fat over that Fern bloke. Living at your beloved's parents' bloody hotel and all.'

'So I won't try and tell you.'

53

He chortled. I could hardly see him for the cloud his breath made. 'Get in, old lad. Too effin' cold to hang about.'

Bing and I accepted his kind invitation. But not for warmth. Gus's jalopy hasn't even heard of a heater. And even if it had one, its colander coachwork would have defeated it ten-nil.

Gus graunched into a gear.

'Where are we going?' I enquired. Oh, it wasn't fair.

'Well, I ... er ...' he stammered and kept his boot on what was left of the clutch. I slapped him on the back, as Bing jumped on to the wrecked Rexine of the back seat.

'All right, Gus, but it's a bit early, you know. Whatever the weather.'

His craggy old face put on its familiar hurt look.

'Wouldn't dream of it, old son. Not at this hour. Not on your life. I'm not a ruddy alcoholic, you know.'

I laughed. Which he took as assent to the destination. And with a jerk that shot Bing to the floor, we were off. To nowhere, of course, but back home.

Boy, I don't know what Bing and I would have done without that stiff five-second walk.

It's always funny seeing Gus overwhelming my sitting-room without a can or jar in his hand. He kinda doesn't know what to do with his body. Arms swing around, shoulders get hunched, mouth twitches, legs cross and uncross. St Vitus should be proud of him. However, nine-forty-five a.m. is a shade before yardarm time, even for Gus Tribble. But I did offer him coffee or tea.

'Naah, old mate, just had a cup. Any road, the quacks say now too much ruddy char can be bad for you.'

'The same doctors say ...' I began, and then quit. Gus was a medical law unto himself. I had to admit, if you wanted an advert for 'Beer is good for you', Gus could just about pass muster. No beer belly, no broken veins to beetroot his face, no shortness of breath (Aroma, yes. Shortness, no.) and none of the aches and pains most elderly people either suffer from or invent to grumble up a bit of attention.

54

Gus was still built the way he was made. Massive. Perhaps the mortar between the bricks of the proverbial privy is starting to crack here and there and the paintwork is more grey and grisled than pristine, but there seems to be plenty of life left in the old structure yet.

Suddenly Gus punched a thick finger at me. 'This 'ere Fern. Knew his dad, I did, years ago. Was coming up to tell you.'

'Tell away,' I invited.

He relaxed back in his chair. Bing leapt on to his lap to start the sniff survey of his sweater.

'Well, it's like this 'ere. When I was a nipper, I knew his dad's dad.'

Gus's explanations are often borderline explanatory.

'Dad's dad?'

'Yer. See. He used to let me play over at his farm. With that dead chap's father, who was his son, see?'

Did I see?

He continued, notwithstanding. 'He must be a year or two, forget how many now, younger than me. But didn't matter.'

'This dead Fern's father?'

'Right. But we kids got on all right.' Gus gave a giant sniff. Bing froze his own. "Sides, my mum's place didn't have no garden, see. So the farm was just dandy, even though I had to walk miles to get there. Always something going on. Things to do. Places to hide. They had one barn up there – probably just the same now – with a hay loft. One time, gor . . .' he slapped his thigh. I wonder Bing didn't die of coughing for the dust. '. . . almost burnt it down, we did. See, his dad, old man Fern, had given him a magnifying glass for his birthday and one day when the sun was out, we – '

'Gus,' I interrupted rudely, 'I hate to cut short your everyday story of arson folk, but old Digby Whetstone may turn up any minute. So right now, I'd rather clue up on the dead son, than Father Fern's flaming childhood.'

He fixed me with his eyes. 'Flabby old Whetstone coming, is he? Well, well, well. What for? Pick your brains or pick

on you for having a girlfriend whose ruddy mum and dad
are staying at the same rotten hotel?' He frowned at his
own suggestion. 'That's no crime, though, is it? And not
anything to do with you, neither.'

'Right, Gus,' I sighed. 'Ma and Pa Trench booked in
where the dead Fern hung out is not the problem.'

'So what is, old son?'

'Where Fern's body was found.'

'Wireless said it was in a graveyard. St Mary's.'

'Right.'

Gus held up his hands, unsettling Bing. He had just been
sniffing the sleeve.

'So? You're not the ruddy vicar.'

'True.'

'Out with it, old lad. What's your . . . ?'

'The grave he was found on. Headstone reads "Marklin".'

'Marklin?' He scratched his stubble, then his eyes suddenly Osrammed. 'Oh no, old mate. Not your old aunty's
grave?'

'Very same.'

'Shit,' he breathed. 'Now who on earth would want to
do a thing like that?'

I shrugged. 'That's what I suspect will be Digby's first
question.' I leaned forward in my chair. 'Now, Gus, tell me
all you know about the dead son, before Whetstone's car
flashes round.'

He thought for a second. 'Can't help too much about the
son, old lad. See, I've more or less lost contact with the
Ferns over the years. Me being a fisherman, see. Didn't
have much time. Keeping up with their doings over at the
farm.'

'Well, just tell me what you *do* know.'

Gus looked down at Bing, who had just extended his
nasal survey to his cord (now worn cordless) trousers.

'Mainly hearsay, old son, 'fraid. Seems Ted's son – '

I stopped him. 'Ted. That's Ted Fern, the father farmer,
whom you used to play with as a nipper?'

'Right,' Gus glowered at me, as if I was knee-high to a

moron. 'And Ted's son is the dead one on your aunty's grave. Get it?'

'Got it.'

He didn't add 'Good'. Don't suppose Danny Kaye's old films are high up on the Tribble hit parade. Only thing I've ever heard him mention watching on TV are weather forecasts. And he hates those.

'Where was I? Oh yeah. This Ted's son, the dead one, I heard grew tired of the farm years ago. Too ruddy dull and dirty, I wouldn't wonder, for the likes of him. Any road, heard he buggered off to London, I think it was, and changed his name to something daft. Wanted to be a poncey actor, so I heard.'

'Jason Brand,' I chipped in. 'And he was a male model, not an actor.'

Gus raised an eyebrow, thick as dune grass. 'Oh . . . so you've already done a bit of homework on him, have you, old love?'

'No. Just heard a bit about him when I went to dinner at Dendron Park with Arabella's folks.'

He looked as if he didn't quite believe me, but went on nevertheless. 'Bleedin' actor or model. Makes no difference. Can't have pleased his old man too much, can it? Farmers reckon on their sons carrying on their farms, now don't they? If they don't who else will, I ask you? Specially these hard times.'

Bing, by this time, had no doubt decided Gus's trousers smelt more of diesel from his old boat than stale fish and had settled down for a lap nap. Gus rested a giant paw on his back and I winced for Bing's ribs.

'But his son came back,' I pointed out.

'Yeah. But not to the farm, now, did he? What use would he have been to his father hanging around Bournemouth, I ask you?'

I pondered, then queried, 'Don't happen to have heard what he did in Bournemouth, I suppose?'

Gus's face broke into a lascivious look, worthy of Benny Hill. 'Didn't they tell you at that hotel? Ladies, old son.

57

That's what he did for a living, so I've been led to believe. Older ladies, who should know better.'

Gus held up an admonitory digit. 'Sharp-looker, I gather he was. Like his dad in his youth. But good looks can be your ruddy downfall, if you're not careful.'

'I'll be careful,' I promised and for once Gus got the gag.

'Yeah,' he chuckled. 'Never quite had that problem, us two, thank you very much. Any road, traded on his looks, he did. His son. Stead of bloody working for a living. Women should have more sense than to let 'em get away with it. Even if they are flattered out of their knickers at having a much younger bloke chatting them up.'

'You know he wasn't just a guest at Dendron Park, then?'

'Wireless this morning more or less gave the game away. "Friend of the proprietress, Mrs Whatshername".'

'Robbins.'

'Yeah. That's it. Not too ruddy hard to read between the lines, now is it? Even without knowing the bloke's reputation aforehand.' He leaned forward, shadowing Bing. ''Ere, what's this Mrs Robbins like then? Bit of a looker still, eh? And well off with it, seeing as how she owns the ruddy place, they said.'

'She's still attractive, yes.'

Gus threw back his head. 'Cor. There you go. Reckon he must have thought he was on to a good thing there, don't you? Living in a posh hotel for free and, no doubt, a good chance later of inheriting the blasted lot. Not too bad an old deal, is it? When all you've got to do is open your perishing flies once in a while.'

Who could argue? So I didn't. 'Not such a good deal now, though, is it? Ending up on a slab, subject to a police surgeon's scalpel.'

Gus winced. 'Should have stayed on the farm, he should have. Then none of this would have happened. 'Tisn't even as if he'd have needed to live with his dad, neither, if he'd wanted a bit of freedom. There's a cottage at the end of the farm track that I dare say old Ted would have let him have, if it meant he'd stay.'

'Cottage?'

'Yeah. I mean, it's not a palace, mind. But it's quite good enough. And he could have done it up, couldn't he, if he wanted it a bit smarter.'

'What do you mean, "at the end of the track"? Which end?'

He frowned. 'Road end. Why d'yer ask?'

'This farm of Fern's,' I frowned back, 'wouldn't be just off the Corfe road, would it?'

'Yeah. That's it. Laid back a bit. Can't really see the farmhouse itself from the road. But you can just about see the cottage.'

Gus shuffled around in his chair and Bing called off his zizz and jumped down to the floor. 'Why, what do you know about it, old son? There's something, isn't there? Don't hold out on yer old mate.'

'I bought something there the other day. That's all.'

Gus was dumbfounded. 'Bought something from old Ted? You're kidding. What could he have that you'd be – ?'

I cut in. 'Nothing. I didn't go up to the farm. Just the cottage. The woman living there had a pedal car she wanted to sell.'

'Woman?' Gus ruminated for a second, then added, 'Oh yeah. Well, I have heard that since his cowman moved out a year or two back, Ted lets the place.'

'So you know nothing about the present tenant?'

Gus shrugged. 'Why should I? I'm not a bloody 'cyclopae-dia, you know. Anyway, what's the woman in the cottage what had the pedal car got to do with anything?'

'Nothing, really,' I conceded. 'Just that she was acting a bit strange.'

'Some women do that for a living, old mate,' Gus guffawed. 'Love to see the looks on our faces, they do. If I worried every time a woman acted funny, I'd be in a loony bin by now.'

And on that typical homily from Gus, we left it. A moment later, I heard the ding of my shop doorbell. It was time to open up.

But this was no customer about to gawp and touch my stock. Nor that much rarer breed, an actual living, breathing, cash-in-hand buyer. I saw that the moment I went in to the counter. Punters very rarely turn up in white Rovers with red flashes down the sides.

I wearily dragged myself to the shop door and unlocked my cop-commendable precautions against burglars who hate the sound of breaking glass.

'Morning, Digby,' I breezed. 'What brings you here on this frosty day? Besides your white wagon, that is?'

His red moustache curled slightly at the ends – the nearest dear Inspector Whetstone ever gets to a genuine smile. But a verbal response to my sally, gave he not. Just brushed past me into the shop. Par for his course. I followed him up to the counter and dodged behind it. The only thing I welcome between me and Digby is a plank of solid mahogany.

He folded his flab on to and around my customer stool.

'You can probably guess why I'm here,' he pursed at me.

'The Fern fellow.'

'Miss Trench fill you in?'

I smiled. I couldn't help it. The idea of a trench filling in . . . ? Oh well, never mind.

'This is no laughing matter, Marklin.' No 'Mister', you note. We're real buddies. 'This is a murder investigation, not some media sideshow to entertain the public.'

I ignored the knock at Arabella and her crime-buster TV programme.

'Sorry, Inspector. Back to your question. Yes, I did guess you'd be round. Hardly difficult, though. What with my aunty having an unwanted overnight guest and Dendron Park having as wanted guests my beloved's beloved parents.' I held my hands up smugly. 'Ergo. You'd be here.'

The red moustache curled again. But this time only on one side. 'Your ergos are up the creek, Marklin.'

I frowned in disbelief. 'They are?'

'Right up.' He took a deep breath to savour his enjoyment of my ignorance a little longer, then went on, 'Let me ask you a question first, if I may.'

'As if I'd stop you.'

His beadies tried to fix on mine, but I pretended to play with the nearest toy on the counter, a Minic fire engine. It has a little bell that swings.

'I have reason to believe you've met the deceased.'

I flicked at the bell.

'What makes you think that?'

'Answer me first.'

'I've never met him. Okay.'

I saw the shake of his head from the corner of my eye.

'I say you have, Marklin.'

I looked up. 'And I repeat, I haven't. But if you're widening the meaning of the word to include "seeing through a pane of glass", then I've met him. By the same coin, of course, I've met the Queen, the Prince of Wales, Princess Di, James Callaghan, Barbara Cartland and countless hookers in Amsterdam.'

I shouldn't act this way. But there's something in Digby Whetstone that . . . well, I suppose one should count oneself lucky there's anything in dear Digby that produces anything at all.

'Don't split hairs with me,' he spat at me.

'Especially heirs to the throne.' There I went again, but I hurriedly moved on. 'Let me explain. As you have probably discovered, I had dinner the night before last at the hotel. Arabella and I were with her parents. And I saw this Fern fellow through the dining-room window. He was helping an old lady out of an ancient Daimler.'

'That it?'

'That's it. I swear to you. I've never met him, talked to him or anything to him. Why should I have?'

Digby reached into an inside pocket and produced a small leather-bound address book. I watched him as he flipped through the pages to the letter 'T'.

'Toy Emporium, Studland 33943,' he read. 'P. Marklin.'

I pointed to the book. 'Whose is that?'

He spread it before me. 'The murdered man's. We found it in . . . their room at the hotel.'

I closed my eyes.

Digby oozed on. 'So you see, Marklin, I was almost willing to ignore the fact that the body was placed on your aunt's grave. Even the coincidence of your... girlfriend's... parents staying at the very same hotel. But when one of my men discovered your name and address in the dead man's diary, why...' He held up his podgy arms in a 'what-else-can-I-do?' mode.

I held up my own arms in traditional surrender mode.

'Okay, Inspector, it's a fair cop. Or, in your case, a copper-headed one. I murdered Fern. And bundled the body on to my aunt's grave and wrote my name in his diary, just to throw you off the scent. Would never have contemplated any of it had the Trenches not been in the same hotel, of course. Would have been madness, now wouldn't it?'

My salvo obviously took him completely by surprise. He shuffled around so much on the stool that he almost tipped it over.

'Marklin,' he at last managed, 'I don't know what game you think you're playing.'

I decided not to quit whilst I was winning.

'Haven't you heard of it, Inspector? You do surprise me. It's called "Extra-Trivial Pursuit". The aim being to stop cardboard cut-out coppers invading your square on the board. Your opponent can choose from a stack of stock questions. You from a stack of stock answers. Each question and answer card has a value and the winner is – '

A freckled fist suddenly slammed down on my counter. The Minic fire engine leapt at least half an inch, releasing its clockwork motor to whizz through the last of its tension.

'Marklin, I'm warning you,' he snapped, a vein at the side of his reddening forehead pulsing like mad. 'I didn't come here to be insulted or to indulge in some pathetically childish form of verbal fencing, but to ask you why your name and address should be in the murdered man's address book.'

Again he spread out the 'T' page in front of me. I looked at him.

'Does – sorry – did the dead man collect old toys, by any chance?'

His eyelids flickered. 'No, not exactly.'

'Come on, Digby, that means approximately yes, now, doesn't it?'

'No, Marklin, it does not. Fern has a collection of Porsche models in the hotel, I admit. But that's because, apparently, he was Porsche mad. Even rebodied a Beetle like yours in a plastic look-alike Porsche body.'

I knew the type. More than one manufacturer offers vintage Porsche-style bodies for Beetle chassis.

He went on. 'But none of the models are old. They are all ones you can still get in ordinary toy shops, so one of my men tells me.'

'Maybe he was thinking of branching out into older and obsolete models. And heard of my shop from someone, so made a note of it in his book for the future.'

'Maybe. Maybe. And Maybe not.' I almost expected him to start pulling petals off a flower to find out which. Then freckled sausages reached for the book, only I got there first and started to flip through its pages. I soon found what I prayed were there.

'I see I'm not the only toy shop listed.' I looked across at him. 'I see under "B" there's Bugatti Models. Don't be fooled by the name. They sell all marques of cars. Then under "F" there's Fairground Toys. They specialise in white metal kits and foreign models. Under "M" I see Magic Motors is listed. And that's after just a cursory flip through. There may be more.'

'All right,' Digby conceded, 'so there may be more. But the ones you mentioned all sell new stuff, right?'

'Yes, but . . .'

'You are the only one there who sells, exclusively, vintage toys.'

'As I've already hinted, many vintage collectors start off as new-model buyers. Then, finding the selection is finite and ultimately rather boring, move on to embrace older – '

'We have no evidence,' he cut in, 'that Fern contemplated any such thing.'

'You have no evidence he didn't.'

Stalemate. Digby rubbed his sausages together whilst he fired up for a new barrage. I waited and flicked the pages back to 'T'. The sight of my name penned by the dead sent a shiver through my soul.

'Marklin,' Digby said at last, 'all that might just be plausible, if it weren't for two other things. One, the murderer chose a grave marked Marklin on which to leave Fern's corpse. Two, the dead man lived in a hotel which you have admitted to visiting only twenty-four hours before his death and at which your girlfriend's parents are still resident.'

That made three not two 'other things' in my book, but I let it pass.

'So, what are you implying, Inspector?'

Notice the 'Inspector' bit, not just 'Digby'. I throw it in occasionally, when I want to remind the idiot I may know him and have sparred with him from of old, but I still have the rights of any ordinary citizen of the land.

He shrugged. 'Am I implying anything? Dear me, I thought I was just laying a few facts before you, that's all.'

I blinked very slowly.

He retrieved the address book and continued. 'Even you must see that this little volume isn't the only thing that's spelling out the name Marklin in regard to poor Jacob Fern.'

There was no answer to that, sod it. An omission he picked up.

'You're very silent suddenly, Mr Marklin.' (Gee, a 'Mr'. I guess in reply to my 'Inspector'.) 'Not like you.'

'Perhaps I'm my own look-alike,' I tried.

Ignoring me, he droned on. 'I won't ask you where you were around two a.m. yesterday morning. Because I already know. From Miss Trench. I asked her this morning, when she and her TV team returned to the hotel. And I'm sure your story will be the same as hers.'

Oh, how clever. Gee, he'd got me.

'Don't ask away,' I invited. Whilst he was in mid-squirm on his stool, I sped on: 'So two a.m. was when you reckon Fern was killed, is that right?'

I could see he was about to issue a routine 'Keep off the grass' warning, so I kept going: 'I hear his poor man's Porsche was found burnt out in a lay-by.'

Thank God, in my ignorance I'd made a factual error, otherwise I'm sure that question too would have come up against KOTG.

'Wrong, Mr Marklin. His Porsche is still alive and well or almost well in Brankdean's Garage in Sandbanks.'

I frowned.

Digby laughed. No, laughed is too generous a word. 'Fern had taken it in because it was misfiring and he hadn't got it back before he was killed.'

I tried to make what I'd heard square with Digby's latest. 'So he borrowed or hired a car whilst it was being mended and it was that one your boys found burnt out by the wayside?'

'If you must know, it was a Ford Fiesta from Avis.'

Good Lord. Digby offering a nugget of info. Wonders will never cease. But that was all I got out of him that morning, for he then swivelled his mass off the stool and stood up.

'I have to get back now. I have the rest of the hotel guests to interview.' He leaned towards me. 'Wouldn't want to keep your ace TV researcher's parents waiting, now would I?'

I nodded him forward towards the shop door. Be he hadn't quite finished with me.

As I opened it wide, he said, 'So you still maintain you've never officially met Jacob Fern.' He patted the doorframe. 'He hasn't ever come round here as a customer.'

'We've been through all this, Inspector. It's "Yes" to the first question. And "No", as far as I know, to the second.'

He frowned at me. 'This is new. The "as far as I know" addition. What do you mean by it?'

'Nothing, really. Only once in an odd while, the shop is open when I can't be here.'

'And then ... ?'

'Someone holds the fort for me.'

'Always the same someone?'

'Yes.'

'Who, may I ask?'

'You've met him. Quite a few times. Gus Tribble.'

Digby breathed deeply. I'm sure to hide his true reaction to the name. For Gus and Digby always got on like a house on fire – Digby's.

'Would you know whether Mr Tribble will be at home during the day? I obviously would like to ask him the same question I've asked you.'

Suddenly a giant 'No' boomed out across the shop. Megaphonic source – from behind us. I whipped round to see that Gus, like some massive genie from a bottle, had emanated from behind the counter. I'd completely forgotten I'd left him in the sitting-room when Digby had first dinged the doorbell. And no prizes for guessing he'd overheard every blasted word that had passed between us.

When Gus was sure we both had our ears bent, he reverberated on: 'No. Never seen him in me life. So don't bother your helmet to come round.'

Digby had now recovered sufficiently to ask, 'How can you be so sure, Mr Trib – ?'

'Knew his dad, didn't I?' Gus interrupted. 'And saw the bleedin' pictures on the telly news this morning, when I turned on too late for the forecast, sod it.'

Gus moved out from behind the counter. I must say he can look a shade menacing when he wants to.

'The young Fern's never been in here. So don't you try and tell me,' he prodded a digit towards me, 'or my friend here that he has. Understand?'

Exit Digby Whetstone pretty pronto, with only a half-stifled oath. Gus grinned at me as the Rover pulled away past the windows.

'Well, old lad, that got rid of him.'

'He was going anyway, Gus,' I pointed out. Gus's face fell.

'There's gratitude,' he grumbled.

I knew what gratitude he was after. And it didn't come out of a mouth, but out of a can.

I patted his shoulder. 'Come back in then.'

66

He must have noticed the weariness in my voice, for he instantly said, 'Worried, aren't you?'

I nodded and started propelling him back into the sitting-room.

''Bout your aunty?'

'About the whole thing. Graves, diaries, hotels, you name it, someone seems to have it in for me, don't you think?'

He stopped by the pedal car. 'This the thing you bought over at the cottage?'

I nodded and he walked and talked on. ''Ere, don't let that Digby get to you. He only came here to get you going, because he'd found half a ruddy excuse. The name of this 'ere shop must be in diary after bloody diary. And I don't suppose the murderer hung about to read headstones when he dumped the body. And as for that stuck-up hotel, hundreds of people must go to eat there, like what you did. It's only prize berks like Digby who'd go making anything of it.'

As I slid in front of him and into the house, he slapped my back. No doubt it was a generous gesture of encouragement. All the same, it almost felled me. Gus doesn't know his own – anything.

After I'd emitted an 'Eaghhh . . .' I went on. 'Could be you're right, Gus. Let's hope so, anyway.'

I was just starting to feel a little easier about things when I hiccuped over something I'd completely forgotten. My time at Dendron Park hadn't all been spent in the Trenchs', so to speak. There'd been a little old lady who had hijacked me about another little old lady's break-in. And the first LOL, what's more, I'd seen with my very own eyes Daimlerising with with yer actual deceased.

The Heinekens hissed not a moment too soon.

5

After Gus had eventually upped stakes there was not much of the morning left. And it seemed the weather had frozen all but one old-toy nutter off Dorset's streets. A raincoated and baggy-trousered oddity who didn't look as if he had a penny piece to bless himself with, let alone the eighty-five pounds he claimed he was willing to pay for a mint boxed Dinky 'King's Aeroplane'. (Produced in 1938/9, it was basically Dinky's Envoy tarted up most decoratively in red, blue and silver to depict an aircraft used by King George VI.) Sod's law, of course, decreed that I was fresh out of King's Aeroplanes and he turned his slightly crooked nose up at a mint green Envoy of similar vintage. (Going rate well under half that of the royal version, such a difference doth a lick of paint make.)

Because of my curtailed morning I kept open until a quarter to two, but no more punters shivered in to blow on their hands. So I slipped the bolts on the door and was about to slip round to the local just up the road for a quick bite – there were plenty of bite-worthy goodies in my fridge, but I felt, *après tout*, that I needed a change of scene – when the telephone rang in the hall. Thinking it was probably Arabella with an update from Dendron Park Hotel, I trotted to answer it without a qualm.

It was a female, all right, but, alas, not my brush-haired beauty.

'Mr Marklin?' Even from those meagre two words, I could tell something was up. I was instantly armed with the most comprehensive set of qualms you can get from the worry shop.

'Yes. Speaking.'

I racked my brains to remember where I'd heard that accent before.

'Mr Marklin, you must help me.' The tension in her voice was even more marked now.

I cleared my throat. 'I'm sorry, but I need a little help right now. Like how about letting on who you are first.'

'Oh . . . er . . . yes . . . I'm Mrs Sandle. Linda Sandle.'

'Should I know you?' Then, the split second before she replied, I realised where I had heard her voice before.

'We met the other day. You came round about a pedal car.'

'Yes, I remember. But how can I help you?'

My first thought was that perhaps she'd sold the car when she actually had no right to it – hence the furtive manner – and now she was about to ask for it back. But how wrong can you be?

'It's my husband . . .' Big gap, so I filled it with, 'Your husband? What about your husband?'

'It's the . . . police, see.'

Did I see? Not right then. And the non sequitur that sequitured hardly helped.

'If it's money you're worried about, don't. I'll pay you–'

I had to break in. 'Mrs . . . er . . . Sandle. I'm sorry but I don't quite follow. Perhaps it might help if you began again. Take your time.'

Another gap, I heard her take a deep breath, and then she restarted, all in a rush. 'I need your help, Mr Marklin. Because of the police, see. They've taken my husband in. And he didn't do it. I know he didn't. But with his record, he doesn't stand an earthly. I've got the money, Mr Marklin. You just say what you want and I'll ruddy make sure I get it together–'

I stopped her. 'Mrs Sandle, before you go any further, where did you get the idea that I was some kind of professional private eye? Because I'm afraid you're mistaken. Sorry.'

'You do help people, though. I know that for sure.'

'Who told you?'

'Remember that ice-cream chap?* I know his aunty. She said if it hadn't been for you . . .'

*Wind Up (1990)

That's the trouble with being an amateur sleuth. Those you help can well have motor-mouthed relations.

I sighed. 'Look, Mrs Sandle, I'm sure you shouldn't be so worried about your husband. If he's innocent of whatever, then the police will soon release him and he'll be back home with you in no time.'

'No, he won't. Because ... well ... he doesn't live with me, exactly. We're separated. Have been ever since–' She stopped abruptly.

Like a fool, I stepped in the breach. 'Ever since what?'

'Since ... well ... since he's been inside.'

Oh Lord, here we went. 'Inside? But he can't *still* be inside if you say the police have taken him in again.'

'He isn't. He did his time, he did. Came out a couple of weeks back. But once a con, no one believes you, see? That's why I rang you. They'll try and nail it on him, if they ruddy well can.'

'Nail what?'

'Oh ... but you must have heard about it. Been on all the news, it has.'

Now I knew for certain what was coming. She went on, her voice in a quieter gear, no doubt out of respect for the dead.

'That boy, Fern. The one they found in the graveyard. You must have–'

'Yes, I've heard.' Far, far too much already.

'Well, just because my hubby ['hubby' now] knew him years ago, they reckon he must be the one who done him in. And I know he didn't. Couldn't have. My old man's never been a saint. But he's not a bloody murderer. Burglary's about the limit with him, honest.'

'Is that why he did time? Just burglary?'

She hesitated before replying. 'Burglary with ... er ... violence. But it wasn't violent violence, if you know what I mean. Just knocked out and tied up the owner of the jewellery shop, that's all.'

That was all. Nothing. Told you so, Marklin. I suddenly decided the water was getting decidedly too deep and icy for me, so I cut for shore with, 'Mrs Sandle, I really am

70

very sorry to hear about your problem, but I'm afraid I must ask you to leave it to the law. They're not nearly as biased as you are inferring. They know there's a helluva difference between burglary and murder and the minds that can commit them. Besides, they've probably only asked your husband to go to the station so that they can quiz him about Fern and not about himself. After all, they're probably interviewing all those who've known Fern over the years and not just your husband.'

She didn't respond immediately, which I took to be reflection on my very valid theory. But wrong again.

'A thousand pounds, Mr Marklin,' she said at last. 'A grand. And I might be able to raise a bit more.'

I was somewhat amazed at the amount. After all, when I'd met her in Chez Tumbledown she looked no more capable of raising a bean than a smile.

'No, it's not a matter of money, Mrs Sandle. I've never helped anyone for payment. Now I must ask you, once again, to leave it in the hands of the police. Anyway, it's far too early yet for you to start worrying–'

I stopped when I heard the click. There was no need to enquire whether she was still on the line. I knew already that Mrs Sandle wasn't like that. To her kind, people were only born to be used. And if they wouldn't or couldn't play, then wham, bam, she'd cut 'em dead.

Mrs Sandle certainly cut dead my 'change of scene' mood. Somehow a bustling pub, even with a roaring open hearth, no longer fitted the bill. So I made do with the fridge fare. Not that I really had much of an appetite, after a dose of Digby and a slice of Sandle. And a huge potful of Fern. Hell, I couldn't quite believe what was happening. And yet I knew I had to, if Marklin was to survive it all sane and vaguely in one piece.

By the time I'd double-swallowed my last knob of Brie-bedecked French bread, I felt like opening up shop and beaming at customers, were the weather to thaw some out, like a grouse looks forward to the glorious twelfth. In the end, I postponed the evil hour by trying to get hold of my beloved at the TV studios. But no luck, dammit. She and her team were still out. I left a message instead. And not just about ringing me back.

So the evil hour enjoyed a big ha-ha as I slid back the bolts on my door and slouched towards my counter to await the onslaught that I knew was unlikely to come. Crusts have to be earned – especially as I'd just downed the last of the French bread.

But my mind was toying with Sandles and Digbys, rather than Schucos and Dinkies and all that infinitely preferable jazz. As far as Whetstone was concerned, I couldn't get much further than the non-conclusions Gus and I had come to earlier. Sandle, however, was a whole different bag, if you'll pardon the expression.

The more I thought about her call, the more giant question marks it raised. Samples: Did she really hear about me from the ice-cream guy's aunty or had she got my number, if you understand me, from some other connection? If so, like who or what, for Christ's sake? What's more, if she had been separated from him all the years of porridge that he must have served for robbery with violence, then why was she suddenly so concerned about his welfare now? What's extra more, if she and he were really separated, how did she know he hadn't killed Fern? *And* what would it be to her if he had?

Then, suddenly, I remembered she lived in a cottage rented from the dead man's father. Curiouser and curiouser. Maybe she was scared that old man Fern would throw her out of her tenancy if she couldn't prove her husband had absolutely nothing to do with his son's death. After all, who would want the wife, estranged or not, of a murderer living at the end of your drive as a reminder of your son's tragedy every time you took car or tractor on to the road. Certainly not me.

But the real humdinger amongst all the questions that bugged me, was how the heck a lady living in a rented, neglected cottage could claim to be able to lay her hands on the kind of spondulicks she bandied around on the blower. All I could imagine was that she must have been lying, just to get me going. And then hope to trade on my good nature (the aunty of the ice-cream guy might just have intimated to her that I actually had one) when the time eventually came to live up to her promise. Who knew? God, I hoped somebody did.

Just before three the telephone dinged me out of my doldrums. I picked up the receiver cautiously, just in case I got booted by another Sandle. But praise be, it was Arabella. She got straight to the point.

'Sandle. Dennis. Age forty-three. Sentenced to eight years for robbery with violence. Released just over two weeks ago. That's all our computer's got on him,' she rattled off before asking, 'Now, my darling. I've answered your question. Now try mine. What on earth's prompted the question?'

I brought her up to date with my whole day, which was starting to feel more like a whole week.

'That's the second assignment you've turned down in as many days,' she reminded me, trying to cheer me up. Then she went on, 'In a way, it would be a great relief if this Sandle person is found to be the murderer and then Digby will get off your back and you can forget about it all. Little harder for me, as I think my parents are going to be reminding me of this holiday for ever and a day.'

'Heard from them since they were interviewed?'

'They called and left a message. They want to move out of the Dendron Park.'

'Don't blame them. Did they say where they're going?'

'No. I'm going to ring them the moment I put down on you. Then I've got to settle down here to sort out my notes and try to make them add up to a pithy news item for the six-thirty slot tonight.'

'Been out all day?'

'I had an interview with poor Mrs Robbins. And the chef. And one of the waitresses. Usual stuff. Oh, and despite what the boys in blue said, I tried to get hold of Fern's father. But his housekeeper said he was still too cut up to see anyone. Not surprising.'

'Well, I'll let you get back to it. Thanks for ringing.'

73

'Thank *you*, my love. You've given us a brand-new lead in this Sandle fellow. When the police have finished with him, I'll try to track him down. We've only his old address listed on the computer. And his wife moved out of there yonks ago. Must go now.' She blew a kiss down the phone. I'm not about to tell you what we call that practice. 'Won't be late tonight. DV.' She signed off.

The gods were kind. And she wasn't.

Arabella stretched her long legs out across my knee. I stroked a hand across the smooth nylon. Calf love, you could say.

I rested my head back against the settee cushions, glad, at last, to be back in the serene world of just Arabella, me and the ticking of the Napoleon-hatted clock on the mantelpiece.

After a delicious silence she observed quietly, 'By the way, my parents are thinking of moving into the Royal Bath tomorrow. They've discovered they have rooms.'

'Quite a few,' I smiled. 'It's some contrast to the small and so-called exclusive Dendron Park.'

'They say your little old lady was very upset when they told her they might be going.'

I opened my eyes and turned my head towards her. 'She's not *my* little old lady. She doesn't own me.'

'I think she may think she owns you. Like . . . er . . .'

'Like er . . . what?'

'Well, I didn't want to tell you the minute I got in the door, but she says she's talked to her break-in friend and the verdict is that she'd like you to go over and see her yourself. Like you promised, apparently.'

I exhaled my irritation. 'I only said I'd go if she couldn't convince her that the police were the best people to call in, not me.'

'I guess she couldn't convince her.'

I made the low grumbly noise a dog does when he's just been told 'walkies' have been cancelled.

'I'd better pop over first thing in the morning and get it over with.'

74

She reached across and patted my hand.

'Good boy,' she grinned. Now I felt even more like a canine. Then she went on, her big eyes brightening. 'Hey, you don't think Fern might have had something to do with the break-in, do you? I mean he obviously knew this Bessy Meade, so he could well have known her friend.'

'Why've you made the connection? Have you heard something abut Fern I haven't?'

'Not really. It's just that both the chef and a waitress at the hotel more or less hinted that Fern was not all that their boss, Mrs Robbins, imagined him to be. The chef, a man called Alistair Frame – I didn't like him much – garlic-breathed that he wouldn't be surprised if Fern's past wouldn't bear too much scrutiny.' She crossed her legs, trapping my hand between them. Who am I to complain? She continued, knowing full well what her action was causing. 'And I was just putting this together with what you've told me the Sandle woman said about her ex-con husband knowing him at one time.'

'Could be making five,' I pointed out.

'Could be. But all the same, it's an interesting coincidence, isn't it?'

I changed tack. 'Digby's press conference this morning. From the fact that you haven't brought it up, I take it that he had nothing but the usual police platitudes to offer at this stage.'

'That's more or less it. There weren't even any suggestions as to possible motives, let alone leads as to who might have done it.'

'Weapon been found yet?'

She shook her head. 'Not that they're telling. About the only thing Digby ventured was the theory that the murderer probably abandoned and then burned Fern's hire car *after* dumping the body on your aunty's grave.'

'The burning to defeat the forensic boys?'

'Exactly.'

'That the lot?' I hoped.

'Only one thing and then I'll shut up,' she grinned, scissoring my hand with her calves. 'I feel very sorry for Mrs

75

Robbins. And not just because she's lost her toy boy, either. She'll lose a lot of business. Bound to, with all this shock-horror publicity. After the last two bad seasons, I wouldn't have thought she could afford it. She certainly seemed a very sad woman when I interviewed her. Unfair, isn't it? Suddenly, out of the blue, she could have lost everything.'

Arabella's comment triggered a thought.

'Perhaps your parents should rethink their plans to move, in case it encourages a mass exodus. You know how sheep-like people can be.'

My beloved pondered on't, then lowered her lids to dissect the expression on my face.

'A little bird suggests to me, my darling, that your suggestion may not be a hundred per cent selfless.'

I shrugged.

She went on. 'Would I be right in thinking that, in the back of your mind, you have an idea that my dear old parents might just come in handy to you at Dendron Park? Like, if by any chance you were to get dragged deeper into all this mess?'

Sometimes I hate George Washington. So I could not but reply: 'The thought must have some merit for you and your crime-busting programme, too, I would imagine. Spies in the camp and all that.'

'I hate you,' she frowned and fretted her legs against each other and, worse, my hand, like some grasshopper.

'So you'll try to get them to stay?' I suggested, when I'd stopped wincing.

'For Mrs Robbins.'

'Of course. Who else?'

She blinked in slow motion. I extricated my hand, fast forward.

'What did you do that for?' She pulled herself more upright. I smoothed the skin on the hand in question. It felt very warm.

'Scissoring is one thing. Grasshoppering is quite another.'

Arabella swung her legs off my lap and folded them neatly beneath her. She then kneed herself right up to me and whispered in my shell-like, 'Don't you know why grasshoppers rub their legs together?'

'No. Tell me,' I lied.

So she told me, midst lobe-nibbling. We didn't eat that evening until really quite late. Food, that is.

Next morning, soon as I'd seen to my post, I kept my promise and rang Bessy Meade at the hotel. She seemed over the moon to hear from me and we made an immediate arrangement for me to come over.

'Like to drive my old Daimler?' she invited. 'We can go over to my friend's in that, if you'd care to.'

I cared to, not often having the opportunity to get behind stately old steering wheels like that of her Conquest.

Whereupon she added happily, 'Oh, and I'm so glad to hear that Mr and Mrs Trench have changed their minds about leaving here. I feel we should all try to show our solidarity behind poor Louise Robbins in this her time of travail, don't you agree?'

Good old Arabella. She'd obviously woven her magic. Mind you, the tale we'd both concocted for her to spin to her parents wasn't half bad: that they could well be aiding her professional TV career by staying put and keeping eyes and ears open and akimbo. I heard later from Arabella that her father had seemed actually to relish the idea of being an amateur spy and had even staccatoed the initials 'MI5' at her, under his breath.

Anyway, five minutes after putting down the phone, I was out by my Beetle. I had half thought of asking Gus to mind the store in my absence, but had come to the conclusion that all the inevitable kerfuffle and complication weren't warranted for the short time I intended to be away. So, muffled up to the eyeballs against the frigid chill, I started scraping away at the frost on my windscreen with an old plastic spatula pinched from the kitchen. I had just about cleared enough to be able to spot at least the bonnet when I heard the clump, clump of heavy feet behind me. I didn't need to look round.

77

'Okay, Gus. So what have you heard on the wireless now?'

'Nothing, old son. Been too bloody busy, I have, to bother about no wireless.'

I couldn't believe my soon-to-be-frostbitten ears. Gus busy at this early hour? I turned towards him. Now I didn't believe my eyes. There was hardly any Gus to be seen. Just a blue/purpling nose and a pair of what passed for peepers. The rest can best be described as a walking ragbag of woolly and hairy garments that must have been over a foot thick and covered him from head to toe.

'Gus, where are the dogs?' I asked in amazement.

'Dogs?' he muttered, in a cloud of condensation.

'Yes, dogs. Those husky things. You'll never get to the North Pole without them. No one has.'

He tried to swing a dismissive arm, but the restriction of the overcoats (yes, plural) he was wearing rather limited the gesture.

'Get away, you berk. No laughing matter what I've had to ruddy deal with this morning.'

'Okay, I'll listen. But make it snappy. If I stand out here much longer, the brass monkeys will leave home.'

'Pipe, see. In the roof. Bloody went and burst now, didn't it? Been up half the night swabbing up the water, other half in the roof trying to mend the sod.'

Well, that partly explained the tonnage of his apparel. I'd had to go up into my attic a few days before to fish out two sets of Britain's lead soldiers to send to auction and had felt like Amundsen by the time I'd returned.

Knowing Gus was no plumber, I was silly enough to ask, 'How on earth did you fix it?'

'Haven't yet. Had to turn the water off in the end.'

'In the end? You're kidding. You're meant to do that before you start.'

'Any road,' he went on, glowering at me, 'came up to see if I could use your phone, so I can get a rotten plumber.'

I laughed at his choice of plumbing adjective. 'Course you can. But what's wrong with your own phone?'

'Water ruddy got in it, what d'yer think?'

I repressed a further laugh and escorted the rag mountain into the house. Some five minutes later he trundled back into the kitchen with a rich assortment of oaths.

'What's wrong?'

'Can't ruddy come till this afternoon, can they? Trot out the excuse that mine isn't the only pipe wot burst last night.'

'Well, it was minus ten centigrade, Gus,' I reminded him. Hardly a helpful remark, but what can you say? If it hadn't been for my central heating and my keeping the loft door open, I too could have been paddling up Gus's particular creek. So I followed up quickly by offering him a hot drink of his choice.

He instantly plumped for Heineken. I didn't join him.

No prizes for guessing who came with me to the Dendron Park Hotel. Once I'd updated him on the Sandle phone call and Arabella's news, let alone on the somewhat odd request of Bessy Meade, he insisted. I, in turn, insisted that he doff at least half his clothing before daring to set foot out of my Beetle. Walking ragbags can play havoc with old ladies' pacemakers.

Though the sun tried sneaking through the pinky greyness of the clouds once in a while, the air temperature was still below freezing; and my Volks's heater was more or less defeated by the draughts that percolated through my leaky soft top. The Sandbanks ferry didn't exactly help, forcing us to sit, engine turned off, for the crossing of the Poole harbour entrance.

To keep my mind off my frozen fate, I asked Gus if he had any bright ideas about any part of the Fern affair, because I sure as hell didn't.

He blew on his mittened hands, then ran his tongue around the stumps of what teeth had miraculously survived his neglect. He countered my question with a question of his own.

'Jeweller, did you say, that woman's worse half knocked about and robbed?'

'That's what I said. Why?'

'Oh,' he sniffed. 'Well, I was just wondering, see, if he robbed a jeweller, what happened to what he stole.'

'The loot?'

'Yeah. I mean, did the rozzers get it all back or just some of it or none of it or what?'

I kicked myself for not having thought to ask Arabella.

'I have no idea. Sorry, Gus.'

He looked round at me through the eyeslit of his umpteenth scarf, which, had it been white, would have rendered him a dead ringer for the Invisible Man.

'Don't tell me, old mate, your great brain's slipping.'

'Must be the ice,' I smirked. 'But you're right. I should have thought of it. Might be important.'

He sniffed again. 'Just what passed through my mind. Might explain the whole ruddy shooting match, mightn't it?'

'Clubbing match, actually. Fern wasn't shot.'

'Figure of speech, old son. Figure of speech.'

I failed to suppress a smile. It's not often you can get one over on Gus. He went on, staring out of the misting windscreen towards the Sandbanks landing ramp. 'Any old road, if the loot was never recovered, see, perhaps Fern got to hear where it was stashed and half-inched it, while this 'ere bloke was in the nick. Bingo, once he's released, he goes to where he had it hidden and it's gone. He gets mad, reckons Fern was behind it and does him in.'

Gus's theory wasn't half bad. That's the thing about Gus. Sometimes he can come up with a real gem. (In this case, almost literally). Trouble is, you never know when he's going to mine one out of the wild and woolly workings of his mind.

'Could be,' I readily admitted. 'What's more, it's just possible that Fern could have been in on the robbery itself. Or perhaps acting as a fence or whatever.'

The ferry, by then, was clanking the last hundred yards to the ramp, so our theorising was cut short. By the time I had started up the engine and accelerated up on to dry land, Gus and I were just concentrating on thawing out our

80

frames, so that we could save poor Bessy Meade from chipping us out of the Beetle at Dendron Park.

Praise be, as we pulled into the hotel forecourt, I saw a plume of condensation issuing from the old Daimler's rear end. Someone had obviously had the sense to get the car out and warmed up before our arrival, to prevent us dying of hypothermia a second time.

That someone turned out to be Bessy Meade herself. She had enlisted the services of the chef, Alistair Frame – her usual unofficial chauffeur – who was sitting in the driver's seat, foot on the accelerator, and looking none too pleased with life.

I left Gus in the Beetle and went over to the high and, by today's standards, dumpy-looking veteran. (The Conquest had been Daimler's 'cooking' product in the first half of the fifties. Priced not far off a Rover, but offering the crinkly radiator and well-furnished image of the horseless carriage then preferred by your Royals. Respect, not adrenalin, raising was both its aim and effect.)

A rather sallow, surly face eyed me through a closed window. Under a heavy dark smudge of a moustache, I saw lips mouth something. I had to go right up to the door to hear what they were actually saying.

'Mrs Meade is in the lobby.'

As it was quite clear that smudge-face wasn't about to risk pneumonia by lowering the window, I pointed a finger towards the hotel entrance and mouthed back at him, 'I'll go and get her.'

Receiving a half-hearted nod, I waved my hand and went on in through the hotel's revolving doors, where the heat hit me like an oven door.

Bessy Meade rose from the lobby's rather ornate settle the second she saw me and greeted me with a buss on the cheek, as if she'd known me for ever. She seemed even more minute than I remembered her.

'So very good of you to come, Peter.' She had an already gloved hand to her mouth in mock apology. 'Oh, I may call you Peter, mayn't I? But I should have asked first.'

81

'You may.'

'And I'm Bessy.' She picked up her handbag from the settle and took my arm.

'You may have seen, I've got Alistair – our chef, you know – to warm up the car for us.' She lowered her voice and looked up at me. 'I think he's a bit put out. I haven't asked him to do the driving to Muriel's.' She squeezed my arm. 'But I thought you might like the experience. Ever driven a Daimler before? Mine's got the funny Fluid Flywheel.'

'Yes, I've driven a Daimler. Got an old one myself. But a bit younger than yours. A 1966 V8. The one with the Jaguar-shape body.'

'Yes, I remember it well. If I'd had the money, I'd have bought one to replace my old thing.'

I let her precede me through the revolving doors. Once outside, I saw her eyes searching the forecourt.

'Where is it?' she enquired. 'I can't seem to see your Daimler.'

I pointed to my yellow Beetle.

'Use a Volkswagen for every day. Drive the Daimler only once in a blue moon. I keep it in a friend's barn and the battery always seems to be flat when I think of taking it out.'

She looked a trifle disappointed. 'Anyway, we'd better be off to Muriel's. She'll be all agog watching through the curtains for us already.'

Bessy knocked on the Conquest's window and Alistair Frame opened the driver's door and got out. I was quite surprised to note how tall he was. Bessy Meade looked like some elderly pixie beside him. She did the introductions and his handshake almost crippled me. Besides the regular 'How d'you do?' his only other repartee was, 'Careful with the brakes.'

'Right,' I said, without a salute and he strode off back into the hotel. Bessy was just about to trot around to the front passenger door when she spotted the giant shape huddling in my car.

'Oh, have you brought a friend, Peter?'

I nodded and beckoned to Gus.

'I hope you don't mind. If you do, I'm sure he'd be happy in the hotel until we come back.'

What a liar I can be at times. I only said it because I'd have bet money Bessy wouldn't quibble.

'No, I'm sure Muriel won't mind. The more brains on her break-in, the better.'

As Gus, sans one layer of clouts I was relieved to see, shambled out of the Beetle, Bessy asked in a confidential whisper, 'He your Watson?'

I had to laugh. 'Not quite. But sometimes his intuition is amazing. He's helped me quite a bit in the past.'

I think that perhaps, as the ragbag of Gus came nearer, Bessy found it all a bit hard to credit. I explained he was a martyr to the cold. However, she was most effusive in both her greeting and her thanks for his coming along. To all of which, Gus grunted his usual diplomatic, 'Yeah . . . well . . .'

'It's Gus's barn that I keep my Daimler in,' I explained, to cover the hiatus, and then we all clambered into the Conquest. The interior, with the chill off, smelt of old saddle soap with a whiff of lavender. (She always kept a sprig of the latter in the glove box, she told me later. 'Not merely for luck, Peter. To sweeten the oil smell, when the engine gets really hot.')

I slipped the steering wheel lever into first, depressed and released the clutch, and off we whined into the road. Everything felt very loose and strange after the relative tightness of my Beetle and the bonnet seemed as high as a church and almost as long.

'Managing, Peter?' Bessy smiled across at me. I caught Gus's eyeslit in the rear-view mirror. The pupils looked none too restful.

'Fine, thanks. No problems.'

I discreetly tested the brakes, just in case. Nothing seemed to happen. I tried again, this time less discreetly. There was a squeal and the steering wheel twitched to the right. Third time I put my foot right to the floor. We started to slow. Given the length of an aircraft runway, I dare say we would have eventually come to a stop.

'I should, perhaps, have warned you, Peter, the brakes are not quite as sharp as they were. But not to worry too much. Poor old Oddie [its registration number started with ODD] can't get up to any speed these days, can you my love?' She patted the cracking wood veneer in front of her affectionately.

Well, that was all hunky-dory then, wasn't it? I drove from then on as if I were following a funeral cortège. Might save my being its star turn. Bessy gave me an elaborate set of directions to her friend's bungalow, which, at my and Oddie's snail's pace, took some little time to reach. To pass some of said time, I asked her how Mrs Robbins seemed to be surviving.

'Oh, as well as can be expected, I suppose. I saw her only briefly this morning and she still looked very pale.' She sighed. 'It's all such a terrible business. Terrible.'

'I take it she was very . . . fond of Mr Fern,' I probed.

'Dear, oh dear, yes. I suppose she must have been.'

Her distaste for the idea was not hard to discern.

She went on, 'If only you'd known the late Mr Robbins, Peter. Now there was a fine, fine man. Such a tragedy that a heart attack should have taken him from us in the prime of life.' She was silent for a second and then resumed. 'I can so understand why, after his death, Mrs Robbins felt she needed someone . . . well, to help her in the running of the hotel. To be a trusted friend and companion. No doubt this Mr Fern, when he met her, must have recognised this need and, well, not to put too fine a point on it, decided to exploit it for all it was worth.'

She looked across at me, a slight flush of embarrassment evident on her cheeks. 'I shouldn't speak ill of the dead, Peter, I know I shouldn't. But somehow, there was something about Mr Fern that none of us at the hotel liked. His selfishness and motives were always so apparent. To everyone except, I suppose, poor Mrs Robbins. If only she'd realised that he was only out for what he could get.'

'His dad wasn't a bit like that,' Gus grunted from the back seat.

Bessy swivelled her head round. 'Really, Mr Tribble? I take it you must have known him.'

'Off and on. From when I was a nipper.'

'Yes, I did hear that the older Mr Fern is quite a pillar of his local church. Such a pity that his son did not follow in his footsteps.'

She looked back at me. 'You turn right at the next lights, Peter.'

I nodded and to my horror, saw them suddenly turn red. I instantly slammed my foot right to the floor and prayed for the souls in the brand-new Fiesta in front of us. But a second later I knew I and they would never make it. In desperation I resorted to the old scrubbers' technique I'd perfected when, yonks ago, I owned an Austin Pearl. You swing the car to the left and let the kerbstones scrub the side of your tyres to a stop. It worked. Just. By an overrider's breadth. Or rather, depth.

After, heart still in mouth, I'd turned right, I said, 'It will, no doubt, be quite some time before Mrs Robbins can start to forget–'

'And the police aren't exactly helping,' Bessy cut in. 'That Inspector Whatshisname – the one who needs to go on a diet–'

'Whetstone,' Gus offered from the rear.

'Yes, that's it, Mr Tribble. Whetstone. Well, he was back to see Mrs Robbins again, would you believe, before nine this morning. We were all still at breakfast.'

'Any idea what brought him back?' I asked, glancing across at her.

She put on her naughty-little-girl look again. How come little old ladies are so good at it?

'Well, I might have just a teensy inkling of what it was about this time.'

I responded to her invitation. 'And what's that?'

'Well, I was just going up to my room when Mrs Robbins' office door opened and the Inspector came out. I overheard him say something like, "Well, Mrs Robbins, I just wanted to double-check, that's all". And then I heard Mrs Robbins' voice – I couldn't see her; she didn't come out – say "If

I'd gone out at all, Inspector, you can be sure I'd have told you". Something like that, anyway.'

I brewed on it, then asked, 'Do you think she was talking about the night of the murder?'

She looked at me. 'Don't you?'

'Sounds a bit like it.'

The Daimler's engine coughed as I tried to coax it up a slight incline. 'I know old Whetstone quite well,' I went on. 'It's typical of him to check and double-check and fret over detail. He's often so busy doing that, he misses the main point entirely.'

Bessy made no reaction. I looked at her and I could see she was still worried.

'What's the trouble? Thought of something else?'

She shook her head. 'No, same thing, Peter, really.'

'Tell me.'

She took a breath. 'Well, it's just that . . . you see, if Louise, that's Mrs Robbins, was referring to the night of Fern's murder, then she wasn't . . . er . . .'

I came to her aid. 'Speaking the truth?'

'Oh dear, I shouldn't really be saying all this, perhaps. But I do so want to help poor Louise . . .'

I looked in the rear-view mirror. 'Gus and I won't say a word. Promise.'

'All right then. I appreciate it. Well, it's like this. I have awful trouble sleeping sometimes, you see, Peter. And that dreadful night it was so bad that I got up around two to get some aspirin. As I was passing the window, I thought I heard a car pulling in outside. It seemed a little strange at that hour, so I peeped through the curtains to see who it might be.' She reached across and lightly touched my knee. 'After my friend's break-in, I've become a little more nervous, I suppose.'

'And it was Mrs Robbins?'

'Yes. I keep asking myself since whether I saw right. But it was her car. I know that little Peugeot well. She gives me lifts in it sometimes, though in the summer when she's got the top down I find it a little blowy.'

'And she was driving it?'

'Well, not when I actually looked out. She'd parked it by then and was just getting out of it. She was wearing that new red coat she bought herself for Christmas.'

I probed a little further. 'Did you recognise her just by the coat? Or–'

'I know what's going through your sleuthing brain, Peter. That it might have been someone other than Mrs Robbins driving her car and wearing that coat.'

'And it definitely wasn't?'

She sighed. 'I do so wish it had been. But she looked up, you see, just as she was coming in. And the light from the lobby – well, unless Louise has a twin sister she's never told anybody about or I'm going senile or dotty or something . . .'

I negotiated the last left-hander into Simpson Close, at the far end of which was our destination, a bungalow going by the name of 'Tra-La', would you believe?

'I take it you've not mentioned any of this to Mrs Robbins since?'

She shook her head vigorously. By a miracle and a lethal-looking pin with a peacock on its blunt end, her hat remained in situ.

'No, of course not. I wouldn't have dreamt of it. Anyway, until this morning I didn't imagine it might have any significance. Louise Robbins has always been the most honest and straightforward of people. I've never heard her utter even a half-truth before.'

By then I was far too busy to comment. Concentrating on stopping the old Daimler before it didn't just call at 'Tra-La', but sailed right on in to her dear Muriel's living-room.

Despite the cold, Muriel Purkiss was already waiting at the front door by the time we'd climbed down from the Daimler. Just from a glance I could see why Bessy Meade would wish to be her minder in times of trouble. No, she wasn't even more minute than Bessy, nor more aged. Quite the reverse, in fact, Muriel was tallish and I guessed her to be a handful of years younger than her friend. But there was a frailty about both her physique and manner that showed a mile off. As my old mother would have phrased it, she looked as if a puff of wind would blow her away.

Bessy wisely suggested we did the introductions indoors in the warm. Muriel's handshake was literally that. A shaking hand that dithered in my grasp.

'I'm so very grateful to you for sparing the time, Mr Marklin.' Her voice sounded like Spike Milligan taking off Edith Piaf. 'And you, Mr Tribble.' I smiled and Gus 'yeah, welled'.

We all doffed our coats and Bessy led us through into the small, bay-windowed sitting-room. Again the contrast with Bessy Meade was well marked. For where Bessy's rooms in the hotel were highly personal in their furnishings and effects and general clutter, Muriel Purkiss's bungalow could have been anybody's – of her general age, anyway. Everything was neat and tidy to a fault, but the shine seemed synthetic and not the result of years of labour and love. The walls cried out for pictures or some form of adornment to give life to the room. Even the patterns of the wallpaper and the loose covers on settee and chairs were so bland, with tiny, tiny blossoms on a beige background, that I almost felt breathing might be too much of a statement for the environment to handle.

We all sat down, I opposite Muriel, Bessy beside Gus amongst the bloomers on the settee. It was she who started the bowling.

'Now, Muriel, as we don't want to waste precious time, why don't you tell Peter right away about the break-in?'

A bony, loose-skinned hand hovered in the air. 'But shouldn't I see if anyone would like a cup of tea or coffee first?'

Bessy looked at me and then at Gus. We both shook our heads.

'How about telling your story first, Muriel, and then we'll see about any refreshment?'

The hand fluttered down to a lap. I could smell mothballs even from where I was sitting.

'Well, Mr Marklin, I don't know quite what to say.' Her

fingers started knitting themselves together. I could hardly take my eyes off them. 'You see, I just came down the other morning and went straight to the kitchen to put the kettle on. I thought it was a bit colder in there than the rest of the house. And then I saw ... oh dear ... where the draught was coming from. One of the panes of the window had been smashed. And the catch wasn't secured, so that the window was flapping.'

She took a deep breath, then looked at me. 'That's it, really, Mr Marklin. I don't know what else ...'

Her voice quavered away to nothing, so I stepped in to save any embarrassment.

'From what Bessy has told me, nothing seems to be missing. Is that right?'

I saw her eyes flick across to her friend, before descending to her lap and the still knitting fingers.

'No, no, no,' she said quickly. 'I mean, I suppose, yes, yes ... Oh dear, what I mean to say is that yes, you're right. But no, there's nothing missing ... that I can see.'

I wondered how much reliance I could really put on her assertion, in view of her dithery nature and, perhaps, therefore, rather uncertain recall of what she might or might not have owned over the years. However, to question her claim right that second would hardly have constituted a diplomatic start.

'So there was nothing missing. But what about damage other than the window? I gather from Bessy that drawers had been opened and stuff strewn about a bit.'

Muriel blinked at a rate of knots. "No, it wasn't all that bad, Mr Marklin. Not all that ... well, Bessy very kindly came over as soon as I rang her and we soon got things straight again.'

I felt I had to say it, just in case the intruder returned.

'You shouldn't have, you know. You should have left everything as it was and called the police.'

She shook her head and a hairpin dislodged itself from her thinning greyness and fell on to the cushion behind her.

'I know, I know. But I just . . . no, I didn't feel I could cope with . . . all that.' She closed her eyes.

'The open drawers and stuff thrown about must mean the intruder was looking for something,' I pointed out rather needlessly, 'and you say that nothing was stolen. So presumably the search was in vain. Now, do you have any idea what he or she might have been after? I mean, do you have any valuable jewellery or money in the house? Something that someone might, perhaps, have heard about?'

Eyes still closed, she replied in barely above a whisper. 'No, I've never been very well off, Mr Marklin. So you see, my jewellery, such as I have, consists of just costume pieces.' She extended a finger of her right hand. 'Except for this ring, which I never take off. It was my mother's.'

The three rubies in their claw settings shone like beads of blood against the almost transparent whiteness of her skin.

'It's very nice,' I smiled, then, after due pause, continued, 'So you have no idea what this intruder can have been searching for?'

'No . . . no, no idea.'

I looked at Bessy. She shook her head. 'No, nor have I.' Then she turned to Gus. 'Any theories, Mr Tribble?'

Gus was obviously taken on the hop, as he guffawed and then, for our further edification and entertainment, started on a seemingly endless clearing of his throat. This finally completed, he asked, 'Footprints. Didn't see any, did yer? Like in the garden, outside the window. Or even indoors.'

'No. I'm afraid I was too upset to think about things like that, Mr Tribble. But you're right, I suppose I should have gone out to see straight away.'

'I looked soon after we'd cleared up a bit, Mr Tribble,' Bessy chipped in. 'But the ground is so hard after all these days of sub-zero temperatures, there were no obviously new impressions. Besides, right outside the kitchen window there's a largish paved area that goes right across the back of the bungalow.'

I tried a wild one. 'Think back a moment, Mrs Purkiss. When you first came downstairs and went straight into the kitchen, was there anything besides the cold that struck you as somehow different?'

She frowned. 'How do you mean, exactly?'

'I'm not quite sure, really. But for instance, did the house smell slightly different or–'

'Smell?' she interrupted.

'I only meant that had the intruder been a heavy smoker, his clothes might have given off a tobacco-y scent. Or had he or she been wearing oily work clothes, then . . . Oh, I recognise I'm clutching at straws, but otherwise there seems to be absolutely nothing to go on.'

She thought for a moment, her fingers momentarily forgetting to fidget. 'I can see what you're getting at. Everyone has a sort of different aura, now don't they?'

I loved the euphemism for odour.

She went on, 'But no, I can't say I remember noticing anything like that. The only thing slightly odd I noticed on my way to the kitchen was that the door of the grandmother clock was ajar. And I recall castigating myself for obviously not having shut it properly that afternoon when I wound it. You see, I always open the door to watch the weights go up, to make sure I never overwind.' She smiled weakly. 'But that was before I'd realised about the break-in and that almost everything else in the house had been opened.'

'So now you think the intruder was the culprit and not yourself?'

'I like to think that. Otherwise it might mean I'm getting more . . . well, gaga' – her face took on colour for the first time – 'than I'd realised.'

I looked across at Gus, who must have picked up my thought.

'Grandmother clocks are much smaller than grand-fathers, aren't they?' he grunted, half in statement, half in question.

'Yes, that's right, Mr Tribble.'

I let Gus pursue our thought. 'Right then, so whatever this 'ere burglar was looking for, can't be all that ruddy big, now can it? Otherwise there'd hardly be room for it in the bottom of your grandma clock.'

I looked back at Muriel Purkiss. But she gave no reaction. Only her fingers seemed to have got any message – knitting knots had now been upped.

'Mmm,' Bessy intervened. 'I think Mr Tribble may have a point. Do you remember, even the silver cigarette box in which you keep the needles of your old wind-up gramophone was lying open?'

Muriel suddenly seemed to wake up. 'I don't remember that. No . . . you must be mistaken, Bess.'

I looked at Bessy. She looked at me. And the look only said one thing.

Muriel carried on. 'No, so many things were disturbed and left open. Some big. Like the drawers in that chest in the spare bedroom. Some smaller, like the grandmother clock. It seems to me that this somebody had no fixed idea about how big the thing he was after was.'

'He?' I queried.

'Oh, sorry, I didn't mean to suggest anything by that. But most burglars turn out to be men, now don't they?'

I had to admit they did. Maybe it's the night work that puts the women off. But I was a trifle surprised and dismayed by Muriel's ready dismissal of the only ruddy theory Gus and I could come up with. Still, even I had to admit that it was a million miles from being a case-solving stroke of genius.

I tried another line of enquiry.

'That night – I take it you didn't happen to hear anything? After all, all the opening of drawers and things must have caused a bit of a ruckus.'

'No, I'm sorry, Mr Marklin, I didn't. Not a thing. You see, I'm not like Bessy. I sleep like a baby the moment my head touches the pillow and nothing seems to wake me until morning.'

'Clear conscience,' I smiled and then suddenly realised my flattery of Muriel's state of mind could be taken as a condemnation of Bessy Meade's. But good on 'er, Bessy took it in her stride, and with a smile, commented, 'It's my sinful past catching up with me, Peter. But I wouldn't trade any of it for a second's more sleep.'

'He didn't mean–' Gus began, but I stopped him by asking Muriel the only question my mind could muster.

'All right. So you didn't hear anything that night. But the previous day, or the previous week for that matter, did you have anyone calling at the house you've never seen before? Like someone claiming to be selling something like double glazing? Or brushes? Or wanting to cut down trees? Or do gardening? Or odd building jobs or anything?'

She frowned. 'No, I can't remember anyone of that description. No . . . no. You're right though, we do occasionally get people like that around here. But I suppose the present terrible weather has put people off tramping the streets and knocking on doors.'

I was stuck for further questions, so glanced across at Gus. He, blast it, was picking an ancient piece of debris out of his sweater and didn't catch my help-me look. But Bessy did, bless her.

'Well, Muriel,' she smiled. 'I expect we've given Peter and Mr Tribble quite enough to digest for the moment.' She turned to me. 'I'm sure if they come up with any useful thoughts, they'll be in touch with one or other of us, won't you, Peter?'

I nodded. But not in any hope that we could really be of any help. I'd only agreed to come to try and calm two LOLs, one of whom I was now starting rather to admire. That and to stop Bessy pestering my common-law in-laws any more than necessary.

'Well, Gus,' I said, rising from my chair, hoping that the sound of his Christian name would distract him from his sweater rather more successfully than his surname had, 'we'd better be off.'

It took, however, a slight nudge from Bessy to do the trick. Gus started like a rabbit and looked around as if someone had shouted 'Fire'.

'Sure you won't stay for a cup of something?' Muriel offered as she too got to her feet.

We all three declined as gracefully as each one of us was able and, preceded again by Bessy, went out into the tiny hall. I pointed to the rather charming walnut grandmother clock and asked, 'Is that it?'

'Yes,' Muriel replied quietly and didn't seem to want to look at me. Gus, without any invitation, suddenly opened the door of the clock and took a quick peek inside.

'Like what I said,' was his verdict.

'Thank you, Gus,' I muttered under my breath.

"Sall right,' he muttered back.

I took his half-ton coat off the hall peg and handed it to him. Well, pushed it at him, to be more precise. He climbed into it, puffing and blowing, as I helped Bessy into hers. All winter wear donned, I turned back to Muriel Purkiss, who was still hovering in the sitting-room doorway.

'Look, Mrs Purkiss, if you're really worried about this intruder returning and you won't go to the police, I'd advise you to get in touch with some burglar-alarm people right away. Nowadays there are all sorts of electronic devices that don't cost the earth and which can even warn of intruders when they're still just prowling around outside. And others can be linked direct to your local police station. You don't need to tell the law that you've already had a burglar if you don't want to. Just say you want the link-up because, living alone, you're afraid you might be visited some time or other.'

She held on to the doorjamb and gave a weak smile. 'Yes . . . thank you, Mr Marklin, I might just do that, mightn't I?'

Her words carried little conviction and I glanced at Bessy.

'I suggested more or less the same when it first happened,' she sighed. 'Perhaps now, Mu, that Peter strongly recommends an alarm system, you should get going on installing something.'

And that's more or less how we left it. But before we actually hurried out back to the Daimler, I gave Muriel my address and telephone number, just in case. Of what, none of us right then could be sure.

94

6

We were about halfway back to the hotel when the thought occurred to me. I guess it was fostered by the uneasy feeling I had about the whole Muriel Purkiss meeting.

I turned to Bessy in the front seat and said, 'It wasn't your friend who really wanted to see me, was it?'

Bessy put on her naughty-little-girl face once more.

'Oh, you've guessed, Peter. I should have realised you would.'

'Wasn't too difficult, ' I forced a slight smile. 'Now tell me the truth, Bessy.'

'Oh dear, you're right. I'm much more the worried one. Muriel, as you obviously noticed, is a bit vague about things these days. Sometimes I wonder if she's still got her feet firmly on the ground. I mean, even her memory is starting to go. Fancy not recalling that silver cigarette box was opened, for instance.'

She reached out and touched my arm. 'You will forgive me, won't you, Peter? I hope you can see that if Mu won't look after herself, somebody's got to do it for her. Things like break-ins can't just be ignored. And what with Mu not being willing to call in the police, as she should have done, I agree, well, what options did I have?'

'Me,' I replied, to which Gus grunted a ditto.

Bessy turned round to the back seat. 'I'm terribly grateful to you both for your bother. I really am.'

''Sall right,' Gus nodded into my rear-view mirror, then added, blast him, 'Now me and my mate can get back to who did that bloke Fern in.'

'Oh . . .' Bessy's voice lilted upwards, a bit like Frankie Howerd's. 'I'm so pleased to hear you two are going to put your brains to work on that one.'

I glowered into my mirror. 'Don't take my friend wrong, Bessy. Gus and I are not – '

But Bessy was not going to give up and cut in, 'Your involvement is exactly what I was going to raise when we got to Dendron Park. You see, I'm so worried about poor Mrs Robbins. As I mentioned to you coming over, I think she may be in some kind of trouble. Otherwise, why should such a thoroughly upright and honest person not tell the truth to the Inspector about where she was that night?'

'I don't know, Bessy. Your guess would be far better than mine, as you've known the lady for so long. I've not even really talked to her. And only ever seen her once, the evening I came to dinner.'

Hell, I wish I'd kept my mouth shut. She instantly exploited my words to issue an invitation. Even double-glazing salesmen could learn a lot from our Bessy Meade.

'So let's right that the minute we get back, Peter,' she beamed. 'I'm quite certain poor Louise Robbins will be only too relieved to have someone on her side that she can really talk to. I mean, you can't really do that with a police-man, can you? Even when they wear plain clothes. They've always got their pens poised to take down everything you say. I'm sure even the innocent feel guilty sometimes when face to face with them. Don't you agree?'

'That may well be so, but you must remember I'm not a professional investigator,' I pointed out.

An ancient Cortina suddenly pulled out of a side-road some way ahead and I slammed my foot to the floor. Thank the Lord, he then accelerated away sufficiently fast for the even more ancient Daimler's overriders to miss his exhaust pipe by a gnat's testicle.

Bessy seemed not to recognise imminent death when she saw it and rattled on, 'Does it matter, Peter? I mean, I know it's asking a lot of you, especially after your and Mr Tribble's kindness with Muriel today, but I would be so very grateful if you could just have a word with her. If you're worried about being away from your shop too much, if you get involved, then I do have a little money put by and I'll be only too happy to recompense you and Mr Tribble – '

This time, it was I who interrupted her. 'It's not a question of time. Or of money, Bessy. It's a question of . . .'

Whilst I was hunting for the right words to sum up my reluctance to become next door to a public property, Gus jumped in with, 'If my friend 'ere can't spare the time, I'd be only too happy to see this 'ere Robbins woman.'

I exhaled my frustration and the windscreen misted over on my side.

'Why, thank you, Mr Tribble,' Bessy enthused. 'How very kind.' I could feel her looking across at me.

I preselected third, and then pumped at the clutch pedal as if it were Gus's face. As I swung into the Dendron Park drive and forecourt, I prayed that Mrs Robbins would have had some reason for going out. But no, Bessy spied her Peugeot 205 in the rank of cars almost immediately.

'Oh good, Louise will be in.'

I pulled the Daimler to a reluctant stop, using both foot and handbrake, then glanced at Bessy.

'Sure you can't spend just a second, Peter?' she smiled mischievously at me. God preserve me from LOLs. If there were only more of them, I'm sure they could rule the whole ruddy world.

Louise Robbins had certainly changed from the proprietorial, confident woman I had glimpsed at dinner. No, she hadn't by any means gone to pieces and there were no signs of sackcloth or ashes. On the surface she was still the same smartly dressed, rather generously curved and sensual woman I had originally noted. But now the look in her eyes had gone beyond weariness into a kind of despair and hopelessness. Her confidence in herself and her attraction had all but vanished. I wondered if Fern had taken it all with him to his grave (not that he had one of his own yet) or whether there were other things we knew not of that had eaten away at her soul.

Even her handshake was less firm and positive. But I'm running ahead of myself. Let me go back a bit and say how Louise and I came to be standing alone in what she described as 'Jason's study' – a smallish room on the first floor, one door up from her own private suite.

Bessy Meade had, indeed, gone to see Mrs Robbins in

97

her office, almost immediately after we had left our coats, scarves and gear in the cloakroom. She was not gone more than three or four minutes. Upon her return, she suggested as tactfully as possible, that as Mrs Robbins was still feeling very distressed, it might be desirable for only one of us to go in and see her. No prizes for guessing who her little eyes lit upon.

I duly knocked and entered said office. I only had time to note the change in her appearance and handshake before she suggested it might be better if we went up to her private suite, while her secretary moved into the office to protect us from interruption or phone calls.

I must say her private accommodation was an improvement on the rather glitzy aura of the hotel proper. Obviously she considered hotel guests to be a race apart. The one room I saw – the living-room – was beautifully furnished in a combination of modern and antique pieces that worked surprisingly well. The walls, washed in a very pale lilac, were hung with a similar contrast in styles: old Victorian rural scenes in oils and watercolours rubbing frames quite amicably with modern abstracts and early twentieth-century portraits that I took to be of members of her or her late husband's families. On an inlaid folding card-table in the far corner by the window was the only souvenir I could see of her relationship with Fern – a silver-framed photograph of the murdered man wearing the kind of skimpy trunks that are made for posing rather than anything to do with swimming. And Louise Robbins, around whose waist his hand was curling, was hardly overdressed either. Even from where I was in the room, I could see her bikini owed more to a length of string than to a loom.

I accepted Mrs Robbins' invitation to take a seat, but she then threw me a little by preferring to remain standing herself.

Neither of us spoke for a moment or two and then I broke the ice with, 'I'm very sorry that all this has happened.' (Note my precise choice of words. What else could I say? No one except her and Fern's father seemed too unhappy that Fern had been plucked from the earthly scene.)

I heard her sigh. Then she looked away towards the window and said, 'Bessy Meade says you might be able to help, Mr Marklin.'

'I don't know that I can,' I had to admit. 'I don't know, in fact, quite what any of the problems might be yet – if there are any problems, that is.'

What a wet, soggy comment. Gives some indication of my mood right then, though.

She slowly turned back towards me, her eyes seeming to search mine. For what? I asked myself. To see if I could be trusted? Or relied upon? Or maybe, even . . . duped? Then she came out with a statement I'd not really been expecting.

'I want to clear his name, Mr Marklin.'

Not the 'I want to discover his murderer' that I'd been awaiting.

'Clear his – Mr Fern's name?'

Her eyelids closed for a second. 'He was always Jason Brand to me,' she said quietly, then went on, 'But yes, I want to stop all this crazy speculation about Jason. I knew him far better than almost anybody, Mr Marklin, and I know that he was not up to anything the least shady. All right, when he was just a kid he may not have chosen all his friends too wisely, but what kid does?'

'This speculation – who is actually behind it?'

She held out her hands. 'Oh, just about everybody, I wouldn't wonder.'

By that I assumed she must have overheard some of her guests rabbiting amongst themselves.

'Can you be a little more specific? I mean, have the police, for instance, tried to link Mr Fern – Mr Brand with anything that might have happened in the past?'

Superfluous question, in a way, as I knew the answer from what the strange Mrs Sandle had told me on the telephone. That the police might be trying to put the murder on her ex-con husband, because he knew Fern/Brand yonks

99

ago. But I wanted to hear how much of this Whetstone had been willing to divulge to others.

'They've asked a number of questions that lead me to believe they're thinking in that direction, yes.'

'Like what, for instance?'

'Oh, they keep trotting out names and asking me if I've ever met any of these people or heard Jason speak of them. But of course I haven't. So I say "No". But that Inspector Whetstone, he looks at me sometimes as if he thinks . . . well, that I'm lying. And I assure you, I'm not, Mr Marklin.'

I had to ask it. 'Amongst those names, do you remember a man called Sandle? I think his Christian name is Dennis.'

Her eyes gave me the answer long before her mouth.

'Dennis Sandle? Yes, his name has come up most often. But how would you know – ?'

I waved my hand. 'I heard a rumour, that's all,' I lied.

Louise Robbins looked as if she believed it as much as I did. I hastily went on with a question of my own.

'Did the Inspector tell you anything about this Sandle fellow?'

'Not much. Just something about his sources of information leading him to believe Jason and Sandle had once been very friendly years ago. Oh, and he did mention that Sandle had done time.'

'For burglary,' I added. 'He was released only a couple of weeks back or so.'

She came towards me. Now I could smell her scent. Balenciaga, if I wasn't mistaken. How did I know? Arabella had been given a free sample at a PR shindig some months before. And had sploshed some on herself that evening. I smelt of it all next day. Beats oysters, all hands down, up and around.

'Now I'm starting to understand things a bit. You see, the Inspector didn't tell me he'd only just been released. I imagined it must have been some longish time ago.' She thought for a moment, then asked, 'You don't think he reckons it may be this Sandle who murdered Jason?'

'Maybe.'

She sighed and looked away. 'Oh God, it just makes the

whole thing a thousand times worse. He's trying to concoct some crazy theory that this Sandle murdered Jason because of something he imagined Jason had done while he himself was locked up.' She whipped back to me. 'That's it, isn't it?'

I shrugged. But only not to aggravate her pain. She hid her face in her hands and cried out, 'Oh why, oh why do people seem to hate Jason so?'

'I don't think it's anything to do with hating or loving, Mrs Robbins. The police are just following up every possible line of enquiry, that's all.'

She dropped her hands and glared at me. 'No, it's not just the bloody police. It's everyone. I know. I've heard people talking. Even my guests. None of them liked Jason.'

She stabbed a manicured finger at me. 'And you know why? They're jealous, that's why. Consumed with jealousy. Jealous of his looks. His charm. His cleverness . . .' She took a deep breath. 'Oh God, why do people always hate to see someone with more damned gifts than they've been doled out? They should be pleased, not jealous, that someone can actually hit the jackpot sometimes.'

She relaxed her finger and then, to my relief, subsided into the chair opposite me. Hell, from what I had heard of Fern/Brand, he didn't deserve such intensity of love as this.

'And you know something, Mr Marklin? The jealousy of these ants – they don't deserve to be called people – wasn't just directed at Jason. Oh no. I know damn well it was of me, too. Me, a widow of forty-two, still being able to attract such a young man. Oh, I know what they called him behind my back. So did Jason.' She mouthed the next three words slowly and precisely. 'My toy boy.' She snorted. 'I guess it pleased their tiny minds to reduce our relationship to sex and sex alone. God, I pity them.'

By this time I was starting to feel a little hot under the collar I wasn't wearing. But, in a way, I was glad that Louise Robbins had at last found a way of venting her pain, even if it was I who was caught in the passionate draught. For, right then, she must have felt the loneliest woman in this whole, to her, goddamned world. And running a hotel full of whispering, conjecturing guests could only have heightened her isolation. I decided to try to get her into a less emotionally charged topic. Me. After a pause to allow her to wind down a little, I cleared my throat and said, 'I wonder if I might ask you a question, Mrs Robbins, about something that Inspector Whetstone put to me.'

She exhaled, as if it were the last wind her sails would ever feel, and said quietly, 'I'm sorry, Mr Marklin, I should never have sounded off like that. Will you forgive me? It's just that . . .'

'I know. I know,' I smiled sympathetically.

'Thank you for being so understanding.' Her mouth made a stab at a smile, but her now damp eyes would not quite sanction it. 'Now, what's your question?'

'It may sound very trivial, Mrs Robbins – '

'Please call me Louise.'

'And I'm Peter. Well, it's just that the Inspector wanted to know how my name came to be in Jason's address book.'

She frowned. 'Jason had your name written in his book?'

'Not only my name. My address and phone number. I just wondered if you might know why. He wasn't a customer of mine at the shop. And I haven't heard that he was ever into old toys.'

She crossed her long legs and caught the line of my look. For a second I saw a flash of her sexual confidence return.

'No, he wasn't. But he did collect models. Mainly of Porsches. They were his passion.'

Amongst other things, I thought to myself.

She continued. 'Maybe someone told him your shop sold toys and he imagined they'd be new ones or, at least, that some of them would be.'

'Possible, I suppose. Did Jason, by any chance, mention my name to you?'

She shook her head and a lock of dark hair fell across one eye, softening her face.

'No. Not that I can remember.'

'I couldn't, by any chance, see his address book, could I?'

'Unfortunately, no. The Inspector took it away with him after his first visit.'

So that was that. Suddenly Louise rose from her chair.

'Like to come and see Jason's Porsche collection? They're just in the next room. He used it as a kind of study.'

I don't know whether she asked because she thought they might interest me, being a toy nut. Or whether she just wanted some company whilst she attempted, at last, a visit to memory lane. Whatever the motive, I accepted.

And that is how I found myself standing in a modest-sized room, dominated by a rather hideous, gilt-laden desk and two glass-fronted cabinets brimful with Ferdinand Porsche's miniature offspring. In fact, there was little space for anything else. As a result, Balenciaga had a Grasse-field day. If it didn't, as with Arabella, make the earth eventually move for me, it sure as hell rocked the room round a bit.

Louise pointed to the cabinets. 'Everywhere we went, Jason would track down the nearest model shop to see if they stocked some rare model Porsche or other that he was after.'

I knelt down and spent some time inspecting his collection. I had to admit, it was quite impressive. I recognised models from almost every manufacturer under the sun and more than an odd few I couldn't source at all. But then I'm not all that hot on the very low-production, cottage-industry, white metal offerings. Or some of the more esoteric, Far Eastern factories, for that matter.

But Porsche types there were aplenty. In almost every scale imaginable. From grand one-eighteenth, right down to micro-jobs the size of a fingernail. And the types ranged from cooking 911s all the way up to the highly specialised Le Mans racers. Certainly there seemed to be no current cars not accounted for. An observation that prompted my next remark, as I got up from my knees.

'Now I can see why Jason might have thought it worthwhile to have noted down my name. There's only one way to go when you've got almost everything new that's made. Into obsolete and vintage stuff.'

Louise blinked hard. 'However that might be, Peter, Jason won't be going that way now.'

I tried to take my foot out of my mouth by asking, 'Did you know Jason's family at all? I mean, like his father. I gather he doesn't live too far away.'

Again her eyes quizzed me. 'No, I never met any of his relations. Jason talked about his father a few times but made it rather plain, I'm afraid, that he was unlikely to approve of . . . well, our relationship.'

To cover her embarrassment, she pretended to flick a speck from the slopes of the well-stretched top of her tailored suit.

'The difference in our ages, you see. And the fact that we weren't married. I gather his father is somewhat puritanical. I think that's why Jason left home in the first place. No mother, you see, to be the buffer between them. Such a great pity. And the housekeeper his father took on didn't really help matters. Jason said she was a kind enough soul, but tried so hard to win him over that he felt utterly stifled by it all. So he upped and left.'

She closed her eyes tightly. 'Oh God, why do people have to be like they are?'

There was nothing a mere mortal like myself could say, more's the pity. So I pretended to be eyeing more of the models in the cabinets until she had recovered somewhat.

After a moment or two, she took a deep breath and said, 'I had a call this morning. From the garage. To say that Jason's car was ready for collection.'

I could imagine what emotions that simple call had raised.

'That's a Porsche replica, isn't it?'

She nodded. 'I suppose Jason would have been pleased it was a hire car the murderer burnt and not his beloved machine.'

At last I'd been given a cue, albeit slender, to pop a question I'd been anxious to ask from our first moment together.

'Louise . . . tell me, have you yourself any idea who that murderer might have been?'

She rested back against one of the cabinets and replied

softly, 'I only wish I did. And then this whole thing could be cleared up quickly and Jason's reputation . . .' She stopped and looked at me.

'Please, Peter, if there's anything you can do to help stop the police muckraking up totally the wrong path . . . I'd be only too ready to pay you. Just name a figure and I'll – '

'Louise, that's very kind of you,' I cut in, 'but I'm not a professional investigator and never have been.'

Hell, this whole Fern case was getting ridiculous. How many more people would be offering me bread (and jam) to get involved.

I continued. 'Don't misunderstand me, I have enormous sympathy for your feelings at the moment. And what's more, if anything does occur to me that might help find the murderer or clear Jason's name [note the "or" and not an "and"], I will naturally get in touch with you instantly.'

She placed a hand on my shoulder. Somehow, I felt a trifle uneasy about this physical contact, slight as it was. Maybe it was the claustrophobic room. Maybe the Balenciaga that was rocking it and me. Or maybe her pent-up passions were vibing down her fingers. Either which way, I felt cornered.

'And I promise to do likewise, Peter.'

I nodded and then thought it was time to make a move towards the door. She removed her hand to let me pass.

As we went out, I remarked as nonchalantly as I could, 'Jason didn't happen to say where he was going that night, did he?'

She blinked. 'Our relationship wasn't like that, Peter. We didn't keep tabs on each other. Nor did I expect Jason always to be around when I had the running of the hotel to do. Evenings are our busiest time, being open to non-residents, and quite often he used to go out then. To the pub or for a run in his car or to see a friend.'

'So you don't actually know where he went that night?'

'Not exactly, no.'

Then I tried a real googly. 'Do you think he might, by any chance, have come back in the early hours and you missed him?'

I could see the bails fly off, mirrored in her eyes.

'Er . . . what do you mean, "miss him"? How could I have done that? Had he come back, he would have come right up to our suite.'

'But you were out, weren't you? At least for a little while.' She avoided my gaze.

'No, no, of course not. What on earth gave you that idea?'

'It's just that someone said that they thought they saw your car in the town in the early hours.' Then I added quickly, 'But it must have been another 205 convertible, I guess. After all, there are quite a few of them around. Just the thing for a seaside place like Bournemouth. Except in this weather, of course.'

'Yes, it must have been somebody else, Peter. Besides, why on earth would I want to go out into the freezing cold at that godforsaken hour? And if you're thinking I might have gone looking for Jason – '

'I'm not thinking anything,' I lied with a calming smile, and followed her down into the lobby.

Downstairs there was a sight to make my eyes sore. Gus was seated at one of the tables used for morning coffee, holding court with not only Bessy Meade, but yes, yes, not one, but two Trenches.

I quickly bade farewell to Louise Robbins outside her office and went over to discover what the hell was going on. Needless to say, really, it was Gus who was going on. I caught him in mid-flight.

'. . . would never have ruddy happened if he'd stayed on the farm. See, I reckon that's the whole trouble. Him leaving home. Wouldn't have got no fancy ideas, he wouldn't, if he'd worked for his father. Nothing like the good earth to keep you on the straight and narrow.' Gus lifted a digit in true guru style. 'I mean, how many ruddy farmworkers do you hear of in court for robbing or mugging people? Let alone had up for killing someone? Read any list of criminals [where can you get one, pray?] and you'll find ninety per cent will be city folk.'

Clement, I could see, was now almost asleep and even

Bessy Meade looked as if she was coming unrapt. I decided to give Gus only a minute or two more, before intervening on behalf of the RSPCA (Not 'A' for Animals, but Adults.)

'And if he'd stayed on the land, he'd have met some nice country girl and settled down. After all, his dad had a nice cottage ready and waiting for him. Instead he upped and left for the glitter of the big city life and Lord knows what bad company he got into. Especially in that there London, where he ponced around having his photy taken every minute.'

I held up a hand. 'Gus, I hate to interrupt, but I really need to get back to open up shop.'

He uttered what sound like 'Gor', but at least that was all.

Bessy caught my eye. 'How did it go, Peter?' she asked quietly.

'All right,' I said, letting the tone of my voice indicate that nothing world-shattering had happened between me and the hotel owner.

'Oh, well, thank you so very much for taking time out to see Louise. And of course poor, dear Muriel.'

I rose from my chair. It was then that Julia touched my hand. 'Got a minute before you're off?'

'Guess so,' I could only comment.

She nudged Clement, who snorted and looked up. 'Yes, what, old girl? What?'

'Just going to have a word with Peter before he goes.'

Clement looked distinctly minussed.

'You know,' she prompted.

Suddenly his eyes lit up like lamp bulbs.

'Oh yes. Of course. Silly me. Forgetting.'

I waved to Gus. 'Won't be a minute.' And the three of us moved out into one of the lounges. Save for a blue rinse and a bald pate pulled as close to the roaring log fire as you can get without actually being consumed, the room was empty. We stopped by the big bay window.

'Sorry to keep you, Peter,' Julia kicked off, 'but Clement and I thought we ought to let you know what one of the waitresses told us, when she brought breakfast to our room this morning.'

She looked at her husband. 'Do you want to tell it, dear, or shall I?'

'Better you. Didn't catch every word. Myself. Girl's accent. Bit thick.'

I took it the 'bit thick' referred to the accent and not to himself.

'All right.' Julia turned back to me. 'I'll make it quick. Clement asked her if there was any more news this morning about that boy's death. You remember, you and Arabella asked us to keep our eyes and ears open?'

'I do, indeed.'

'Well, she said there wasn't anything new, really, and instead of then going out, she seemed to sort of, well, hover, as if she wanted to say something. So to encourage her, I asked her what she herself thought about it all. She went a trifle red and said it wasn't really her place to go talking about it, especially to guests. Well, I said "Nonsense" and said she was as entitled to air her views as anybody else.'

Julia stopped and looked at me. 'And then she said a funny thing. That she was "in a way, more entitled". I immediately asked what she meant and she went even redder and said something like, "He wasn't any good, that Jason, and poor Mrs Robbins is well rid of him". Of course I asked what made her say that. And she went on that no girl or woman was safe from him, if he thought he could get anything out of them.'

Julia hesitated, and then slightly blushed herself as she went on: 'I think she wasn't meaning just money, Peter, if you understand me. And she came out with it all with such vehemence that I guessed at once that she must have suffered from his attentions herself.'

'Bit near home,' I muttered.

'Just what Clement and I thought. But I dare say he wouldn't have tried anything on with her actually in the hotel.'

'Did she say anything else?'

'Not really. And I didn't like to ask her outright whether

108

he really had propositioned her or what-have-you. Maybe another day, when she's grown to trust us a little more, we'll be able to find that out.'

'Hmmm. Nice character this character's turning out to be.'

'Poor Mrs Robbins,' Julia sighed. 'By the way, how did it go with her? Learn anything?'

'Not really,' I parried. 'Except that she seems more interested in clearing Jason's reputation than in finding his murderer. From what you've just told me, the first might be a task beyond the powers of even a Hercules.'

'Oh dear, yes, you could be right.'

I looked at my watch. 'Well, I'd better go and rescue Bessy Meade by whisking Gus away.'

Julia smiled and I was just leaning forward to give her a farewell buss, when I felt Clement's hand on my arm. I looked round and saw he was proffering a small card towards me.

'Her address. Digs. Where she lives. Got it from the porter. Case you want to see her. You know. Privately.'

I took the card and popped it into my pocket.

I didn't take it out again until I handed it to Gus on the Sandbanks ferry, halfway home.

He took a little time to decipher Clement's rather cramped handwriting, then knocked me back with, 'Know where this 'ere waitress digs down, old son? Not so bloody far from your old aunty's graveyard, that's where.'

7

Gus and I had little time to brew on our morning once we were back. I genuinely had to open up shop, just in case some toy fanatic wanted to brave the weather. And Gus, realising that Heinekens would thus not be in the offing, immediately decided he had to check on his pipes and do some more swabbing up before the plumber arrived. I did fill up a largish plastic container with water, though, and dropped it down with him to his cottage, to tide him over until he could turn on his stopcock once more.

It was well after twelve by the time I parked the Beetle round the rear of the shop. I hurriedly let myself in the back door and went straight through into the shop to turn my 'Closed' sign to 'Open'. To my surprise, there was what I took to be a punter already waiting outside. I prayed he had not been there too long, otherwise he might be too frozen to get his wallet out of his pocket. However, through the window he seemed to be built after the style of a concrete bunker, so I hoped for the best.

Hell, he was impatient, brushing past me before I'd hardly straightened up. I'd had eager customers before, but nothing quite like this.

I closed the door and followed him up to the counter. Whereupon he startled me by whipping round and asking, 'Got somewhere where we can talk?'

'Er . . . yes,' I replied. 'Right here. It's called a shop.'

Flippancy was quite clearly not his bag right then, for he bristled (wasn't difficult with his decidedly non-designer stubble) and stated rather than asked, 'You're Marklin.'

I'm a fool. I should have read the signs.

'At last count,' I half smiled.

His eyes condemned me and then did a tour of my shop. It was then, a bit late, I admit, that I realised he was no toy fanatic. Fanatic, maybe, but the look from those almost

110

indigo peepers was one of caution and fear, not interest in my stock.

A rough-hewn finger jabbed towards the still open door behind the counter.

'Can't we talk in there?'

I took a good look at him. He was somewhere in his mid-forties, around five foot ten, but even through his rather scrubby anorak you could detect the kind of muscles that no amount of clerical work can give a man. His head was the spitting image of a cube, seeming to have the same measurements whichever side you might choose for your ruler. Not that he was downright ugly or anything. The features were regular enough and geometrically neat like his head. I could see that to a female aficionado of, say, all-in wrestling, he could be said to have an uncertain attraction. But the most off-putting of his characteristics was his pallor, which the dark stubble seemed only to accentuate. It was this pallor that suddenly gave me the clue as to who he might be. I mentally shivered.

'I take it you're not after toys,' I sighed.

'Toys? No, don't be daft. I'm here to get what you wouldn't give my wife.'

Now I had the final confirmation.

'You're Dennis Sandle, aren't you?'

A hand shook me by suddenly reaching for mine. Then shook again.

'Pleased to meet you, Mr Marklin.'

I wish I could have said likewise. But I just winced and lifted up the hatch of my counter.

I took him through into the sitting-room, but didn't offer him a chair. For what I had to say wouldn't take long.

I was about to kick off when he said, 'My wife has told me all about you.'

I was not sure I liked the sound of that, but I let him go on.

'How you've helped people and that, when the police have got the wrong end of the bloody stick. Like they have with me right now. Shit, have they got it wrong.'

111

I made the mistake of saying, 'Have they, Mr Sandle?'

His eyes lasered into mine. 'Don't tell me you bloody think I killed young Fern too.'

'I don't think anything, Mr Sandle. One, because I don't know anything. And two, because it is a police matter and really nothing to do with me.'

He reached into an inside pocket of his anorak, produced a wad of notes and proffered it to me.

'There's a thousand there, Mr Marklin, in fifties. Count them.'

I waved my hand. 'Please, Mr Sandle, I've already told your wife, I'm not for hire. Never have been. Never will be. I only get involved in those cases where I'm pretty certain an injustice is about to be done – '

'Well,' he interrupted, bunging the wad back in his anorak, 'you'll be bound to help me then. I didn't kill Fern, but just because I've done time they're trying to nail it on me.'

I looked at him. He was pleading now and his indigos had changed their aggression for desperation. Even so, his vibes were still ambiguous. I decided my jury was still out and arguing about the verdict of 'guilty' or 'not guilty'.

'You have no alibi for that night, I assume.'

'Yes, I do,' he came back in a flash. 'I know I have an alibi, anyway.'

Oh great. A secret alibi. Only known to the accused. As cast-iron as a packet of Jello. But my curiosity was now aroused, if only by his audacity.

So I asked, 'And what's that?'

'I was in bed.'

'In bed? Alone?'

'Yeah. More's the bloody pity.'

'Where are you living? Not with your wife, I gather.'

'No. Not yet.' His eyes brightened for the first time. 'But we'll be back together very soon now. All being well, that is.'

I wondered if his wife had heard about it.

He continued. 'No, I'm renting a little chalet place for

112

the time being. Well, it's more like a caravan really. Except it hasn't got wheels. Belongs to an old mate of mine.'

'And where is it?'

'In a field, back of Wareham.'

Hey ho, I thought. Popular place to live. What with corpses opting for it. Aunty having chosen it as her last resort. And waitresses digging it. And now Sandle. I wondered if the Wareham tourist office could make any mileage out of the new-found craze.

'Let me guess,' I said. 'The chalet isn't overlooked by any other houses, right, so no one can vouch for your being there that night.'

'Oh, don't bloody mock me, Mr Marklin, I'm in enough trouble without you – ' He stopped, as he realised what he might be about to say.

'I'm not mocking you, Mr Sandle.' I took a deep breath and pointed to a chair. 'Look, you'd better sit down and tell me all the rest.'

He looked at me expectantly. 'Does that mean you're going to – ?'

'Listen, that's all,' I quickly cut in. 'Just listen.'

He bit his lip and then sat himself down on the very edge of the seat of the armchair. He looked about as relaxed as a fox who has smelt the hounds.

'All right, then. I'll tell you all I know.' He sniffed and went on, never looking up from his tightly clasped fingers.

'I tell you straight away, I'm no saint. Least, I used not to be. But those years in the slammer have taught me a thing or two since. Anyway, when I was younger, I did get up to one or two . . . well, things that I'd never be so stupid as to get up to now . . .'

Like robbery with violence, I thought of saying, but was afraid of interrupting his flow.

'. . . like a bit of burglary and that. Thought I was doing rather well, I did. Bought myself a fancy car and cruised around pulling the birds. That's how I got to meet my wife, Linda. She was a cashier in a petrol station. Well, anyway, before that, whenever I had a bit of money, I used to blow it on girls and parties and things. Anything to have a good

113

time. It was at one of those parties I met Jason. That is, you know, Fern, the bloke who was murdered.'

He looked up for the first time. 'He was ever so young then. Fresh off his old dad's farm, he was, but thought he knew everything, even at his age. Lord help me, if Trev grows up like that.'

'Trev?' I queried.

He narrowed his eyes at me. 'Yeah, Trev. You know. My son. Well, mine and Linda's. He's seven now. That's why the sooner Linda and I get back together the better. He needs a dad, he does.'

'Most children do.' At least now I could see why his wife might have had a pedal car. Though by its condition, little Trev couldn't have given it much use.

'Yeah. Right. Well, about me and Fern. See, about that time he knew a girl in Poole. Ever so young she was. Couldn't have been more than seventeen. She was besotted with him. Kept him, in fact, for ages before some photographer bloke he'd met said with his looks he should go up to London and try his luck as a model.'

'Kept him? At seventeen?'

He blinked hard. 'She was earning quite a bit, see. Working the docks and that. She was a . . . you know . . .'

'Prostitute?' I offered. Extraordinary that such a tough guy couldn't get his tongue around such a word in front of a stranger.

'Yes, if you like.'

I didn't like. Not at all. Any of the scene. Teenage hookers or fresh from the farm exploiters.

He continued. 'This girl, see, came across quite a few of the operators around here in her course of work. And one night, when we were both a bit the worse for wear, I, like an idiot, told Fern about my latest . . . job, and that the fence I'd been relying on had just been picked up by the fuzz. So he suggested that, through this girl, see, he could shift the stuff but it would cost me a bit off the top. Well, to cut a long story short, I let him get rid of a couple of pieces. Not the really expensive stuff, mind you. I didn't trust that to an inexperienced couple of kids like those two were. Still, he kept his side of the bargain and that was that. Soon after, I heard he'd upped and gone to London. And we've never seen each other since and that's the honest truth, Mr Marklin.'

I looked across at him. He averted his slightly bloodshot eyes and I just couldn't tell how much reliance I could put on what he'd told me.

'I take it, Mr Sandle, that you've told all this to the police.'

'Course I have.' He rubbed his hands together nervously. 'But I can tell they don't reckon I'm speaking the truth. Especially that Inspector . . .'

'. . . Whetstone?'

'Yes, that's him. I can see from his piggy little eyes that in his book, I'm dead. Stone bloody dead. He more or less came out with it, he did. And I don't reckon I helped myself by telling the bloody truth about me and Fern in the old days. Should have kept me bleedin' mouth shut, I should have. All because the fuzz are narked because they never found the stuff from my last job. Trying to take it out on me now, they are.'

'What happened to the stuff?' I asked, not really expecting to be handed a map and a set of directions as to where it was stashed.

'How do I know? It's years ago now. The house where I hid it has been torn down to make way for a new housing estate. I expect some sodding demolition merchant is laughing all the way to several banks by now. It was all jewellery, high-class stuff, so he could have walked off the site with it all stuffed in his anorak and no one would have been the wiser.'

I didn't comment. My mind was playing around with what role his wife might have played in all this. Like, surely he would have told her where it was hidden, so that she could find some way of retrieving it before the guys with the big swinging balls demolished the haven. What's more, he'd only been out a couple of weeks and yet had a grand in notes to offer me. Sandle took my silence as either disbelief or indifference to his plight. Or both.

'It's the honest truth, I swear to God. I didn't have nothing to do with Fern's murder. Nothing. You must believe me.' He reached across, as if to grab my hand, then obviously thought better of it. 'Please, Mr Marklin. Help me.'

His gravelly voice was starting to jump octaves.

'And if you don't want to help me, think of my poor innocent wife. And Trev . . . little Trev . . .'

I stopped him before he verged on the falsetto.

'Answer me this, Mr Sandle.'

He leaned forward, white-knuckled fingers now clutching the arms of the chair.

'Anything. Anything, Mr Marklin.'

'First, why did you and your wife become . . . estranged? And two, what makes you think your wife is now willing to consider taking you back?'

He seemed to find my questions surprising.

'Er . . . why did my wife and I . . . ?' He sniffed. 'Why d'you think? All those years without a man, while I was inside. She couldn't stand it, I suppose. At first she used to visit me regular. But then, after a while, it grew less and less. Especially after Trev started school. Said she didn't have the time any more. But I know she hated admitting to people where she was going those days. Ashamed, see? Don't blame her, neither. That's why she kept moving around. Never stayed in no place long. That is, until she was offered that cottage, a couple of years back, now.'

'Offered?' I frowned.

'Yeah. See, my wife got to know a social worker quite well. One of the ones who used to visit to check up that she was looking after the kid properly and that. Well, he's a great churchgoer, from what she's told me, and knew the cottage's owner, Fern's old father, as it turned out. Both members of the congregation, see.'

I nodded.

He continued. 'This social worker knew old Fern had just lost his last tenant, so told him that my wife was looking for a cheap place for herself and the kid, where people wouldn't know about her past, like. Being a couple of do-

116

gooders, I reckon they thought Linda needed saving from the likes of me, I wouldn't wonder. Anyway, old Fern let her have the place for a joke rent, which is nice of him. And she and Trev have been happy there.'

He stopped and stared down at his knees. 'So she tells me now.'

'She didn't tell you before?'

'Well, no. See, it was almost immediately after moving up there that Linda stopped visiting me altogether. So I never knew then whether she was happy there or not.'

I brewed on't for a second, then went on to the second part of my original question. 'Okay, so that's how you drifted apart. Now what makes you think she'll want you back?'

He hesitated before replying. 'Er . . . she said so, see? She's just waiting until I can get myself together a bit, that's all.' He felt his stubble. 'She'd hardly be happy in that there cottage any longer, anyway. Nor would I be. Not with old man Fern as the landlord, now his son's . . . dead. I wouldn't be too ruddy surprised if he asked her to leave, anyway, if I suddenly moved in.'

'Because he might have heard about the police taking you in for questioning?'

'That. And the fact I'm an ex-con. Do-gooders like him and that social worker would think Linda's far better off without me, I'm ruddy certain of that.'

Again I made no comment. Fern and his church mate could well be right. Who was I to know?

Sandle leaned forward anxiously. 'So, Mr Marklin, I've answered your questions. Now will you help me?'

It was crunch time. I knew it. But not because of Sandle alone. I had now heard *cris de coeur* from four separate throats – first Sandle's wife, then Bessy, then, via her, Louise Robbins, and last but not least, the ex-con himself. That's without chucking in poor aunty's feelings about having an unwanted overnight guest. Or, indeed, my own thoughts about that, or my being marked down in a dead man's address book. Or my common-law in-laws' sentiments about their hotel's owner and her likely financial plight if things weren't sorted out soon about Fern's death.

Never before on any of my previous sleuthings had I felt the fates had so got it in for me. To be absolutely honest, I had really had that sodding feeling right from the second I'd heard the grave news from Arabella about aunty. So, irrespective of any feelings I'd had about Sandle's guilt or innocence, I showed the white flag to my fates and replied in a tone that was as un-chipperesque as you can get: 'I'll see what I can do, Mr Sandle.'

He stood up instantly and extended a hand. I raised one of my own in caution.

'Now, hang on, Mr Sandle. This doesn't mean to say I have any views on your innocence or guilt. It just means I will be making some enquiries of my own over and above anything the police may be carrying out.'

I rose from my chair and saw his hand reach into the inside of his anorak once more.

'Put that money away, Mr Sandle. I'm not working for you. Or your wife. Or any one person. Except myself, that is.'

'All the same, Mr Marklin, I don't know how to thank you.' He again tried to pump flesh, but by that time I was past him and opening the sitting-room door.

'I haven't done anything yet,' I reminded him.

'But you will, you will,' he pronounced, his relief softening the square, stubble-ridden cube of his face. 'And if you want to see Linda or anything on your own, go straight ahead. Don't mind me. I'll have told her about our little meeting.'

'Where can I reach you?'

'Oh yeah, I forgot. Either leave a message with my wife or call the Cock and Wagon in Wareham. The chalet's not on the phone, see. But they'll get a message to me. Anyway, I'll drop by there every day, just to see, like.'

And that is how my first meeting with Dennis Sandle ended. But more importantly, how my first real personal commitment to the whole Fern case began. Oh lordy, lordy, had I but known . . .

Although I kept the shop open until five, my mind was

elsewhere. So much so that when a balaclavaed, scarfed and duffle-coated figure dinged through my door, I was hardly aware of his presence until he was actually at the counter, clutching a boxed Wiking Vulcan bomber from my stock in one hand and sixty pounds in fivers in the other.

I pulled myself together to take the money.

'Collect Wikings?' I asked, just to pass the time of day.

'Got quite a collection. Only plastic models I like.'

I agreed with him. Wiking, a German company, had built up quite a reputation during World War II as a maker of aircraft recognition models for the German forces, so their products had to be extremely accurate, otherwise German gunners might have been rat-tat-tatting away at their own planes. After the war, Wiking continued their tradition when in the fifties they were commissioned by NATO to bring out aircraft recognition models of the main combat types. The Vulcan was one of the best, biggest and most collect-able of this latter group.

'Got any wartime ones?' I enquired, as he placed the Vulcan box gingerly into a side pocket of his duffle.

'Most of the main types. Heinkel 111, JU 88, ME 109, Thunderbolt, Fortress, Blenheim, Fulmar, Stuka. That kind of thing. But I prefer the fifties stuff. You don't have a Canberra, by any chance?'

I shook my head and offered to take his name and number, in case one flew my way, but he declined and, with a weak smile, shuffled back out of the shop. Funny how some collectors will be only too open about their obsession, but shut up like clams if you get too personal. As I watched him cross the road, he reminded me of Gus. I guess it was his ungainly gait. And general size. But mostly the way he was swaddled up from head to toe against the bitter wind.

It was soon after balaclava that I shut up shop. The reminder of Gus prompted me to put Bing on a lead to take him for a constitutional down sea lane, otherwise known as Gusland. My excuse to myself was that both my and Bing's brains could do with the invigoration of a massage from frost's icy fingers. In reality, I actually wanted for once to be hijacked by Gus as we shivered past his cottage. One, so that I could update him on Sandle's visit. And two, to brew (quite literally, no doubt) on some plan of action for the morrow.

But, sod's law, there was nary a light from the old cottage windows and equally nary a black upright menace rusting away in the drive. I turned back instantly and even Bing looked miffed at being robbed of a roam around Gus's sweater. I assumed that Gus, having had his fill of cold houses, plumbers and the reek of blowlamps, had trotted off to warm his bones and innards in some hostelry or put up his feet in front of a hot, roaring lady friend. On a night like this, I didn't blame him.

Back home, I fed Bing, then pulled my own self up before the TV weatherman, just in case he had some good news for once. But no. The winds, he seemed to take relish from saying, would remain from the east and blow further Siberian weather across the southern half of the country for the following few days. Whilst, of course, the more northern counties, including the Trenchs' beloved homeland of Shropshire, would enjoy temperatures in the mid-forties. Great. I poured me a Scotch against the prospect and decided to try to sharpen my wits by starting on the big grown-up's crossword in the *Independent*.

Arabella returned around seven. And to a blunter than blunt-witted man. She saw the discarded page of the paper and remarked, 'Clues defeat you?'

I shrugged, as if totally indifferent to such a petty problem as a newspaper crossword. She laughed and put her arms around me.

'Never mind, darling. At least you won't be getting a cross word from my parents now.'

I blinked.

She went on. 'I popped into Dendron Park on my way home, just to say hello to them and they told me all about your seeing Mrs Robbins. They're most impressed.'

'Didn't learn much,' I muttered.

'It doesn't matter. It's the fact you bothered to see her at all that counts with them. Especially after having only

120

just come back from Bessy Meade's friend. By the way, how did that all go? I gather Gus went with you.'

I pulled her down on to the settee beside me and brought her up to date with my day. The only bit she'd heard before – from her parents, obviously – were the remarks from the waitress. This, put together with Sandle's account of the murdered Fern's pimping past, produced the inevitable 'Poor Mrs Robbins', followed by, 'What a bastard.'

Arabella then looked at me and asked, 'Want to work on my clue?'

'What's that, pray? Eight letters. Let me think. "Middle Eastern, Italian beauty shares Western alphabet number two".'

'Eh?' she recoiled.

'Get it? Middle Eastern – Arab. Bella – beautiful girl. Second letter in the alphabet – B.'

'Arab sharing a "B" with Bella. God, what kind of a mind have you got?'

'I'm not sure I've even got one, right now,' I laughed. 'Anyway, back to your clue. What is it?'

'Oh, I'm having you on a bit. It's probably not really a clue at all. It's just that my parents came upon another snippet of gossip this afternoon.'

'What's that?'

'Well, that waitress in the hotel. She has a regular boy-friend, apparently. By the name of Firestone. I only remember it because I thought it funny his having a name like that and working in a garage. Same garage, in fact, that serviced Fern's or Jason's whatever you want to call him – car.'

'Well, there's no law against waitresses having mechanic boyfriends.'

'Shut up, idiot,' she said tactfully. 'That's not the point. The reason my parents latched on to it is that this Firestone seems to have spent quite a long time this afternoon quite literally locked away with Mrs Robbins in her office. Some-one, I think it was the chef, tried to get in, apparently, and the door was bolted.'

'That's it?' I queried, in case there was more.

121

Arabella nodded. 'Bit funny, though, don't you think? Now what would Mrs Robbins be doing – ?'

I cut in. 'Do your parents know whether Mrs Robbins has ever met this Firestone before? I mean, it's just possible she has her car serviced at the same garage.'

'No. That's the point. She doesn't. My father was very proud of having checked that out with the barman. Her Peugeot goes to a Peugeot garage, surprise, surprise. But Fern always insisted his Porsche look-alike went to the Volks agent, where Firestone works.'

'Hmmm,' I reflected. 'I can see now why Mater and Pater thought it might raise a question or two. Number one, for me, would be whether it was Firestone or Mrs Robbins who called the meeting.'

'My money is on the mechanic.'

'Why?'

'Well, it would appear that he just turned up out of the blue.'

'How do we know that?'

'Bessy Meade saw him in the lobby and, apparently, he asked her where he could find Mrs Robbins. She showed him to the office and as she left heard Mrs Robbins say something like, "Why do you want to see me? We've already picked up the car".'

I thought for a moment, then said with a smile, 'Know something? I'm starting to regret having asked your old mum and dad to start sleuthing. The more they discover, the more ruddy perplexing the whole Fern affair becomes.'

'I'll tell them to wear eyepatches and earplugs until further notice,' she gagged, then got up from the settee. 'Now I'd better go into the kitchen and get a little food for our thoughts.'

I pulled her back down. Onto my lap. 'Why don't we go out somewhere instead? It would save you and I feel like a change of scene. Besides, I actually had a real half-alive customer this afternoon. In this weather, that's something to celebrate on its own. Shelled out twelve fivers for that Vulcan that I bought a month ago for seven pounds fifty.'

She made a that's-not-a-bad-idea face, then gave me a

long, lingering kiss. An hour and twenty-three minutes later, we were on our way.

That evening, we chose to go to the Jug and Hare. No, it's not a pub. But an almost twee-ly thatched cottage near Wareham, just off the Bournemouth road. Thomas Hardy could have been born in it (he wasn't though) or Tess of the d'Urbervilles loved amidst its beams. But neither, I suggest, could have enjoyed such sophisticated fare under its eaves. Nor, sure as hell, have paid such a price for victuals of any description.

We went in my Beetle. I had suggested Arabella's Golf. Though still a convertible, the top, unlike mine, both fits and touches, and the heater, ditto unlike mine, does actually do what its name implies. But she said it had been playing up the last couple of days, with the engine occasionally cutting out and she'd booked it in the next day for a service. But if I liked to risk being stranded late at night in the Arctic etc . . . I didn't like. So we clambered into the Beetle, muffled up to our eyeballs and phut-phutted off, Wareham-wards.

It was on the A351 out of the town that I first noticed the headlights in my rear-view mirror. They belonged to a Ford Escort that I had just passed. When the lights started flashing I assumed the driver must have been miffed at my manoeuvre and was just venting his frustration, if not anger, by flicking his switch.

So I ignored it all and accelerated to try to lose him. But lo and behold, he did the same. What's more, he was still trigger-happy, flicking from high to low beam and back again, disco style.

Arabella looked behind. 'Someone should tell that berk there's no law against passing,' she observed, then turned to me and asked, 'Unless he's trying to tell us something. Like one of your rear lamps is out. Or we're on fire. Or have lost a wheel . . . two wheels . . . three wheels?'

I slammed my foot to the floor and the Beetle dredged up a few more b.h.p. But our edge over the flasher still didn't lose us all the dazzle from his lights.

123

'Shit,' I mumbled, 'there's one born every minute.'

'And he came right on time,' Arabella smiled across.

It was then that the light show changed its act into a light and horn show. After twenty seconds or so of this further entertainment, Arabella remarked hesitantly, 'Sure we aren't on fire?'

'Well, if the car isn't, I am,' I shouted above the din and switched a heavy foot to the brake. I saw the lights of the Escort dip down in my mirror as it too slammed on the anchors. But then, surprise, surprise, it suddenly pulled out and accelerated to run alongside me.

I wound my window down and was all set to hurl a few choice expletives into the night air, when I suddenly saw a pudgy arm gesticulating and fleshy lips mouthing at me from the Escort's passenger window. Both seemed to be saying, 'Pull in.' Now that wouldn't have been the end of the world, if I hadn't recognised to whom the arm and lips belonged; and as I duly slowed and swung on to the verge, I wondered what the hell he was doing in a lowly Escort, and what's more, accompanied by two portly, middle-aged women, one driving, the other goggle-eyeing from the rear seat.

As I stopped the Escort pulled diagonally ahead of me, in true cop style. Arabella and I unified our sighs as we sat and watched Digby Whetstone almost roll out of the Escort door and approach us.

'Ten out of ten, Digby,' I smiled. But he frowned, so I put him into his misery by explaining, 'Greatest undercover trick I've seen for years. Anonymous little car. And aboard, a couple of middle-aged frumps in mufti. Jesus, Digby, the Dorset force needs more people like you. Why, you could fool anybody into thinking it's just a down-the-line family outing – '

'Marklin,' he held up a gloved finger. I missed the freckles. 'Just you keep your smart comments to yourself and listen to me.'

I cupped my ear.

He went on, 'I got my wife to flash you down – '

124

'Wife?' I breathed, as I heard Arabella try to stifle (none too successfully) her mirth.

'That's right, Marklin. Directly you flashed past us. I recognised your car instantly. And though it's my wife's birthday and we've just picked up her sister to come out to dinner with us – '

My heart sank. 'Jug and Hare?'

'Yes. As a matter of fact . . .' He stopped as he suddenly twigged. 'God, Marklin, don't tell me I'll have the highly dubious pleasure of your company . . .'

I looked round at Arabella. She shook her head.

'No, I won't tell you,' I smiled at Digby. Shit, there went our dream dinner. 'So why've you stopped me, Digby? What is so very urgent that it won't wait until the sparrows start to fart again?'

Before he could reply I heard a rather imperious shout from the Escort in front.

'Digby!'

'Coming, my dear,' he shouted back.

Oh, even if I had now lost a dinner, there were a few compensations to the flagging down. Domesticity à la Whetstone. And already plain as a pikestaff who wore the helmet.

His face now red from more than just the cold, he condensated on: 'I thought I'd be doing you a favour, Marklin, warning you now rather than dragging you down to the station tomorrow for your bollocking.'

'Bollocking? What on earth is it this time that makes me bollock-worthy?'

'You know damn well.' Again the digit was raised. 'You are up to your old tricks again, aren't you? Don't deny it.'

I shrugged. I had always known it would only be a matter of time before Whetstone cottoned on to my probings at the hotel and elsewhere. But the sand had run out somewhat earlier than I had been expecting.

'We're keeping our tabs on Sandle. So we know you've seen him.'

So that's how he knew so fast. Hey ho. Thank you, Mr S.

'He came to see me. I didn't go to see him,' I pointed out.

'And how did he get hold of your name?'

'Must have heard about me from someone, I suppose.'

I wasn't lying, now was I? But I wasn't going to complicate matters by admitting I'd already both met Linda Sandle and had her try to hire me. Wouldn't have gone down a treat, right then.

'Heard you're willing to stick your nose into affairs that should be left to us professionals.' He hunched his loud check overcoat higher around his neck. 'So what was Sandle wanting, eh? No, let me guess. He tried to feed you some bullshit about what a saint he is really, and how he'd never hurt a fly. And how bloody rotten we in the Force are for picking on him and detaining him for questioning.'

'No,' I correctly asserted. 'He didn't.'

'Pull the other leg.'

'Can't reach from here,' I smiled, then went on: 'Okay, he said he wasn't guilty of Fern's murder. But he didn't pretend he was whiter than white or whinge about the treatment you boys are giving him.'

'So what did he want?'

'He asked if I'd help him, that's all.'

Digby was about to comment, when again his name rang out from the driver's window of the Escort.

'Just finishing, my love,' he rang back. 'All right, Marklin, I can't spend all night arguing the toss with you here. And I can't afford to waste time on you in the morning either. I'm up to my ears in this Fern case and only took time off tonight because it's my wife's birthday . . .'

And there would have been another murder if you hadn't, I thought to myself.

'. . . so just you listen to me. Whatever Sandle has asked you to do, whatever anyone anywhere may ask you to do at any time in regard to the murder of Fern, forget it.'

He stooped further down and peered across at Arabella.

'Same goes for you, Miss Trench. Remember your TV programme only exists because of the co-operation of the police. Step over the line and . . .' He karate-chopped his

126

gloved hand on to the sill of my door. The steel positively rang with the blow. I determined to chop his Rover down to size next time I saw it.

'Understand me, Miss Trench?'

'Happy birthday to your wife, Inspector,' Arabella beamed. Clever girl.

'DIG-BEEE,' echoed through the icy ether.

'Right with you, my love.'

'Ever drive yourself, Digby?' I asked nonchalantly.

'What do you mean by that?' he glared. But he knew what I meant by that, even if he gave a literal reply. 'Oh, I see what you mean. No, that Escort's my wife's car. And when I'm dead tired, like I am tonight, I'm only too happy to just sit back and let her take the helm. But that's beside the point.'

'The point being . . . ?' As if I needed to remind him.

'That you stay in Toyland, Mr Marklin, and Miss Trench within the guidelines we have agreed with her studio. Simple. And keep a million miles away from anything to do with Fern's murder. We may well be near to cracking this case now and the last thing I want is for anything to start muddying the water at this stage.'

I raised my now freezing eyebrows. 'Oh, so does this mean it won't be long before you make an arrest?'

He fluttered his hand. 'Too early to say. It all depends on what forensic think of a discovery one of my men made late this afternoon.'

I made a quick guess and asked bluntly, 'Wouldn't be the murder weapon, now would it, Digby?'

He smiled, hugging his little secret to his chubby checkered chest, then made quick tracks back to the Escort of his life.

Arabella and I, after a speedy conflab, decided on quick tracks back to our nearest Chinese takeaway. Somehow, the magic of eating out had disappeared with Digby.

8

After we had sweet-and-soured and crispy pancake-rolled, Arabella asked, as she crumpled the last of the little foil containers into the kitchen swingbin, 'Where are you thinking of starting, 'Ercule?'

I shrugged. She came over to me and put her arms around my shoulders.

'I wish you'd for once obey old Digby and not start at all. You know how I feel about you sticking your neck out.'

I nuzzled at her neck. Balenciaga still lingered in the down at her nape.

'From what Digby implied tonight, it may all be over tomorrow, anyway.'

'Saved by a blunt instrument?'

'If that's what his men have actually found . . .' Nuzzle, nuzzle. '. . . he must be making some headway, because you must have noticed he's stopped getting at me about Aunty's grave and address books and your parents . . .'

She pulled away and smiled. 'Know something? If Whetstone does solve this one all on his ownio, then there are going to be two very disappointed people in town.'

'Ma and Pa Trench.'

'They're really hyped up, you know, about being involved in a real live murder case.'

'Live murder. I like it,' I grinned.

'No, I'm being serious. Father has actually said to me that he's looking forward to seeing you in action – which is more than I am. He thinks it beats farming up in Shropshire all hands down.'

'Talking of farming,' I commented, 'perhaps that's where I should start. With one in Devon.'

'With old man Fern?'

I nodded. 'I'd like to know a little more about his son from someone who hasn't got some axe to grind. All I've heard so far are the dodgy bits about him. I think it's time to hear the other side.'

'He wouldn't see me,' Arabella grimaced.

I thought for a moment. 'Gus knew him years ago.'

'You're going to ask Gus to try to make an introduction?'

'Why not? Gus can explain that I'm only trying to speed up finding his son's murderer, so that this whole sad affair doesn't run on and on like *The Mousetrap*.'

'How about seeing Sandle's wife while you're up there?'

'Yes. Might as well kill two birds whilst we're at it.' I ran my hand through the brush of her hair. If only Kleeneezee could capture the way it flicks back through my fingers, they'd clean up, so to speak. 'So what have you got mapped out for your day tomorrow, Miss TV Trench?'

'First, I'm taking my car in. Thought I'd use the VW dealer that serviced Fern's mock Porsche. Good idea?'

Silly question. 'Ask for that fellow Firestone who was shacked up in Louise Robbins' office.'

'Of course. Who else.'

'Then what?'

'In the guise of interviewing people who knew Fern, I could see if that waitress would be willing to play.'

'She might, if you asked her up to see the studios or something.'

'Right. I'll try it on.'

'That it?'

'For the moment. Don't forget Digby may call a press conference later tomorrow, if he has actually found the murder weapon. I'd have to attend that. If he doesn't, then I was hoping you might put in a good word for me with old man Fern. My producer is very anxious to get an interview with him. I realise he'll still be feeling God-awful about his son, but we have held off quite a time already.'

'I'll see what I can do. But I can't force him to see the media. And wouldn't want to. Grief's not public property.'

'I know . . . I know,' she sighed. 'Sometimes I don't like my job at all.'

'And other times you love it, don't you?'

129

She came back into my arms. 'But not with a passion,' she whispered. Hell, there went that Balenciaga again.

I phoned Gus the second Arabella had left in the morning.

To be greeted by, 'Must be pathetic, old son.'

'Oh, why?' I responded, not being blessed with 'pathetic' insight, like my giant granite friend. (I kidded him once he should get himself tested for radon. To my amazement, he knew what I was talking about, laughed, and reminded me his name was Gus, not Gas.)

'Come on, I was just about to ring you.'

'About what, Gus?' I hesitated but asked.

'What happened yesterday evening,' he replied and stopped right there.

'I'm not "pathetic", Gus. Though I popped down last evening and saw you were out, I have no idea what you were up to.'

'Oh . . . yeah . . . well, I done you a favour.'

Hell, there was another six-pack signed for.

'You got rid of your car?' I tried.

'Get off it, old son. I went up to old man Fern's, now didn't I?'

Hell again. I prayed he hadn't screwed up my own plans for that morning.

'You might have told me, Gus.'

'Why? You don't know him, old mate, and I do. Or did.'

'Did he see you?'

'Yeah. Course. In the end.'

My heart dropped bootwards. 'And what, pray, happened in the beginning?'

'That woman of his. That's who happened.'

'Woman?'

'Yeah. Woman . . . housekeeper . . . what have you. Stupid old tart. Stupid old name too. Quaintance. Would you believe? Madge Quaintance.'

I believed. I'd met the name before. In Cornwall.

'What did she do that merits your two-part description, Gus?'

'What she didn't do, more like. Stood at the door and

130

wouldn't even go and tell his nibs that I'd called. Now, I ask yer.' He sniffed. 'Wasn't until I got a bit stroppy and said things like she'd only have her ruddy self to blame if her employer's son's murderer was never found that she deigned to go in and pass on me message.'

Well, that was going to be a lady's face to watch when, and now maybe if, we two went up to the farm in an hour or two.

'So then you got in to see him?'

'Right. Cor, old son, it was quite a shock, I can tell you. He looked a hundred years older than when I last clapped eyes on him.'

'It's some years, you said, since you two have met.'

'Yeah, but he looks treble that. Easy. All shaky and white, he is. I tell you, his son's death has really knocked all the stuffing out of him.'

'Not surprising,' I muttered. 'Explains why this house-keeper woman doesn't welcome visitors right now. Wants to give him a bit more time to recover.'

He snorted. 'Yeah. I s'pose so. But I reckon she's a possessive old cow, too. Could see it in her eyes. The way she talked to him. Almost like he was a ruddy child, rather than a grown man. And him her bleedin' employer, too.'

When Gus takes agin someone, watch out.

'Any road, she made it plain as a pikestaff she wanted to stay while I talked to Ted. But I wasn't having any of that and said so.'

Exit housekeeper swearing oaths and making strangling gestures with her hands, no doubt.

'Come on, Gus,' I said impatiently. 'Get to the point. What's this big favour?'

I heard his proud old chest inflating with air.

'I've got old Ted to agree to see you, that's what,' he exhaled.

'You're really "pathetic" yourself, Gus. That's why I was ringing. To see if you could arrange something like that.'

'Well, I done it, haven't I? He didn't agree right away, mind. Not by a long chalk. Not until I'd told him a few tales about how you and I have tracked down the real bloody

131

criminals when the police were stuck fart-arsing about on false trails. At the end of all that, he seemed to take my point . . .'

I didn't blame him. Gus in full flight is something else. My worry was that old man Fern may just have agreed to see me to shut Gus up. But what the hell?

'. . . and said he'd give you a few moments. Though he did add he didn't reckon he could help you much, seeing as how he hadn't seen much of his son since he upped and left the farm.' Gus paused, then added, 'Began crying then, he did, when he said that. Terrible to see a grown chap like him in such a state. I left soon after. Hell's bells, old mate, we've got to find who did his son in. Old Ted will never be at rest till we do.'

It was at that point that I updated Gus on Digby's highway hijacking of the night before. Cheered him up no end, it did. And I don't mean the chance that the murder weapon may have been found, either.

'Cor . . . Get a glimpse of her?'

'Not close up,' I chuckled. 'Didn't really need the video. Sound said it all.'

'Well, well, well,' he digested. 'Still, it's all that berk Whetstone deserves, in't it? Makes up a bit for all that earbashing he gives other people.'

'Be that as it may, Gus, you didn't happen to arrange a time with Ted Fern, by any chance, did you?'

'Said it'd probably be some time today, that's all.'

'I was planning that you and I should run over there this morning. Like in the next hour. And perhaps pay a little call on Sandle's wife on our way back.'

'I'm free if you are, I suppose,' Gus said pointedly, to remind me I'd taken his agreement and freedom to accompany me for granted. I went through the ritual.

'Sorry, Gus. Can you make it?'

He sniffed. 'Mean putting off me meeting with the sodding Emperor of Ethiopia . . .' (To Gus, the world is still populated by figures from the distant past. He still, for instance, won't really believe Hitler is dead or that there are any Germans who don't wear helmets.) '. . . but there y'are.'

'About ten, then?'

'Yeah. All right. My car or yours?'

The sod; he only asks that to get me going.

I whipped past the cottage rather smartish. I didn't want Sandle's wife warned that I was in the vicinity by the sight of my yellow peril. But I did cock an eye cottage-wards en passant. Round the back I could see some washing on a line. She must have been some optimist, unless, that is, she equated freezing stiff as a board with drying and airing.

Ted Fern's farmhouse proved to be a rather bleak affair and would have looked far more at home on some blasted Yorkshire moor than amongst Dorset's cosy countryside. I almost expected Heathcliffe to be toiling away in the yard. Its proportions weren't so bad. Its length and lowness disguised its quite considerable size. And I guess a coat of Snowcem over its dark and discoloured cement facing would have banished most of the brooding Brontë-tude.

I pulled the Beetle to a stop outside a small decomposing gate let into the stone wall that separated the private property from the frozen ruts and hummocks of the working farmyard.

Gus must have read my thoughts.

'Not so bad inside,' he muttered. 'Real working farm, see? Not yer tarted-up ponce of a place doing bed and breakfast.'

We got out of the car and I was almost floored by the stench of cow dung that emanated from the buildings two-siding the yard. Gus made no comment on't, so who was I . . . ?

By the time we were halfway up the weed-ridden garden path a rather cuddly figure had appeared at the front door.

'That's 'er,' Gus muttered out of the side of his mouth.

I looked again and could hardly believe that this round-faced woman with her apple cheeks and down-the-line aunty aspect could be the obstructive harridan of Gus's

133

earlier description. My fears at making her Quaintance rather evaporated.

Gus did the honours. If you could call the following that:

'This 'ere's me mate, Peter Marklin,' Sweep of hand. 'And this 'ere's Mrs Quaintance.'

We shook hands. She had her sleeves rolled up and the dewlaps on her chubby arms wobbled.

'Mr Fern's in the parlour,' she announced, with a rich 'Darset' burr in her voice. Then, having taken our coats and hung them up on a peg on the back of the door, she said, 'I'll lead you through, shall I?'

Gus and I followed her. In old-fashioned farmhouse style the front door led directly into a big beamy kitchen with stone-flagged floor, brown earthenware sink, and an Aga big enough to cook for and heat the whole of the frigid county. With, thank God, not a fitted cupboard in sight.

From there, we padded down a dark corridor, past a couple of firmly closed doors with blacksmithed latches, until we came to a dead-end door on which she knocked.

'Mr Marklin and Mr Tribble,' she shouted.

I took it by her decibels that Ted Fern must be HARD OF HEARING. I wasn't wrong.

'Right,' was grunted from within the parlour and on that say so, Mrs Quaintance led us in to her long-time employer.

Ted Fern was not quite as I had pictured him, either. But in his case, no one had given me a bum steer à la Gus's description of the housekeeper. What's more, I should have realised good looks in a family often have a precedent. Though the elder Fern had to be over sixty and looked, as Gus had this time rightly described, totally shattered by his son's death, you could still discern the clean-cut features that must have made him quite a catch among the country lasses of his youth. But there was a strength about his expression and bearing that had been missing in the off-spring I had briefly glimpsed helping Bessy Meade out of her Daimler that evening.

The parlour was a long, low, beamed room with only two smallish windows. In the winter gloom, the well-worn velvet coverings of the two chairs and settee looked black rather than the dark green I discovered them to be (or, more precisely, to have been) and the none too recently cream-washed walls took on the hue of cheddar, light years past its eat-by-date. The latter wouldn't have been so bad if they'd been festooned with pictures. But the only two I could see were a framed sampler of 'You're Nearer God's Heart in a Garden' and a rather primitive oil painting of a bull, hung like you wouldn't believe (the bull, that is, not the picture), the ring in his nose secured to a pole held by a gormless-looking yokel wearing leather chaps and a smock. No straw in mouth though. Obviously he was too stupid even to have thought of that.

'Gus has told me about you, Mr Marklin,' were Fern's first tired-sounding words as he shook my hand.

He pointed to a chair to the side of the green-tiled Victorian fireplace. I did as I was bid and sat down. The chair's padding was so worn, the springs shook hands with my bottom.

He went on, in a gruff, yet not unpleasant, voice, whose accent was certainly South-Western, but equally certainly not deep Darset.

'He says you might be able to help find . . . who killed . . . my son.'

I held up my hand. 'I'll give any help I can.'

He looked at me blankly.

I looked at Gus, who instantly cupped his left barn door.

'Oh,' I said, at greatly enhanced volume. 'I can't promise anything, but . . .'

He folded his frame into the settee in front of the fireplace and Gus, with a grunt, sat down beside him.

'I don't want to take up your time, Mr Marklin, so let's get down to what you'd like to know. Not that I shall be of much help, I reckon, because, as Gus knows, me and my son . . .' He blinked and looked down at his brown cord trousers. 'Well, since he left the farm years ago, we haven't seen too much of each other.'

'So you have no idea,' I articulated loudly and clearly, 'what your son might have been doing that . . . er . . . night?'

135

He closed his eyes and was slow in replying. 'God knows what my son might have been doing, Mr Marklin. I gave up all attempt to follow what Jacob was getting up to years ago . . . years ago. Even before he upped and left for London.'

He looked across at me. 'I'm afraid, Mr Marklin, Jacob was a law unto himself.' He sighed. 'Even changed our name, you know. Fern wasn't good enough for him. Nor Jacob, I suppose. They weren't, how do they call it now, "with it" enough or "trendy" or . . . I don't know.'

He shook his head and when he resumed, his voice was barely audible. 'But whatever he called himself, he was still my son . . . he couldn't change that. Nothing can . . .' He put his head into his hands. 'Oh God, if only he'd never left home . . . he'd still be . . .'

I was starting to agree with the housekeeper. It was clearly still too early for Fern to have visitors who would inevitably evoke memories of his terrible loss.

'Perhaps it would be better if we did this at another time – '

I began to get up but he instantly cut in. 'No, please, stay where you are. I'm sorry, it's just that . . .'

'I understand,' I said, but you can't say something like that at a million decibels, so I don't think he heard.

He took a deep breath. 'Well, crying over spilt milk never helped in the dairy, so . . . if I'm to help my son . . . go on, Mr Marklin, don't mind me. Just ask away.'

Gus nodded to me. I cleared my throat.

'What *do* you know, Mr Fern, of your son's life after he left here?'

He thought for a moment. 'First thing he did was to get digs in Poole. I never went there. Never invited. Heard tell he got a job as a waiter in some boarding house or hotel. Any road, he got a girlfriend pretty smartish and soon was running round in a posh sports car. I know only because he came visiting up here in it. Pink it was. He didn't stay long. Well, it wasn't hard to see he'd only popped up to show off the car.'

That certainly fitted with what I had heard from Sandle.

136

Pimping and pink cars seemed to go together like Liberal Democrats and hung parliaments.

He went on, 'Soon after, it was, that he changed his name to Brand. Jason Brand.' The contempt showed in both his face and his voice. 'Next thing I heard, he'd gone to London. Without a word. No goodbye. No nothing. Only wrote once the whole time he was up there. And I know that was only so he could send me some clippings of adverts he'd been in.'

He looked up. 'He was a male model, see. That's why he went up to London, he said. No money in modelling down here in Dorset. No call for it, is there?'

He suddenly looked across at Gus, who nodded, then shook his head. One of the very good reasons I've never been with him to an auction.

'So you don't really know anything about his life up there?' I asked. 'Beyond his modelling, that is.'

Fern shook his head. 'How could I? I didn't have a chance.'

'Haven't heard about any mates he might have made up there, then?' Gus enquired.

'Mates?' Fern repeated, then sighed. 'If you mean male friends, no. Not when he was in London.'

I picked him up. 'What about female friends?'

He closed his eyes. 'Don't talk to me about his women friends, Mr Marklin. It's them who started him on the road to . . .'

I waited, but the word 'ruin' never came. I guessed he just couldn't bring himself to say it.

After a moment, Fern continued. 'It was his good looks, you see. I can't really blame him. But I do blame them.' His voice took on an edge. 'All of them.'

I hesitated to probe too deep in his present mood, but Gus dived right in. 'Stories going round that Jacob was a bit of a . . . whatchermacallit . . . toy boy. That what yer mean, Ted?'

He looked down at his cords once more. 'They toyed with him. Not him with them. My son's failing was that he couldn't say No, that's all.'

137

New interpretation. But it wasn't difficult to see why he had both to believe it and make it.

'Have you ever met the lady who owns the hotel, where he was living last?'

He didn't look up. 'No. Never,' he said, emphatically. 'And I never want to. If she tries to come to the funeral, then . . .'

His eyes flicked up towards mine. 'No God-fearing woman would dare to behave the way she's done. A widow too. Living openly with a boy half her age . . . I wonder she got any guests to stay at all in her damned hotel. The world's come to a pretty pass if no one takes a blind bit of notice any more at such blatant living in sin.'

I decided to change tack, before fire and brimstone were invoked to consume Mrs Robbins and the whole Dendron Park devil's playground.

'Reverting to male friends, for a moment. Did you ever hear him mention a Dennis Sandle?'

He looked at me and then at Gus. 'You been talking to the police?' he asked suspiciously.

'No,' I lied. 'I just thought, with Mrs Sandle living in your cottage, that you might have heard something about him.'

He resettled himself against the arm of the settee, as if trying to ease his mind via his body.

'Mrs Sandle has been separated from that awful man for years now. Otherwise I would never have let her have the cottage. She never mentions him. And I never mention him. What's the good of digging up the rotten past?' He exhaled his disgust and continued. 'Said that outright to the police, I did, when they started asking all sorts of questions about Sandle and that poor woman. Leave her in peace, I said. Last thing she wants is you raking up memories of the terrible mistake she made marrying such a criminal.'

Hell. Fern obviously had no inkling of what Sandle had told me about a possible reunion. But mum was the word right then. One, Fern needed news that his do-gooding might ultimately have failed like a hole in the head, and two, if he knew, her tenancy of his cottage would, no doubt, be terminated *tout de suite*.

'Were the police asking about Sandle because of a possible connection between him and your son?'

He waved his hand. 'They claimed they had known each other. Years ago now, they said. But I told them. My son might not have been a saint, but he wasn't a fool, either. Except, perhaps, with women. So he'd steer a million miles away from a criminal type like Sandle.'

I could see my new tack wasn't progressing me very far, so I glanced across at Gus.

He sniffed and asked, 'So . . . you've had a bit of time to think, like, Ted. Who do *you* think wanted your son . . . out of the way?'

He shook his head from side to side, as if in slow motion. Then, with a look of complete desolation, he said quietly, 'More I think, more I don't understand any of it . . . but I reckon there'll be a woman in it somewhere.'

I wanted to ask whether he meant as the murderess or as the cause, but I didn't want to upset him further. Christ, I haven't had any little Marklins – yet, that is – but I know that if I did and I'd lost one, from whatever cause, I'd just want the whole world to go away and leave me alone. So I acted on my own imagination and stood up from my chair.

'Well, thank you for being willing to see us both, Mr Fern. I know what a terrible ordeal all this must be for you.'

He rose from the settee. 'God works in a mysterious way, Mr Marklin. I just wish I could understand His meaning . . . a little better. Anyway, thank you and Gus for bothering about . . . poor Jacob.'

He led Gus and me to the door, but before opening it turned and asked, 'Do you go to church, Mr Marklin?'

Hell, or rather, Heavens, I wished he hadn't asked that.

'No . . . no, I don't, Mr Fern.'

His eyes, for the first time, exchanged despair for a burning intensity.

'Don't tell me you don't believe in God?'

I had to say something. 'I don't believe in God as represented by any orthodox religion, no.'

139

He looked at Gus, then back at me. The next question, somehow, came as no great surprise.

'Married, Mr Marklin?'

'No.' I held my breath. Little good it did.

'But Gus mentioned an Arabella, I think her name is.'

'Yes. That's my girlfriend.'

Gus suddenly stepped forward. 'Sorry, old mate, I only said how much of a help she's been to us. You know, other times, like.'

'That's all right, Gus.' I turned back to Fern. 'To anticipate your next question. No, we're not married, but we do live together.'

He took a deep breath, then opened the door. To my surprise, Mrs Quaintance was already padding along the corridor towards us. Another one who was 'pathetic', perhaps.

Before he entrusted us to her care, Fern asked one last question. 'You'll be sure to keep me informed of any progress you make, won't you, Mr Marklin?'

'We will, Ted, don't you fuss yerself,' Gus answered for me.

We all shook hands then and that was that. He closed the door and, no doubt, went back to the prison four walls make, when pain is acid-etching your soul.

As we came back into the kitchen, Mrs Quaintance asked, 'Been of any help, has he?'

'Every bit of information at this stage could be helpful,' I parried, with a smile.

'No need to shout with me, Mr Marklin,' her rosy face beamed. 'My hearing's still sharp as a needle.'

'Sorry. I hadn't realised I was still doing it,' I replied. And it was the honest truth, s'welp me.

She stood by the door. 'How did you find him, then?'

'Still very down. But it's only to be expected.'

'Perked up a bit towards the end,' Gus said pointedly at me and winked out of Mrs Quaintance's eye-line.

'Really?' she commented. 'It'll be the very first time, then, since it all happened. Perhaps your visit has taken him out

140

of himself a bit. Perhaps I was wrong, Mr Tribble, to be so unwelcoming to you yesterday.'

''S nothing,' Gus grunted. 'Understood, didn't I? You wanting to protect him and all.'

Since the housekeeper seemed to be not averse to a chat, I asked, 'The tenant in Mr Fern's cottage. Do you see much of her at all?'

She frowned. 'Mrs Sandle? Goodness me, no. Why should I? Who Mr Fern wants to rent his cottage to is his affair, not mine.'

So she didn't like her much. I probed for a reason.

'And her husband, Dennis Sandle. Ever seen him around here? Like recently?'

She folded her chubby arms across her bosom to prepare herself for the high moral stance that followed. 'Him? That dreadful man? No, I'm very glad to say I haven't, from all I've heard about him. Don't want the likes of him hanging around here. Be counting the silver every five minutes if he ever dared to show his face, wouldn't wonder. Shouldn't have been allowed out of prison, he shouldn't. Once a bad 'un, always a bad 'un, I say.'

'Mrs Sandle isn't likely to take such a man back, then?'

'Not if she's got half an ounce of sense or of what's right and fitting.'

'So you don't rule it out completely?'

She narrowed her big round eyes at me. 'What you getting at, Mr Marklin? That now that awful man is out of prison, she'll be thinking of . . . ?' She shook her head. 'No, she's got it all too comfy down there, with her son and the silly rent Mr Fern lets her have the place for. It would take more than a man on his knees to get her to give up all that.'

'Supposing that man had suddenly got hold of money, say?' I watched her face as she pondered on what I was hinting. 'Like a lot of money,' I expanded.

'How would a man like Sandle get hold of – ?' She suddenly stopped, then looked up at me, her eyes light-bulbing at the possibilities. ''Ere, you don't mean that you think that Sandle's up to his old tricks again so soon?'

141

I shrugged. 'Maybe. Or perhaps the money's from some old tricks he pulled. Before he went to gaol.'

Gus looked at me. 'They never found no loot, now, did they? The police said.'

'Right.' I turned back to the housekeeper. 'So what do you reckon his wife's answer would be, if he's really dangling big money in front of her?'

She obviously decided her views on the matter were best left unsaid, for in lieu of a direct reply she asked a question of her own. 'What's all this got to do with Mr Fern's poor dead son, then?'

'I don't know. Maybe nothing. It's early days. Just scouting around at the moment. Trying to find any connections of any kind, with . . . anything.' Hell, that sounded, and was, limp.

She pursed her lips. 'I've got a feeling you know more than you're letting on, Mr Marklin.' She pointed a well-filled finger at me. 'You reckon that there Sandle did it, don't you? Oh, Mr Fern's told me all about the questions the police have been asking about him and poor Jacob in the old days. You're trying to make a connection with what might have happened then and Sandle coming out of prison, now aren't you?'

'Well,' I began, but she went on wagging her finger and her tongue.

'Like, maybe, Sandle thinks Jacob was the reason he got put away in the first place. Like he'd reported him to the police or something. And all these years in his prison cell he's been plotting his revenge.'

Not quite what I had in mind, but none the worse for all that. From what I'd seen of the young Fern, he might well have played all sides against the middle.

'You're clever, you are, Mr Marklin.' She wriggled her nose. 'Very clever. I can see Mr Fern's very lucky he's got you and Mr Tribble here on his side.'

She chewed her tongue for a second, then added, 'Here, you wouldn't like me to keep a bit of an eye on the goings-on down at the cottage, would you? You know, so that I can tell you if I see that dreadful man hanging around.'

That didn't seem a bad idea, so I nodded. 'If it's not too much trouble, Mrs Quaintance.'

'Madge,' she smiled and a finger brushed my arm. 'Call me Madge. Mrs Quaintance is far too formal for someone like you, who's trying to help.'

'So is Marklin. I respond better to Peter,' I grinned.

'All right . . . Peter . . .' She hesitated and then added, 'Marklin. That's the name on the gravestone where Jacob was found, isn't it? Something like that, anyway.'

'Yeah,' Gus grunted. 'That's his aunty's, see.'

'Your aunt?' She looked both puzzled and embarrassed.

''Fraid so.'

'Oh dear, oh dear,' she blinked. 'How terrible for you.'

'Not really,' I said to cheer her up. 'I'm sure my aunty wouldn't have minded too much.'

'Nice of you to say that, Mr . . . er . . . Peter.' She took a deep breath. 'Well, all you can say, I suppose, is that poor Jacob was lucky, in a way, to end up in a churchyard. He could have been burnt in that hire car of his, now couldn't he? Or anything.'

She tried to blink back her tears.

I held out my hand. 'Try to keep your spirits up, Madge. I'm sure, right now, you're the pillar of strength that Mr Fern so badly needs. Without your cheerful face . . .'

She looked up at me. 'Do you really think so, Peter?'

'Sure so,' I smiled and leaned forward and kissed her on the cheek.

9

As we drove the short distance down the track to the cottage I remarked to Gus, 'She's hardly the mean old thing you made her out to be, you know.'

He sniffed. 'Well, she was acting better today than she was yesterday. Old Ted must have given her a talking-to.'

'Gus, all she was doing yesterday was trying to protect him. There's nothing wrong in that. You've seen how frail and vulnerable he is right now. The slightest thing could tip him over.'

'I s'pose so,' he reluctantly agreed.

I stopped the car just a few yards up from the cottage.

'Gus, the only reason you don't go much for Madge Quaintance is that you've never liked – '

'Bossy women,' he cut in.

It wasn't quite the adjective I was going to use, but it would do.

'No, I don't, old mate, 'cos women shouldn't always try to make up men's minds for them. We're not bloody children, you know. And nor's Ted. She should have gone and told him I was at the door and let him make up his own ruddy mind whether he wanted to see me.'

Oh dear. At some very early point in Gus's life some lady must have really got under Gus's skin, and she's been bringing him out in rashes ever since. Not that Gus can't relate with women. On the contrary, he's related with dozens to my knowledge and they seem to love him, with all his warts. But directly they try to mother him – or what he considers smothering – then wham, bam, alakazam, Gus is off to pastures new.

'She wasn't being bossy, really,' I pointed out. 'Just protective and loving, that's all. I bet she carries a candle for old Ted, if we did but know it.'

'Better not carry it too long, old love,' Gus chuckled, 'or

she'll get bloody burnt. Old Ted's never going to marry her in a month of Sundays. Nor anybody, for that matter. Not Ted. Once was enough, I reckon. 'Sides, what would a man of his age want with a wife?'

I reached for the door handle. 'Let's go and see if Mrs Sandle is about,' I said with a sigh.

Well, someone was about. I saw a small face at an upstairs window. It vanished instantly as we walked up to the front door. I rapped my knuckles on the chipped and peeling paint-work. And heard a rattle of what sounded like saucepans in a sink before, eventually, the door was opened by the lady we had come to see, her hands still wet with suds.

Her initial look of annoyance changed to a smile of relief as she recognised me. 'Oh, Mr Marklin, I'm so pleased you've come.' I saw her eye the bundle of overcoats that was Gus.

'Don't worry, Mrs Sandle. This is a friend of mine, Gus Tribble. He's helping me.'

'Oh, do come in, both of you. You must be frozen stiff.'

Like her washing on the line, I thought, but just bowed my head to miss the door lintel and went in to the tiny hall-cum-corridor. Linda Sandle edged past us both (she only just made it past Gus's garmented girth) and opened a well-woodwormed door on the left. We were ushered into what could have been, in the hands of someone who cared, a snug and characterful little room, criss-crossed with the beams and period features so beloved of estate agents' bumf. But years of neglect and heathen hands, who had obviously filled in the original fire-place in the thirties and replaced it with a streamlined tiled job in mottled cream and brown, had taken their toll. Now even the most silver-tongued could only describe it as a depressing mess of a room, not helped by the junk-shop, fifties-style three-piece suite and the children's toys that were strewn all over the worn, wave-patterned, shadow-shaded, warehouse-worst carpet.

'Sorry it's a bit of a mess. I wasn't expecting visitors,' she

145

said, blushing and wiping her hands on her rather skimpy skirt that exposed too much thigh.

I waved my hand. 'Don't worry, Mrs Sandle. We only popped in on the off chance. My friend here,' I pointed to Gus, 'wanted to visit Ted Fern up at the farm.'

'Knew him as a kid,' Gus muttered in explanation. 'Just wanted to say how sorry I was. 'Bout his son, like.'

'So, as we had to pass the door,' I went on, then saw the look of disappointment in her big blue eyes.

'Oh,' she said quietly. 'I thought you'd come round, special. But I suppose you couldn't have heard the news yet. I've been trying to ring you, see. But got no reply.'

I frowned. 'What news?'

'About Dennis.' Her fair hair was not done up in a plait, as it had been on my first visit, and hung loose around her face. She pushed a lock off one eye and continued. 'He's been taken in again. And they're sending a car round for me this afternoon, they said too.'

I looked at Gus. 'No, I'm afraid we haven't heard any news.' The thought instantly went through my mind that her husband's detention might well have something to do with whatever Digby's man had discovered the previous afternoon.

'But you're going to help Dennis – ?' she began, then suddenly switched to, 'Oh, I am dreadful. I should have taken your coats. If you keep them on, you won't feel the benefit when you go outside again.'

Gus and I let her take them, although the warmth emanating from the barely glowing coals in the streamlined fireplace was only just above shiver point.

'It's how Trev got his cold, I expect. That's my son. He's home from school today with it. For the past few days they've let them keep their coats on at school because only part of the central heating is working.'

So that explained the face I'd seen at the window.

When she was back from hanging up our coats in the hall, I had to say, 'I'd better come clean, Mrs Sandle. I'm not here because you and your husband have asked me to try to clear his name. My only interest in young Fern's murder is to help discover the truth. And if the truth goes against your husband [I didn't add "and you"] then . . .'

I could see from her face I had no need to say the rest.

She did not respond for a moment, but then said, barely above a whisper, 'He didn't do it. I know he didn't. I just know.'

'How can you be so certain, Mrs Sandle?' I probed. 'Was he with you that evening and night, by any chance?'

The question seemed to phase her for some reason, for she looked away and stammered, 'Er . . . no, no . . ; course not. Dennis wasn't here. Why should he have been here? No one was here.'

'Because he wants to get back with you again. You know that.'

She sniffed and her fingers, still red from the sink, fretted with the edge of her miniskirt.

'Yes, I know he does. Well, nothing wrong with him wanting, is there? Not a crime.'

'So he wasn't with you. You sure?' I tried to watch her eyes, but she kept them averted.

'No. I mean, yes, I'm sure. No one was with me that night. No one at all.'

Gus suddenly cut in. ''Cept your son, like. Trev.'

She blinked. 'Oh yeah. That's right. 'Cept for Trev.' Then looking back at me, she said, 'I've told all this to the police. So why they want me down at the station again, I don't know.'

'Tell me, Mrs Sandle, when the police got in touch with you today, did they mention any new developments? Like whether they had found the murder weapon or whatever?'

She shook her head and then had to scrape her hair back from her eyes. 'No. Didn't say nothing about anything like that. Why, have you heard something, then?'

'No, as I told you, we've been out.'

The remark obviously reminded her of where we had been, for she looked at Gus and asked, 'You known . . . Mr Fern long? Him up at the farm?'

'Since we were both nippers. Used to play up here, I did. Even been in this 'ere cottage.'

147

'Oh,' was her only reaction, but I could see she was bothered by something.

'Get on well with your landlord?' I asked.

'Yeah, course I do. Why shouldn't I?' was her too immediate reply. 'I'm no trouble. Nor's Trev. Fact, he spoils Trev sometimes. Giving him things, like. Wouldn't do that, if we didn't get on.'

The old light bulb flashed. 'That pedal car I bought off you the other day, Mrs Sandle. Was that something Mr Fern had given Trev?'

She blushed to the roots of her genuinely blonde hair.

'No . . . well, er . . . yes, it was, if you want to know. But I have a right to sell it, if I have a mind.'

'Does Mr Fern know you've disposed of it?'

'No, he doesn't. And don't you two go letting on. I wouldn't have told you if – '

I held up a hand. 'We won't say a thing, Mrs Sandle.'

'That a promise?' Her eyes were on Gus. 'See, it was . . . his son's, when he was a kid. But it was a bit heavy to pedal and it got put away in the attic. Because it was . . . well . . .' She swallowed hard. '. . . *his* and that. Mr Fern might be offended if he knew I'd got rid of it.'

'Why did you sell it? Was it because you'd heard what it might be worth?'

She turned away towards the window. 'Course not. I sold it because . . . well, Trev didn't really like it. And it took up such a lot of room and there seemed no point in keeping it.'

I decided to puncture the balloon she was blowing up.

'You could have given it back to Mr Fern.'

'No, I couldn't. He'd get offended, that's why.'

'Not half as offended, I would have thought, as he'd be if he got to hear that you'd sold it. And not even told him.'

She whipped round. ''Ere, you promised you wouldn't tell.'

'And I won't. Nor will Gus. It's not our business, anyway.'

Having got her somewhat rattled, I probed deeper.

'Both you and your husband, separately, have offered me a lot of money to come to his aid.'

148

I could see she was in two minds as to how to react. In the end, she chose silence.

'Okay. So my question is, where, suddenly, does all this money come from?'

She looked from me to Gus and back again.

'Er . . . well, see, I had a little bit tucked away for a rainy day and Dennis, well, he had . . . had . . . some luck with the gee-gees. Yes, quite a win he had the other day. Always been a bit of a gambler, has Dennis, see.'

I wondered if Linda Sandle had always been a bit of a liar.

'Is that why you might go back to him now, Mrs Sandle? Because he's come up with a bit of money. From the gee-gees?'

She suddenly went into the attack. ''Ere, whose side are you supposed to be on, eh? Coming in 'ere and insulting me with all your insinuations.' She stopped as suddenly as she had begun. I suppose she thought she had better not antagonise me too much, otherwise she might be destroying the last hope she and Dennis had to save themselves.

'I don't mean to go on, Mr Marklin, but I'm just about at the end of my tether right now. So's poor Dennis. If only someone had bloody well seen him that night in his mobile home.'

I noted she, unlike her husband, did not feel the need to flatter his abode into a 'chalet'. I decided the time had come to try a little flattery myself.

'Mrs Sandle,' I said, 'you're an attractive woman. During your husband's imprisonment, you must have had quite a few men who were only too willing to . . . take you out.'

She pulled her sweater down to emphasise, I assumed, the reality – correction, realities – of her attraction. I saw Gus's eyes take in both the gesture and its products.

'Yes, well, course I did. But having Trev, see, and not wanting Dennis to hear I was galavanting around while he was stuck inside, I kept myself more or less to myself.'

I wondered if it was a case of 'less' being more than 'more', if you follow me. Certainly I couldn't imagine someone as patently sexual and extrovert as Linda Sandle living for years closeted away with nothing but herself and her son to hug. But then, in the last two years or so, she'd been in Ted Fern's cottage, which, within the straight laces of his philosophy, might have made having lovers a mite more difficult – and certainly a strictly governed and back-door affair. After all, I was still sore from the moral pasting Ted Fern had given *me* that very morning.

It was at that moment that the woodwormed door creaked open. We all looked round. A second later a boy of around seven or eight was in the room, together with a cough that sounded almost as deep as a horse's.

'Trev, what are you doing down?' his mother admonished, rushing over to him and running her fingers through the reddest shock of hair I've seen since the colour control on my telly once got stuck on 'max'.

'Hello, Trev,' I smiled. Lot of good it did me.

'Trevor,' he coughed as a correction.

'Trevor,' I repeated, not wishing his face to match his hair through rage. He looked up at his mother.

'What they doing here?'

She raised her eyebrows to us. 'This is Mr Marklin and his friend. Just popped in to have a chat, that's all.'

An answer her son found wanting, to put it mildly.

'Weren't chatting,' he sniffed. 'They're 'ere about the murder, aren't they?'

I saw his mother's hand hover around his head, but, no doubt because of us, the backhander was postponed.

'You been outside listening, haven't you, Trev?' Her lips thinned with anger. 'I've told you a thousand bloody times not to spy. Besides, you should have stayed in your bed-room, with that cold. Why do you think I put the electric fire up there? Waste of bloody money if you will catch your death down here.'

I think her homily went in one dirty ear and out the other. Carrot-top said, frowning his freckles at Gus, 'Saw you, yesterday. Going up to the farm. You had a funny old car. Black it was. And all beaten up.'

And black was Gus's expression after such an insult to

150

his pride and no one else's joy. But the boy pressed on regardless.

'Thought you were going up about the cows, didn't I, Mum?'

Mum looked distinctly embarrassed. 'Now, that's quite enough of that, Trev. You'll be in real trouble yourself, if you go spreading nasty rumours.'

Rumours? I perked up. 'About what, Mrs Sandle?'

'Cows,' Gus muttered across to me, but politely refrained from adding the two words 'you' and 'berk' that I knew were hovering on his lips.

'No, don't you take no notice of Trev, Mr Marklin. He watches far too much telly for his own good, he does.'

The sequitur of television from cattle rather escaped me.

Linda Sandle pointed a Damoclean finger at her son. 'If Mr Fern heard just one word of what you're on about, we'd be put out on our ear before you could say knife.'

Carrot-head sniffed contemptuously. Change his accent and he could have been Ginger out of *Just William*.

'What's it matter? You said yesterday we were going, anyway.' He looked up at me. 'Somewhere posh. In Bournemouth. And Dad's – '

The backhander's swipe-by date had at last arrived and the red of his head was almost instantly matched by the red blotch on his left cheek. To my surprise, he didn't bawl out or cringe or anything. Eight years of toughening practice, I suppose. But there were two of us in the room thankful for Trev's big mouth. The gee-gees must have really come in big.

'Cows?' Gus muttered once more. 'What about flaming cows?'

'Yes, Mrs Sandle,' I began, but she cut in.

'Doesn't have anything to do with the murder. Those cows don't. Whatever they've got.'

I suddenly saw what dear little Trev might have been on about. Over the last many months there had been reports of BSE or, as it's unpopularly known, mad cow disease, having spread up from Devon to infect herds in Somerset

151

and Dorset. But up to that moment, I certainly had heard of no cases in the Purbeck area.

I looked down at Trev, whose nose had now started to run rather attractively.

'You think Mr Fern's cows might have got that disease that's been so much on television, don't you, Trev?'

He looked at his mother apprehensively before replying, 'Well, I seen 'em up in the yard, falling about like the ones on the telly.'

'Not them,' his mother corrected. 'Just one.' She looked at me. 'He does exaggerate so. You don't want to take no notice – '

'Three I seen,' carrot-head asserted. 'Last time I saw one I got chased off, otherwise I might have seen more, mightn't I?'

Gus glanced at me. 'All Ted needs now. Bloody mad cow disease.'

Disasters, so they say, often occur in triplicate. I prayed that there wouldn't be one more scheduled in the Big File marked 'Ted Fern'.

As carrot-head thereafter showed no signs of obeying his mother's instructions to return to his upstairs warmth, and Mrs Sandle showed every sign of not enforcing her instructions, for whatever reason (after Trev giving the game away about the posh house in Bournemouth, she might have been distinctly worried about being left alone with further questioning from yours truly), Gus and I soon upped stakes and left. But only after she had extracted a promise from me to try to discover 'what the blazes the police are doing with his dad'.

As we jolted down the hard ruts of the track, Gus observed, 'Trust her, old mate, as far as I could throw her.'

I couldn't really disagree.

He went on, 'Wonder to me that old Ted ever let someone like that have his cottage.'

'Felt sorry for her, perhaps. You know, husband inside, bringing up a child on her own. Besides, I dare say, as he's obviously a tub-thumping pillar of his church, he thought it a Christian duty to try to help others . . .'

'. . . and save her ruddy soul. That's if she's got one.'

'Exactly.'

Gus glanced at me. 'Poor old Ted. First he loses his son. Then, by the looks of things, he's about to lose his battle to keep the devil from that there woman's door and now, sod me, it looks as if he's got mad cow disease.'

'*He* hasn't got it, Gus,' I corrected. 'And we've only got that little horror's word for it that his cows might have caught it. After all, a lame cow can look very much like a BSE victim. Especially if it's sliding about over the icy ruts in the yard.'

'Yeah. Well, let's hope for the best. For Ted's ruddy sake.' He resettled his bulk in the seat, then changed the subject, as I knew he was about to, after such a familiar gesture.

'What we going to do now, old son, eh? Go down and beard old Digby in his den or see that ruddy waitress you told me about or what?'

'We're going home first, Gus,' I said, changing down for a junction, 'and I'm going to give my so sadly sinning lady a ring.'

Gus chuckled. 'Get to you. Ted's remarks. Did they?'

'Not really. But just recently, what with Arabella's parents being down and everything, I'm starting to feel very real sympathy for every specimen that's ever slid under a microscope.'

Gus guffawed, then prodded his layers of clothing. 'Got the perfect answer, mate. Get a thick skin, like mine. Too bloody tough to cut no slices off for any ruddy microwotsit to peer at.'

I smiled. 'How do you get one, Gus?'

He turned to me, a big grin on his rotten face. 'Know that shop in Swanage High Street, just up from the chandlers? Well, they've got lots of them in the window. *And* soddin' telescopes . . .'

Oh, why don't I ever learn?

153

10

One day, no doubt, I'll be pressurised by society and some of my customers into getting an answering machine. But right now, I rank them with car phones, portable phones, bleepers and Digby Whetstone as insidious invaders of the world's privacy. 'Call me old-fashioned', to use one of Edna Everage's immortal prefaces, but I believe electronic communication should be imprisoned indoors and not allowed to roam noisily through our green and, so far, pleasantly tranquil land.

I know, I know. Answerphones are indoors. But when they're in use, I'm not, am I? What's more, I believe I'd dread coming home, if the first thing I'd have to do is replay a tape to hear about all those calls that I might have exited just to evade in the first place.

I only blah on about it all because Arabella's first words, when I rang her, were, 'I've been trying to reach you for the last half-hour.' Becoming a somewhat familiar message that morning, after Linda Sandle's similar comments. But my beloved did not follow it up with a hype for an answering machine. Luckily, she hates the things too. And once played a mind-blowing trick on one of her colleagues by feeding into her machine the following message:

'This is the International Direct Mail Company. We picked your name at random out of the directory to give you the chance of winning a twenty-five-thousand-pound BMW or cash equivalent. All you had to do to win was answer the following question: What is the name of Walt Disney's mouse character? But sorry, you were out, so we must extend this offer to the next subscriber on our list.'

Her colleague, I gather, no longer seems to connect up her machine. Anyway, back to Arabella and why she had been ringing me.

'Digby's got his tail up,' she announced.

154

'Found the murder weapon?'

'So he thinks. At the press conference he said the traces of blood on it matched Fern's blood group.'

'The "it" being?'

'An old car jack. That is, a jack off an old car. Really old. Like Gus's.'

'There's nothing like Gus's.'

'Granted. Digby did mention the model type. Said the police used them years ago. I don't remember them . . . but you might.'

'Thanks,' I said. 'Right this second, I need reminders like that like a hole in the head. However, let me guess. It would be a Wolseley. Either the Six eighty or the Six ninety model.'

'Six eighty. But Digby said some Morris models used a similar jacking system.'

'Oxford and Isis.'

'Told you you'd know,' she teased, then continued, 'It was apparently found on that car dump near Wareham. And guess who's living just up from it.'

'Dennis Sandle.'

'Right in one. For once, Digby seems to have come up with something.'

'No wonder he seemed so cock-a-hoop last night when he, sorry, her at the wheel, flashed us down. By the way, how on earth did his men find it?'

'Digby ordered a thorough search of the whole area around Sandle's mobile home or chalet or whatever he calls it. It seems the jack was lying on the bonnet of a junked Cortina. It caught the attention of one of his men.'

'Sounds a bit too good to be true, doesn't it?'

She took my meaning.

'That's more or less what I commented at the press conference. That the bonnet of a car didn't exactly seem the cutest place to hide a murder weapon. But Digby had a reasonable answer for that. Apparently the dump is to be closed down soon. Environmental pollution and all that jazz. So the owner has already disposed of most of the parts that will fetch anything and has left the place unlocked and unguarded for some weeks now. Result, kids play there and ferret around for old hubcaps and things. So the jack, he says, could have been hidden well away and lost forever, had it not been accidentally unearthed by the local children or whatever.'

'That certainly explains why the police have taken in Sandle again.'

'How did you know they had?'

I told her. Not just the bit about Linda Sandle's concern for her one-time estranged husband, but a précis of the whole morning's shebang. Ted Fern, Madge Quaintance and all.

But I asked her not to say anything about carrot-top's BSE suspicions to anyone, until we had more to go on than a bad cough and a maybe wild conjecture.

In answer to my next question Arabella said she knew nothing more about Sandle's detention than I did, beyond the fact that it had occurred and its likely reason was the discovery of the jack. I then asked her about her Golfing experiences, when she drove down to the VW dealer.

'Ah,' she replied, 'well, there I think I made a bit of a hit.'

'Hopefully not with your car jack.'

She treated that with the contempt it deserved and went on: 'The mechanic, Tony Firestone – he looks a bit like James Dean – seemed terribly flattered that I had asked for him by name to fix my misfire. Naturally imagined his prowess with a spanner has begun to get around. So while he worked on my ignition and took out my plugs and all that, I kept up the flattery. Bit by bit he began to tell me all about himself. How he had never been any good at school until they'd been given a project by the headmaster to make a vehicle that would do a hundred and god-knows-how-many miles to the gallon. Then how he really came into his own, blah, blah, blah. God, I should have won an Oscar for the way I hid my boredom.'

'I don't think there's a category for that. Anyway, what did you learn that might help us?'

'Wait for it.'

156

'Breathless.'

'Then I'll begin. Louise Robbins gave him Fern's car this morning.'

'The Porsche replica,' I exhaled.

'The very same. He said she'd given it to him for having helped Fern build it in the first place and for having looked after it so well for him since. And that she had no use for it, anyway. Keeping it herself would only be a constant reminder of Fern and how he died.'

'Believe him?'

'I do believe he's got the car. Because he showed it to me. But as to the reasons he gave for Mrs Robbins suddenly donating it . . . well, I can already guess what's going through your mind.'

'Blackmail? Proceeds of . . . ?'

'Could be, couldn't it? Fits with what Bessy Meade said about his suddenly being closeted away with Mrs Robbins in her office.'

'Wonder what he knows that we don't.'

'That Mrs Robbins didn't stay in the night of the murder, as she claimed?'

'Or even where she actually went that night?'

We both hmmed in unison.

'That it?' I queried. 'Or is there more?'

'When I asked him what he thought of Fern himself, he said, "Not much. That Mrs Robbins is well rid of him".'

'Did you ask why?'

'Of course. Only I wrapped it up a bit, knowing his girlfriend is that waitress who blabbed to my parents. "Not exactly the faithful sort?" were my actual words.'

'And he said?'

'Nothing at first. Just laughed out so loud that he dropped one of my plugs into the engine bay. While he was ferreting it out he went on that Fern's only interest in life was "the main chance". With women. With anything, he said.'

'He didn't mention his girlfriend?'

'No. Not a word. I didn't like to press my luck right then.'

I thought for a moment, then asked, 'He didn't voice any

opinion as to who might have wanted Fern out of the way, did he?'

'Not specifically, no. But there was one other thing he said that intrigued me – that Fern had been talking a lot recently about going abroad.'

'On holiday?'

'No. Permanently, it would seem. You'll never guess the place he talked about most.'

'In this weather, it obviously wouldn't be Siberia.'

'Rio de Janeiro.'

'Seriously?'

'Seriously. Firestone said he'd been fascinated with the place ever since he'd seen a Michael Caine movie set in the place. Remember the one? We saw it on the box once. Almost made our supper make a return trip. Though, as I recall, you rather liked the topless teenager in it, with the big boobies.'

'Nonsense,' I came back. 'That film had no good points.'

Arabella chortled. 'Anyway, that's it. I must get back to work again now. They're waiting for my write-up of the press conference.'

I was about to bid her goodbye when visions of another, more recent feature film flitted through my mind.

'Hey, remember *A Fish Called Wanda*?'

'Course I do. You can't compare that with the Caine thing, though.'

'Rio de Janeiro,' I reminded her.

'Oh yes. That's where John Cleese was scarpering to at the end, wasn't it?'

'Yes. But not alone,' I said, pointedly.

'Alone. Oh, you mean he had Jamie Lee Curtis with him – '

She stopped abruptly, as the penny dropped.

'Just a thought,' I said.

Gus and I pulled a Heineken and brewed on what we had learnt that morning.

'Well, old love,' Gus opined, wiping froth off his stubble, 'things don't look too good for your Sandle.'

158

'He's not my Sandle,' I corrected. 'But you're right. Digby and his boys are, no doubt, right now trying to screw a confession out of him.'

'Think he did it?'

'He has no alibi for that night. And he might well have had a motive for killing Fern.'

'That Fern had shopped him after the jewellery break-in?'

I shrugged. 'Maybe, or that he'd somehow got his hands on the loot while Sandle was inside. Maybe that's the real reason he went to London. To fence the stuff.'

Gus slumped back in his chair. 'Might be a thousand other ruddy motives, for all we know. Still, if Sandle is telling the truth and that night he really was zizzing away in that place he's renting, then who else we got?'

I held up a handful of fingers and began counting.

'For a start, I'm afraid to say it, there's Louise Robbins. After all, we're pretty sure she's lying about where she was that night. I don't think dear Bessy Meade's eyesight can be so bad that she'd mistake her hotel owner, whom she has known for years, for someone else. But somehow, the finding of that old car jack . . . I mean, it's not the most likely weapon for someone like Mrs Robbins to come across, surely?'

'Yeah.' Gus slurped some more Heineken as Bing put forepaws on to his knee to facilitate the investigation of some intriguing odour on his cords. 'But you can't be sure, old love, that her late husband didn't have an old Wolseley or something, can you? Besides, no one has said yet where exactly they think the boy was killed. I mean, maybe the jack was just lying around on the ground and she just grabbed the first rotten thing she saw. She's got a perfect motive, if all we hear about his larking about with other women isn't a big pack of bloody lies.'

I had to admit that Gus had more than one point. Louise Robbins was a woman of passion, to say the least. And, I felt, of great pride. Hence her stated objective of clearing her young lover's name. Having fallen for a toy boy was one thing. Falling for a crooked, womanising and unfaithful

159

toy boy, quite another. By proving the rumours about young Fern to be false, she would feel she was restoring her own reputation and retaining some dignity for the future. After all, Bournemouth is hardly a Cannes or Antibes, where toy boys are a sou a *douzaine* and toy girls are accepted as the flip side of the declining currency of age.

'Anyway, this mechanic, Firestone – he's got something on her, certainly. I can't see her giving him Fern's Porsche look-alike for the reasons he gave. Dammit, the car had only been returned to her from the garage yesterday.'

'What about this 'ere girlfriend of his? The waitress. If Fern was after her too, then Firestone himself could have a motive for killing him, don't forget old son.'

'I haven't forgotten,' I sighed. 'I just don't see how his blackmailing Mrs Robbins, if that's what it is, fits with him as Fern's murderer.'

Gus downed the last of his lager and pulled himself up in his chair. An only too familiar gesture. I went out to the kitchen and got him another Heineken from the fridge. While I was out there, I fed Bing half a tin of Whiskas. After all, even in Thailand the odd whiff of a pair of trousers hardly constitutes a meal.

Gus's glass now refreshed, we brewed on.

'We ought to go and see that there waitress girl,' Gus offered.

'I suspect she might shut up like a clam if we did, Gus. Probably deny ever having said anything to Arabella's parents. You know, on the "job'sworth" principle. Like she still works for the woman Fern was living with.'

'Could be right, old son. But seems a pity . . .'

'I'll get the Trenches to do a bit more probing. She's opened up to them once. Maybe she'll do it again.'

Gus held up a massive hand and tapped his little (misnomer of all time) finger. 'So, who else we got left? What about Sandle's wife? She's a nasty bit of work, if you ask me.'

'Can't think of a motive. I mean what possible reason would she have for wanting Fern out of the way? Besides, he was the son of her landlord. She'd hardly be likely to – '

Gus waved his hand. I could feel the breeze. 'Yeah, yeah, yeah. Okay, but I still say she's a wrong 'un. Lucky she and Sandle got together, otherwise two other people might have been landed with them.'

I smiled at Gus's logic. 'I'll admit she's a wrong 'un to the extent that I reckon she's more than willing to go back to Sandle to share what the gee-gees have brought in.'

'Jee-jaws, you mean,' Gus grinned. 'The bloody loot they never found.'

'That's what I meant, Gus . . .' Then I saw his face. Hell, not again. Hey ho.

'Wonder where he had it stashed, while he was inside,' Gus went on, his superior look, thank the Lord, gradually receding.

'We can't have it both ways,' I reminded him. 'Fern having filched it and Sandle still having it, can we?'

Gus sniffed. 'All right. So we can't.'

'Rio de Janeiro.'

My sudden mention of the Brazilian playground took Gus by surprise.

'Whatcher mean?'

'Remember what Arabella reported about the mechanic. That recently Fern had been on about buggering off to Brazil. Well, I doubt if he intended going without a bean or two behind him.'

He took my drift. 'But old mate, it hardly proves he had the jee-jaw money, now does it? 'Sides, how can he have had it, when Sandle seems flushed to the ruddy gills with filthy lucre? Like you said just now. Can't have it both bloody ways, can we?'

'Unless there are actually two separate sources of money, no,' I conceded. 'Still, if Fern was serious in his Brazilian intentions and not just bragging to that mechanic, then he must have been anticipating funds from somewhere. And what's more, I doubt if he was planning to go alone.'

Gus fingered his stubble. 'P'raps he reckoned he could get Mrs Robbins to sell up that there hotel of hers and then they could bugger off to Brazil on the old wherewithal.'

'Not impossible. But all the signs seem to be that he was

161

growing tired of Mrs Robbins. Besides, I doubt if she's the kind or of the age who would exchange Bournemouth and the security of her hotel for the great unknown of Rio de Janeiro. And I reckon she'd realise in a flash that she needed the competition of bare-breasted beach bimbos, tanned to a teenage turn like a grouse needs the twelfth of August.'

Gus put down his already two-thirds empty glass.

'Maybe young Fern had pulled some ruddy robbery of his own. Or was about to. Wouldn't put it past him, from all we've heard. Then he could have scarpered with just about any rotten woman, couldn't he? That waitress, for one. And God knows how many others he might have had on the end of a string, sod like him. After all, you've said that there Mrs Robbins didn't keep tabs on him all the time, with her having a hotel to run and all.'

Yes, that was the trouble about the whole Fern case – there were far too many things we, or even God, maybe, didn't know right then.

'Then again,' I sighed, downing the last of my first Heineken, as Gus dittoed with his second, 'Fern could have been simply fantasising. Imagining himself on Copacabana Beach like some Ronald Biggs or other, with a harem of bare-boobed bimbos in his wake.'

'How far away is this place, any road?' Gus asked with a wink.

'Too far for you, Gus, unless you win the pools,' I smiled back. 'And for your perishing Ford Popular – unless that sprouts wings.'

He tapped at his now empty glass with a fingernail. I pretended to be too preoccupied with my musing to notice. The last thing I needed for any sleuthing we might get up to in the afternoon was a Gus up to the brim with canned comments and conversation, let alone laughter.

After a moment or two's silence, Gus came out with, 'Poor old Ted. I hope that ruddy kid is wrong.'

'About mad cow disease?'

'Yeah. Just about bloody kill him, that would, on top of everything. He looks just about half dead already, and no wonder.'

'Pretty horrible child, wasn't he?' I reflected. 'Yet your Ted must like him well enough to have given him that pedal car.'

'Making up for his lost son, p'raps,' Gus said quietly. Well, quietly for him.

'Most likely.' I put my empty glass down on the table next to my chair. 'I hope he never hears that she's sold it. And worse, who she's sold it to. Your friend Ted's opinion of me is not exactly high at the moment without that.'

'Sold it yet?'

'No. And I'm not going to if I'm never around enough to open up shop.'

Gus looked at me. 'That a hint, old son?'

'About what?'

'That you'd like me to mind the store this afternoon or tomorrow or something.'

It was a temptation, even though Gus's views on the role of a shopkeeper are poles apart from mine as he'd proved on almost every occasion he'd stood in for me in the past. To be frank, he makes even Arkwright in *Open All Hours* seem downright generous, lethargic and laid-back. Gus ups most of my prices, weaves fantastic fictions about the background of even the most modest of my toy stock (Examples: Margaret Thatcher once owned the set of Dinky Toy dolls' furniture, would you believe? And Hermann Goering, head of the Luftwaffe, originally bought the pre-war Meccano Aeroplane Constructor outfit), and when he sees a customer hovering, uses bombast and belligerence to clinch a deal, rather than charm and a nice line in flattering chat. All the same, I have to admit that in the short term I've never really lost out with Gus as a locum tenens, as he often does seem to shift stock. Of course, to judge him accurately in the long term, I'd have to keep a tally of how many of those customers ever brave my shop's portals again.

'I'll let you off this afternoon, thanks, Gus,' I decided ultimately, as I knew how miffed he'd actually feel if I 'took him off the case' right at that juncture. Anyway, it would look as if I'd only used him to gain me access to his old mate, Ted Fern.

163

But the morrow was another day. I couldn't afford to stay shut for a whole two days out of the trading week, but by then anything could have happened – like Digby might have forced a confession out of Sandle, now that the murder weapon had actually been found.

Gus rubbed his hands together. 'What are we going to do then, old lad, this afternoon?' He chuckled. 'I'm game for anything, other than another ruddy hair-raising ride in that old lady's Daimler.'

Our trip to Bessy Meade's friend Muriel seemed light years away by then. I was truly thankful that we had received no further word about her break-in problems. The Fern affair was more than enough for our tiny minds to deal with.

'No. I think I can promise there'll be none of that. I would imagine that Muriel will have taken our advice by now and fitted out her bungalow like a miniature Fort Knox.'

'So what's in your head, old lad? I hope you're not thinking of seeing that Digby about Sandle. 'Cos if you are, I'd rather stay here and mind yer shop, if you don't mind.'

'No, I'll leave Digby for Arabella and her TV lot to follow up. Besides, there won't be any news until they've either arrested Sandle or had to let him go.'

Gus sat and gazed at his empty Heineken can as if it held the answer to the whole of life's problems. Maybe, for him, it does on occasion.

'If that bugger Sandle did do it,' he muttered, 'then I'm looking forward to hearing why he left the body on your poor old aunty's grave. Not what you might call very bloody clever, is it? Leaving your victim's body right out in the open, where the first sod who comes along can see it.'

'Maybe the murderer was trying to be clever. Throw people off his scent by, say, taking the body miles from where the killing had actually taken place.'

'Or try to pin the blame on someone else – like whoever ruddy lives round that way.' He looked at me.

I nodded. 'Well, there's more than just Sandle. There's that waitress and I wouldn't be surprised if the mechanic,

164

Firestone, doesn't live in the area too. After all, Wareham's quite a stride from Bournemouth and Dendron Park. And I very much doubt if she can afford a car of her own. Could well be Firestone who brings her in every day on his way to the VW garage.'

'Can't think no one would try to pin it on no waitress. Boyfriend, maybe. And course, Sandle . . .'

'And now the murder weapon has turned up round there. Lying on a bonnet, where you could hardly miss it.'

'Like a body on a bleeding grave.' Gus put a hand to his mouth. 'Oh, I'm sorry . . . no disrespect to your aunty, old lad.'

I looked at my watch, then rose from my chair. 'Let's grab a ploughman's up the road, Gus. I think we might both need some food for thought before we decide where we're off to this arvo, as they say down under.'

Our hostelry hour or so produced no great sensations. And I'm not talking about the French bread, Cheddar cheese and brown pickle, the last-named, to our mortification, tasting more or less like it looked. But about how best our afternoon could be spent.

We eventually settled on a visit to Dendron Park Hotel, and its owner in particular. Gus and I agreed that it was about time we stopped pussyfooting around our considerable list of suspects and started to confront one or two of them with what little we had discovered so far. At least that way we might have a chance of paring down the list.

I rang the hotel first to check that Louise Robbins would be in and willing to see us. Correction. See me. Thank the Lord, Gus took the point that if she were confronted with two accusing faces, she might well decide that preservation of her pride was worth more than any relief she might feel from unburdening her soul. Of course, as Gus pointed out, if she really had killed her toy boy, then she was unlikely to confess to anything, however few the witnesses or inquisitors.

We went off in my Beetle under a claustrophobic sky

165

that suddenly had become that smoky pink which threatens snow.

Gus pointed a digit up to the heavens while we froze on the ferry to Sandbanks.

'Won't get ruddy warmer, old mate, till we get that lot down.'

'I hope it holds off until we've finished motoring around on this Fern case,' I shivered. 'And until Arabella's parents have finished their holiday and gone back home. Because if they'd wanted snow, I hazard they just might have preferred St Moritz to downtown Bournemouth.'

As we had already arranged between us, directly we arrived Gus went off to quiz Bessy Meade, just in case her Miss Marpling about the hotel had produced any new sightings, soundings or rumours.

Louise Robbins, who must have seen my yellow peril parking in the forecourt, was already standing at her office door to greet me. Once inside, she offered me a seat, then, somewhat to my dismay, sat down behind her desk. Now there was something between us, so to speak. The separation of veneered timber, behind which she could take refuge, like so many nervous executives in the world of commerce.

She rested her elbows on its surface and came right to the point. 'You said you'd discovered something that worried you, Mr Marklin – ' She suddenly stopped and smiled. 'Oh, I'm sorry, it's Peter, isn't it?'

Her smile only pointed up how strained her face was looking. If anything, she came over as more racked and tense than at our last meeting.

'Yes, Louise,' I smiled back. 'I just feel that if I'm to be able to help you over Jacob Fern, than I must have all the available facts. And there's a piece of information that's come to my attention that does concern me and it's . . . er . . . about yourself.'

Elegant fingers nail-tapped at the desktop. 'Me, Peter? Something that concerns you?'

'Yes.' I decided to go right in with the actual assumption

166

rather than the facts that had led up to it. 'You're being blackmailed, aren't you?'

To my surprise, she held my gaze but gave no response.

I went on. 'And the blackmailer is the mechanic who serviced Jason's car, Tony Firestone.'

Still no reaction. Still she held my gaze. Not quite what I'd been expecting. I had no alternative but to plough on.

'That's why you gave him Fern's car, isn't it? To stop him from telling what he knows.'

At last she did look away. But said absolutely zilch.

'What does he know, Louise? That you didn't stay in that night, as you claim? That you actually went out in your car and did not come back until the early hours?'

I waited, but she still sat immobile, staring out of the window.

'Where did you go, Louise?' I asked firmly. 'To find Jason?'

Nothing.

I pressed on. 'And did you find him? Because if you did, you must – '

She suddenly swung her head back to me, her big eyes now narrowed by anger or grief, or maybe both.

'Where did you get all this, Marklin?' I noted my Christian name had now gone out the window. 'I asked you to try to clear poor Jason's reputation, not dig around to try to blacken mine.'

I held up my hand. 'Louise, all I'm trying to do is discover the truth, that's all. I'm not trying to get at anybody – '

'It's that Bessy Meade, isn't it?' she cut in. 'She must have seen that bastard Firestone come out of my office. Hell, why can't she mind her own bloody business?'

'She cares for you, Louise. She doesn't want to see you getting hurt any more.'

She looked at me, her eyes slightly softening. 'Peter [Ah! He's back.], please don't ask any more. You must take my word for it that whatever relations I may have with that mechanic have nothing to do with Jason's death. Or with whatever bastard may have killed him.'

'You don't have to prove that with me right now. But you

167

may well have to later with the police.' I leaned towards her. 'Listen to me, Louise. Blackmailers' demands rarely remain static. The appetite grows with what it feeds on. Jason's car is just the beginning, believe you me. If what you say is true and whatever Firestone knows has nothing to do with the murder, then why not come out in the open and expose him for what he is? Surely, what he knows – '

'Will expose me, Peter.' She rose and came out from behind her desk. As she approached me, I could see the moisture in her eyes. 'Please don't ask me to say any more. Just believe me. Can't you see I'm telling the truth?'

'I'd see better if only you'd come clean about where you were that night.'

She shook her head slowly from side to side. 'I didn't kill him, Peter,' she said softly. 'I could never have killed him, whatever he'd done.'

I gritted my teeth. 'If you won't tell me, Louise, I'll tell you where I think you went that night.' She didn't try to stop me, so I went on. 'You took your car out in an attempt to find him. I have no idea all the places you must have tried, but I guess, from the fact that Firestone must have spotted you or your car, that at one point you tried his girlfriend's place – your waitress's digs in Wareham.'

She closed her eyes and a tear escaped down her left cheek. But she said nothing.

'I'm sorry, Louise . . . but you see, I think you'd guessed about Jason and the waitress. Was he there, Louise? Did you find him? Or did you, perhaps, wait in your car until he came out and then . . . ?'

She suddenly fell on her knees in front of me and grabbed my hand. 'I thought he was there . . .' Her voice was barely above a whisper and my hand shook with hers. 'His car was outside, you see. The Porsche . . . I thought Jason must have gone and picked it up . . . I waited and waited and waited . . . I was frozen to death by the time I saw the figure come down the steps. I started my engine, flashed on my lights and revved up.'

She looked up at me and tears were now furrowing down her make-up. 'Peter, I don't know what I thought I was

168

going to do . . . just scare the living daylights out of him, I suppose. But in the lights, I suddenly saw it wasn't Jason. It was Firestone. He must have finished fixing Jason's car and taken it home with him for the night. God . . . when I saw who it really was, I just slammed the car into gear and roared off home, praying he hadn't spotted who I was.'

'Only, being a car nut, he recognised your Peugeot?'

She nodded and lowered her head on to my lap.

'You came straight back here? You didn't go on anywhere else?'

'No. Seeing Firestone like that shocked me into realising what a bloody idiot I was being, letting my suspicions run away with me.'

I looked down at her. Maybe I had been letting my suspicions about Louise Robbins run away with me. I had to ask.

'But if that's all there is, why are you giving in to Firestone's blackmail?'

She lifted her head up from my lap and let go my hand.

'Oh God, Peter, can't you see? Once anyone knows I didn't stay in the hotel all night, it's only my word that all I did was wait outside Mavis Peach's digs. If the police got to know – as that bastard Firestone pointed out – they'd naturally suspect I might have been to all sorts of other places and up to all sorts of other things. Especially with poor Jason . . . being found in a Wareham churchyard.'

She hid her face in her hands. 'I swear to God, all I did was wait outside her place. You must believe me.'

I reached forward and touched her hand. 'It's not the reaction of the police you're really worried about, though, is it?'

She did not look up.

I continued. 'It's that of all the other people, isn't it? Your friends. And the hotel guests. And your staff. Especially your staff.'

She began to cry, like the agonised whimpers of some scared and wounded animal. I did not need any other reply. I got up from my chair, bent down and lifted her up to her feet.

'Louise . . . I leave it all up to you.'

She buried her head in my shoulder and shook with her sobbing.

'But my advice to you is still the same. Be prepared to tell the truth, whatever it takes. It's the only way to get a wretched leech like Firestone from sucking you dry.'

I moved back slightly from her and tilted her chin, so that I could look her directly in the eyes.

'No one will think badly of you, Louise. This time, you must believe *me*. They'll understand . . . in fact, I'm sure they understand already. Going and waiting outside Peach's place was a natural instinct of someone in love. Not a sign of any weakness in you. Quite the reverse. Had you not gone, that would have been interpreted as – '

My next words were abruptly cut off by her lips upon my mouth. But it was the kiss of a survivor to her rescuer. One of sheer relief and gratitude, not of desire.

There was no sign of Gus when I left Louise Robbins' office, though I searched through every public room, with particular reference, needless to say, to the two bars. On enquiry at the desk I was told that Mrs Meade had invited a Mr Tribble up to her rooms. I thanked the rather prim-looking receptionist, who, for some reason, seemed to look at me rather askance. But, with a shrug, I thought nothing of it and plodded up the stairs to where I remembered Bessy Meade's room to be.

My arrival was greeted with a buss on the cheek from Bessy, whose lack of inches or, rather, feet – meant I had to bow very low for the gesture to be accomplished without sending for a ladder. Gus's greeting from an armchair by the window was as enigmatic as ever.

'See yer meeting with Mrs Robbins went well, then.'

I looked at him. 'What makes you say that?'

He pointed to his own mouth and then to me. I glanced at Bessy who put her hand to her face to hide a smile. There was a gilt-edged mirror on the wall to my right, so I went over there to inspect my reflection. As I had by then guessed, Louise's full lips had left their mark, smearing scarlet across part of my upper lip and stubble. I instantly rubbed at it with my handkerchief.

Whilst I did so, Bessy asked, 'Did it really go well, Peter?'

I nodded. 'I hope so. Let's just say, I don't think you need to be concerned any more about what you saw out of your bedroom window that night.'

'Oh good,' she sighed with relief. 'That's one worry out of the way, then.'

I didn't like the sound of that. I glanced at Gus.

''Er friend, that Mrs Purkiss,' he mouthed at me.

I turned back from the mirror and pocketed the now red-stained handkerchief. Bessy took up the story.

'I'm sorry, Peter, I wasn't going to mention anything about it right now, with you and Mr Tribble here obviously so up to your eyes trying to discover the truth about Jason Brand.' She smiled across at Gus. 'Mr Tribble has brought me right up to date, you see, while you were downstairs with Louise.'

I dreaded to think what Gus might have said. But that was water under the bridge.

'Has Mrs Purkiss had another break-in?' I queried, praying she hadn't, as otherwise I could see another trip in that kamikaze Daimler looming and even more hours being spent away from my Toy Emporium.

'No, no, no. Nothing like that, I'm glad to say.' And I was even more glad to hear. 'No,' she went on, 'it's just that, well, not to put too fine a point on it, she . . . er . . . seems . . . in the last day or two . . .'

Gus and I waited with baited breath whilst Bessy looked from one to the other of us.

In the end, Gus exploded with, '. . . to be going round the bend.'

I gulped.

Bessy now rushed in to explain, 'No, Peter, Mr Tribble is right. Muriel really does seem very strange at the moment. I don't know what it is, quite. I've asked her time and again if anything has happened, like another visit from that burglar or such like, and she adamantly assures me that nothing of that sort has happened. But there's something worrying her, that's for sure.'

'Has she had the security-lock people round yet?' I asked.

Bessy nodded. 'Yes, they've surveyed the whole bungalow and she's waiting for their estimate.' She leant towards me. 'If it's too high, I've promised I'll help her out. Living alone like she does, she ought to be sure her place is as burglar-proof as possible. I'm lucky. I don't have that problem, living here at Dendron Park.'

'Well, if there's anything you think Gus or I might be able to do . . .' I began, but Bessy waved her hand dismissively.

'Oh, Muriel will get over it, I expect, whatever it is, thanks all the same.'

'Any news on any other fronts?' I asked pointedly.

'No, 'fraid not,' Bessy sighed. 'I was just telling Mr Tribble that though I've kept my eyes and ears open, there is nothing of interest to report.' She looked up at me apologetically. 'Not being much of a Miss Marple for you two, am I?'

I smiled a 'don't worry' smile and turned to Gus. 'We'd better be off, otherwise we won't be much use to anyone, either.'

As we reached the door, Bessy grasped my arm and asked, 'Do you think Louise is going to be all right now, Peter?'

'I hope so,' I replied, then added, 'Why don't you pop down and see her? I think she might just be in the mood for a chat with an old friend.'

She smiled her gratitude and reached up to kiss me. If this goes on, I thought, one day I'm going to get a slipped disc.

'Sounds as if you believe her, old son,' was Gus's first comment on my time with the hotel owner. We were in my car on the way back to the Sandbanks ferry.

'Got to believe someone, somewhere, sometime,' I muttered, rather uselessly, then corrected myself. 'No, that's not it. I actually do think she's speaking the truth.' I saw his eyes. 'No, really, Gus. And it wasn't just the kiss. And before you think or say any more, she kissed me purely out of . . . well, relief that she'd at last unburdened herself to somebody.'

'Pride's a funny old thing,' Gus mused. 'Someone like Mrs Robbins preferring to tell a ruddy lie to the world rather than admit she's gone running after a bastard like poor Ted's son.' He huddled himself deeper into his over-coats. 'I s'pose she was feeling guilty enough already, without that coming out.'

I turned to him irritably. 'Guilty of what?' But I knew the answer. My question was simply a way of venting my anger at a society that still creates guilt feelings in those who happen to fall for partners of a much younger age. And God really help you if you're a woman.

'You know, old son . . . having a toy boy and that.'

I braked for the run down to the waterside and cursed as I saw the ferry in mid-channel, still clanking its way over to Studland. That would mean a twenty-minute wait in the brass-monkey chill. My dander (whatever that may be) now really up, I barked across at Gus, 'Don't tell me you've never hankered after a much younger woman, you old hypocrite.'

He looked quite taken aback, then, after a suitable pause, said with quiet deliberation, weighting each and every syl-lable equally, 'I'll have you know, my old son, I've never 'ankered after no woman of any age in my whole life.'

I should have known that was coming.

He went on. 'If I like 'em, I say so and get down to it. If I don't, I don't. Bloody 'ankering doesn't come into it.' He took a deep breath. 'And as to age, don't make no difference to me, if it don't make no difference to them. And anybody else – ' He raised a couple of fingers towards the still pinkly leaden heavens. Then, after another pause, he reached across and picked up my own gloved left hand, separated the first and second fingers in a 'V' and jerked my arm in a vertical thrust skywards. I loved him for the gesture, which meant the old bastard really understood. But I loved him rather less for the effing great hole my forefinger made in the frail fabric of my Beetle's soft top.

11

I rang Arabella the moment we got back to Studland. But she reported there was still no news from the boys in blue and that as far as she knew, therefore, Sandle must still be under interrogation. The good news was that she was thinking of knocking off early that night, as the notes she was writing up could just as well be completed at home as in her soulless, seventies glass and plastic office. 'But if you and Gus will still be sleuthing around . . .'

It was then that I told her about my time with Louise Robbins and she asked if it was all right if she passed on the news to her parents on her way home.

'You know how worried they are about her.'

I couldn't see any reason for her not to and went on to say that I could think of little more that Gus and I could do that day with Sandle still detained, so please come on home.

Gus seemed disappointed when I told him, but took the point that a pause for thinking would be no bad thing at that stage. Besides, he said, he'd better go back and stoke up his fires to keep his ruddy pipes from freezing again. He went, leaving me an hour and a half or so's shop-opening time.

To my amazement, it now being black as pitch outside, I did actually get a customer. A guy in his mid-fifties, muffled up to the eyeballs against the cold. He said he'd called earlier but I'd been shut.

I didn't argue with that. Just asked him what his interest was. He instantly pointed a sheepskin-gloved finger at the J40 pedal car.

'That,' he coughed. 'Mind if I look at it?'

I waited whilst he gave it the toy equivalent of an MOT.

'Not bad,' was his verdict. 'How much do you want for it?'

I suddenly realised I was in a dilemma and, for once, wished Gus had not gone. The problem was his old mate, Ted Fern. Maybe, with his son dead, he would, at some time, like the pedal car back. As a tangible memory of the past and what might have been. After all, I was sure that when he'd handed it over to the dreaded Trevor, he'd had no idea that Linda Sandle would then up and sell it. I could have done with Gus as a sounding board as to whether I should now be selling it at all.

'Er . . . it's rather expensive,' I parried.

He fingered the Flying A on its bonnet.

'Oh? How much would that be, then?'

I looked at him. His check overcoat and matching scarf certainly didn't shout poverty. And the white Toyota Lexus parked outside could have been traded in for a small starter home down our Dorset way. So I reached for the skies.

'Nine fifty,' I said.

He didn't even blink. 'Bit steep.' He adjusted his scarf. 'But you don't often see one these days in such original condition.'

'But it's already under offer,' I lied.

He looked at me. 'For nine fifty?'

I nodded. Hell, why had I started all this? I could have just said it was sold the second he'd asked after it.

'Give you a thousand. Cash.'

Shit. Now I knew what Eve felt like in that Garden of Eden.

'Tell you what,' I said. 'Give me your name and telephone number and I'll let you know what the other bidder wants to do. After all, I did give him first refusal. And I hate to just sell it without giving him a chance to match you.'

He blinked his disappointment. Jesus, what was I doing? Giving up a grand on the off chance an old farmer friend of Gus's etcetera, etcetera. With a sigh, he reached inside his coat, extracted a wallet and produced from it his card. I took it from him and saw that he was a business consultant in Bournemouth.

'Don't take too long,' he cautioned.

I promised not to and watched the thousand oncers go

175

out to the Lexus and then quite smartly recede from my sight.

'Marklin,' I said to myself, as I put his card away in my customer index file, 'you need your bloody head examined.'

When the twenty-five-past-six weatherman had finished, Arabella remarked, 'Well, thank the Lord for that. At least the last part of my parents' holiday won't be Siberian.'

'Didn't like that bit about snow tonight, though,' I muttered. 'I hope they've got the sense to grit the roads early.'

'Often get snow before a thaw. Look on the bright side,' she urged. Then, moving closer to me on the settee, she said, 'By the way, when I popped by Dendron Park on the way home, Mother took me aside and asked how things were going.'

I shrugged. 'About dear Jason? Nowhere much right now, as you know. Except for Louise Robbins' confession of where she'd gone that night, that is.'

'Yes., I told her and Dad all about that. They were very relieved and full of sympathy for her. Even Father, would you believe? But my darling, both of them, I'm afraid, are champing at the bit. They've got a taste for this sleuthing lark and want to get more into the action. Be of more help.'

'There's nothing much they can do, really. Except, perhaps, to keep probing away at that waitress. She might open up to them in a way I'm sure she'd never do if Gus, myself or you cornered her.'

'What should they ask her?'

'Just about Jason. What he talked about when they were together. Who his friends were. Like did he ever mention Sandle, and so on. I'd like to know, for instance, if he'd ever mentioned South America or Brazil to her.'

'Right. I'll ring them later this evening. They'll be having dinner right now. But don't forget that Copacabana Beach bit could have just been his sexual bragging or fantasising to another fella. To a girl, he might not have felt quite the same need.'

That weatherman's seaweed hadn't fooled him. We woke

176

up to a blanket of snow. Not deep, mind you, in our part of the world. Only a couple of inches or so. Not like the nine inches to a foot that we heard on the news (grin, grin!) had fallen over the hills in the Trenches' Shropshire. As prophesied, the air temperature had risen by at least enough points for Arabella and me to be able to add sixty seconds to our dressing time that morning.

Needless to say, no gritting lorries had got to our neck of the woods before Arabella had to leave for the TV studios, so I had to give her Golf a push to get it moving off down the ferry road.

The post was late arriving that morning, which wasn't surprising. I was only halfway through packing up the two 39 series Dinky cars, an Oldsmobile and a Packard ordered in one of the letters, when Arabella's assistant phoned through the news about Sandle's release, Arabella herself having, apparently, gone down to the station to see if she could get an interview with old Digby.

My reaction was one of both surprise and, I have to confess, disappointment. Surprise that Digby hadn't found some way of detaining Sandle further, on some pretext. After all, in anyone's eyes, he had to be a prime suspect. And disappointment because, I suppose, the whole affair had not now been brought to a conclusion, and thus my involvement looked like continuing.

I phoned the news to Gus and suggested we might make a call on Sandle later in the day, when we'd had time for Arabella to update us on Digby. Meanwhile, I had a chance to open up the Toy Emporium once more to those willing to trudge through snow and slush to the promised land of childhood dreams.

Lot of good it did me. Or my overdraft. I could have been in the frozen wastes of Alaska for all the customers who dinged my bell that morning. All in all, I was quite relieved to hear that other bell – the telephone – ring about an hour or so after opening up. Thinking it just had to be Arabella, I said, the instant I picked up the receiver, 'Bugger all's happening here. How about you?'

Instead of my beloved's laugh or responding wisecrack, I heard a clearing of the throat.

'Hello,' I said with trepidation.

'Oh hello, is that you, Peter?'

Hell, I recognised the voice instantly.

'Oh, hello, Julia. I'm sorry about the greeting, but I thought you were – '

'Arabella,' she cut in. 'Well, not quite. By a generation, actually.'

I winced. Was that a dig or was I now becoming supersensitive?

She went on. 'Sorry to disturb you, Peter, but we've just heard the news at the hotel that all the guests are wanted for questioning again. This morning actually. The Inspector, it would appear, is taking us in alphabetical order from about eleven o'clock. I asked when "T" was likely to come up, in case we wanted to go out – Clement and I have some shopping we want to do – and he said probably not until around one or so. I'm ringing just to inform you, that's all.'

Obviously Digby had either reached a dead end with Sandle and was starting again or, perhaps, was simply following up something Sandle might have disclosed during interrogation. Either way, I suddenly saw a way of both discovering what Digby was up to and, if necessary, of feeding Digby with lines of enquiry that might not have occurred to him. But all this would be dependent on my common-law in-law's ability to flatter and charm Digby out of his tiny mind. And, of course, her willingness to take on the role of a Bournemouth Mata Hari in the first place.

'Thanks, Julia, for letting me know so promptly. Because it's given me an idea.'

'An idea? Oh, don't tell me, Peter, I may have been of some help?'

'Well, it all depends on your feminine wiles, Julia. Are they in fine fettle?'

She hesitated, then 'oohed' almost like a schoolgirl before asking, 'How do you mean, exactly?'

I cleared my throat. 'Do you think you could think up

178

some reason for having your interrogation upstairs in your room?'

'Upstairs?' I could hear the gulp.

'Yes. Like, say you've got a bit of a chill and don't want to venture down.'

There was a pause, then she asked, 'But what about Clement?'

'Let him have his like the others. Downstairs.'

'Oh . . . What exactly . . . er . . . have you got in mind for me to do, Peter, once I've got the . . . er . . . Inspector . . .'

'. . . under your spell. You've got to mesmerise him, Julia. With your charm and femininity and everything you don't need me to tell you about. I know Digby. He'll be a sucker to a classy act.'

'But, but . . . what do I say? I mean . . .'

'I'll rehearse that with you before he arrives.'

'Really? Oh, well, I'm not quite sure . . .'

'Yes you are, Julia. Very sure. I *know* you can do it. And so do you. Besides, Arabella told me only last night that you were champing at the bit to get involved.'

'But I have agreed to have a further go at the waitress,' she said plaintively.

'Kid's stuff. If you can pull off what I want with Digby, you're in the senior league.'

'Really?' The first note of excitement tinged her tone.

'Really really,' I asserted. 'Really.'

'Oh . . . well, is that it? Anything I should be doing while I'm waiting for you?'

'Only the waitress, really.'

'What time can I expect you?'

'Say twelve-thirty. I'll sidle in the back and come straight to your room. I don't want to be recognised, so don't be alarmed if I'm all muffled up.'

'I won't be, I promise. Anything else?'

'Yes, just one last thing,' I chuckled. 'How big exactly is your wardrobe?'

I was halfway through the 'big boys' *Independent* crossword, waiting for the chance snow-loving punter, when the phone

179

tinkled again. This time it was Arabella with the news that there was no further news. The Law was apparently playing the whole Sandle release so close to its chest, it must have felt the indents of the silver buttons.

'Perhaps letting him go is just a ploy,' I suggested. 'You know the routine. Scare your suspect rigid enough and he might well do something silly once he's free again. I bet Digby has set a tail on him, so they'll know when he blows his nose, let alone attends to any of his other more vital bodily functions.'

'That could well be. But only if he reckons Sandle really is guilty, which we don't know, do we?'

'I hope to, around lunchtime,' I replied and explained the Mata Hari role I had devised for her mother. I asked her if she minded.

'Hell, Peter, no,' Arabella laughed. 'My mother will be tickled pink that you asked her. I can't think of a better way for you to go right to the top of her good books section. Cunning bastard.'

It was some twenty lonely minutes after that call that I saw (having heard the squeal of brakes some moments before) the aged, crinkled prow of the Daimler Conquest try to stop opposite my shop door. Needless to say, it didn't quite manage it, but amazingly, I could just still see one of its rear overriders by the time it did actually manage to come to a halt.

I instantly toyed with the idea of pretending not to be in by quickly locking up and tearing out the back to my own car and scooting off. I needed Bessy's friend Muriel's troubles right then like Harold needed his arrowing experience in 1066. Then I thought that Bessy might not have come about Muriel but about something she had discovered at Dendron Park. So I remained at my counter, like any good shopkeeper.

However, to my horror, a minute or so later Bessy was opening my door, trailing behind her the unmistakable figure of her friend.

'Mind if we both come in?' she smiled.

180

I came forward into the shop to greet them both with as much of a smile as I could muster.

After the usual greetings, Bessy said, 'I'm sorry to be bothering you like this, but I thought it would save you coming over.'

Little did she realise that I was soon to be over at Dendron Park anyway. I looked at Muriel, whose face was almost as ashen as the snow outside.

'Has there been more trouble then? Another break-in?'

Muriel turned away and Bessy answered for her.

'No, no. Nothing like that.'

I frowned.

Bessy went on: 'No, you see Muriel rang me early this morning with some news that had been troubling her.' She turned to her friend. 'I've known something was wrong, Mu. You should have told me about it, you know. That's what friends are for.'

Bessy reached for my hand. 'I've brought Muriel along with me this morning because she says she prefers to tell you all about it herself. Now, dear, where would you like to start?'

'In my sitting-room, rather than the shop,' I interrupted, extending an arm. 'Do please come on through.'

When we were all settled in our chairs, I asked who had driven them over. She said the chef had been kind enough to offer. I suggested that he'd freeze to death if he was left long in the car, but she said he had a cousin who lived just down the road and was going to have a cup of something with her for the half-hour or so they would need with me.

I then offered a choice of drinks to them both, but they declined, saying they'd had 'a glass of Dutch courage' at the hotel before setting off to see me.

'All right, Muriel, now tell it simply, like you told me,' Bessy advised. 'I'm sure Peter will understand.'

Her friend's hands fretted with each other in her lap, and without looking up from my fading Wilton carpet, she began in a voice so frail it almost blew away before it got to me.

'You see . . . I . . . er . . . do the flowers each week at my local church . . .'

'That's in Branksome,' Bessy nodded.

'Yes . . . in Branksome and I always save the best to arrange each side of the pulpit.'

She paused and took as deep a breath as I guess she could muster. 'Well, a good few months ago now, I tripped going up the pulpit stairs and as I picked myself up, I noticed one of the floorboards was a bit loose. About a fortnight later, I suppose it was, my foot caught on it again. I bent down . . . and . . . er . . . tried to see what was wrong with it. I found I could lift one end of the board – it was quite loose – and . . . er . . . I saw there was something inside.'

'Under the floorboard. Hidden away,' Bessy explained. 'Come on, Muriel, speed it up a bit. We don't want to keep Peter all morning.'

'Oh yes,' her eyelids fluttered like netted butterflies. 'No, we don't, do we? I'm so sorry . . . Anyway, I felt inside with my hand and, er . . .'

'She discovered a plastic bag. All covered in dust and cobwebs,' Bessy interrupted. 'And tell Peter what was inside.'

But, somehow, I knew I didn't need telling.

'I just opened up the neck a little. I knew I shouldn't have, but there . . . and I saw that it was . . .'

'Full of jewellery,' Bessy aided, raising her eyebrows and looking away.

'Yes, it was full of jewellery. Rings and . . . and . . . necklaces and . . . pendants . . . and all sorts. Well, I was so amazed, I didn't quite know what to do, so I just replaced the floorboard and tried to forget all about it.'

'Muriel should have reported it right there and then, Peter, I know,' Bessy affirmed. 'But somehow she felt it was really none of her business.'

'I thought it might even be Church property,' Muriel blushed. 'I was so very silly, you see. Bessy has made me see that now.'

'Go on,' I urged.

'Well, another week or two went by and I'm afraid I fell to temptation. I kept looking under the floorboard . . . and then one day I . . .'

This time both of us waited for some moments for the story to be continued, but Muriel's fingers were now going a hundred to the dozen and she looked as near the end of her frail tether as could be.

Bessy gently suggested, 'Shall I go on from here, Muriel?'

The slight quiver of her head we took to be a nod.

Bessy quietly took up the tale. 'To cut a long story short, Peter, Muriel borrowed a diamond necklace from that bag because she had been invited to a rather swank do at the Town Hall by one of her neighbours. And, well, she . . . er . . . omitted to put it back right away.'

'I forgot,' Muriel cut in, without looking at either of us.

'That's right. You forgot,' Bessy responded sympathetically.

'But the once or twice I went to the church afterwards, I did check that the floorboard was back all right,' Muriel said quickly.

'And it was whilst you had this necklace that the break-in occurred?'

'Yes, that's right, Peter,' Bessy answered. 'I've told Muriel she should have explained that to us directly you were so kind as to get involved. But as you can imagine, poor Muriel felt very embarrassed.'

At last most of the questions about her friend's reticence to involve the police were now being answered.

Bessy continued. 'Well, it wasn't until the day before yesterday that Mu felt strong enough to face going back to the church and replacing the necklace in the plastic bag.'

'But when she got there, the bag was gone. Is that it?' I asked.

'Yes, that's right. As you can imagine, it instantly put poor Mu in a bit of a state of shock. So she just dropped the necklace loose under the floorboard and ran out of the church. That's what you did, didn't you, Mu?'

Bessy looked at me. 'And then poor Muriel rang the vicar yesterday and resigned from the group who do the flowers

183

in the church.' She took one of Muriel's fretting hands in hers, for which I was quite relieved. 'And that's about it, Peter. It's been so much on Muriel's conscience that she's been giving us all this trouble, without actually telling us the whole story.'

I held up my hand. 'No trouble,' I lied. 'Forget it, please.'

'Nice of you to say . . .' Muriel began, but her voice soon dissolved into tears.

'Sure I can't get either of you a drink?' I offered.

'Well,' Bessy said rising, 'perhaps we will have just a coffee, after all.' She gave me a knowing look. 'I'll come out into the kitchen, if I may, and help you get it, shall I?'

Once in the kitchen, out of her friend's earshot, Bessy said excitedly, 'Well, what do you think of all that, Peter?'

'I'm so sorry for Muriel,' I sighed. 'Little did she realise what she had unearthed in that Branksome Church of hers.'

'It must have been some burglar's cache, wouldn't you say? What a cunning place to hide it. A church. No one would think of looking there, would they?'

'Sounds a bit like it. Can't think that the Lord would have put it there.' I smiled. 'Or the vicar's wife.'

She poked a finger at my sweater. 'We shouldn't make fun, Peter. Mu is so very upset. Absolutely insisted she should come herself today to put things straight.'

I thought for a moment, then said, 'I guess the thief, whoever he was, must have noticed her mucking about with the floorboard at some point. And followed her home to find out where she lived after he discovered the necklace missing from the bag.'

'Then, after dark, broken in to try to find it. That's what Muriel now reckons.'

'Exactly. By the way, where had she actually put it the night of the break-in? After all, whoever it was made a pretty extensive search of the place.'

She looked around the kitchen, as if to check for eaves-droppers, then whispered, 'In her pillowcase. It was under her sleeping head the whole time.' She came right up to me as I filled the kettle. 'Do you know what I think? I reckon you and I might just be able to work out who the thief might be.'

I lit the burner under the kettle, then went to get the mugs from the dresser.

'You tell me,' I invited.

'Why, that fellow the police have been questioning. You know. Sandle. I've forgotten his Christian name.'

'Dennis.'

'That's it. He knew Jason Brand, didn't he?'

'Before he want to prison for a jewellery robbery, yes.'

'Well, maybe he hid the loot – that's what they call it, isn't it . . . ?'

I nodded.

'. . . in the church and when he came out of prison, went to recover it and, well, found the necklace missing. He suspected that Jason might have taken it, set up a meeting with him and . . .'

She raised her arm above her head and brought it down on my kitchen table with surprising force. Certainly woke up my coffee cups, which did a jig.

I spooned some Nescafé into them directly they'd settled down, then queried, 'Kill just for a necklace?'

She held up a diminutive finger. 'Ah, now, we two don't know, and Muriel doesn't know, what the bag held in the first place, do we? Maybe at one time there was more than one bag. Mu says there's plenty of room under the stairboards. Besides – '

'There are other stairs,' I chipped in.

'Precisely,' Bessy said with some satisfaction. 'Well, what do you think? Or have I seen too many episodes of Miss Marple?'

I went to the stove as I heard the kettle start to bumble away.

'You could be right about the loot being from Sandle's robbery. The dust and cobwebs around the bag would fit with it having been there for some long time.'

'But you don't believe that Mu might have inadvertently caused Brand's death?' She took my arm. 'Naturally I've not breathed a word of these suspicions to her. And nor must you.'

I gave the honest-to-goodness original boy scout's salute. 'Course I would never do such a thing.' I sighed. 'But to be honest, Bessy, I don't really know what to think right now. All I have to go on are feelings. And somehow Sandle killing Brand simply for that necklace doesn't smell right. Mind you, I have no idea what does.'

I took the kettle off the burner and brought it over to the cups. 'Besides,' I went on, 'the necklace killing theory rather clashes with our previous assumption. That the thief must have spotted Muriel herself fiddling about with the stair-board. Otherwise he wouldn't have followed her home, would he? And found out where she lives.'

I filled the cups and Bessy made hay with a spoon to dissolve the Nescafé.

'Oh dear, oh dear,' she smiled ruefully. 'Maybe there's a bit more to being a Miss Marple than I ever imagined.'

Directly they had gone, the old Daimler slithering away on the slushy road, I got my own car out and hurried down to Gus's cottage. I wanted to go over to Sandle's mobile home-cum-chalet right away and beard (or, in his case, stubble) him about Muriel's church find. Then I intended Beetling instantly from Wareham to Bournemouth to be in time for Julia's interview with Digby. For who knew, I might then have more information for my Mata Hari to feed into his shell-like.

To my amazement, Gus was nowhere to be seen when I arrived, although his dreaded Popular was standing in what he cared to call a 'drive'. (In reality, a muddy, weed-strewn area by the side of the house. On that morning, a snowy, slushy, weed-strewn area, etcetera.) In my impatience, I walked round the outside of the house, shouting to him. Not environmentally friendly, I know, but I was in a tearing hurry, otherwise I'd be too late for Digby. It did, at last, produce a result – a grunt or two emanating from the ramshackle barn at the far edge of his garden, or more accurately, bramble patch.

Now, I keep my old Daimler V8 in that barn, so I ran across to see what on earth he was doing out there on such a morning. The sight that met my eyes froze me in my tracks.

Gus was standing by my Daimler looking down at what looked like an H_2O equivalent of an oil gusher. In his hand he held the tap that normally sat on top of the now open pipe that had already spread a lake of water across the barn floor. Correction. Iced water. The ground temperature had obviously still not woken up to that of the air and was freezing most of the flow as it spread across the dirt floor. Which would have just about been acceptable, if the fine spray had not also frozen on contact with my old V8, with the result that it looked like a giant wedding cake ornament of white icing.

'Gus, what on earth . . . ?'

He held up the old brass tap. 'Frozen up, hadn't it? All I did was give it a slight turn with the wrench to free it.'

I looked down. I could just see the dark shape of the wrench beneath the glassy sheet at his feet.

I pointed to my car.

'Don't worry, old love. Hasn't come to no harm. Be right as rain when it thaws.'

I loved his choice of words. But only days afterwards.

'Have you called a ruddy plumber, Gus?' I shouted above the Niagara Falls.

He shook his head. 'Haven't had a bloody chance, have I?'

'God . . .' I began, then asked, 'What's the number of the plumber you had last time? I'll go in and ring him for you.'

''Son a piece of paper by the phone . . .' But by then I was halfway back to the cottage.

The plumber was, of course, out, but luckily his wife said he had a car phone in his van and she'd ring him and say it was an emergency. I thanked her and rushed back to Gus, who was still gazing at the gusher, as if looks could still the flow on their own. I explained that the plumber would be coming a.s.a.p. and that he'd better wait around until he came.

'Then we can go to that Sandle,' he said, brandishing the tap.

'Not without finding the stopcock.'

'Haven't got one out here. Piped straight off the mains.'

'Well, I really have to go right away, Gus. Sorry.' And I took him through at a gallop what I'd learned from Bessy Meade's Muriel and what I planned for Julia Trench.

'Gor . . .' was his main reaction to the news, and 'You should sodding wait for me, in case that Sandle kicks up rough,' to the first part of my plans.

'I'd like to. But can't. Sorry,' I shrugged. 'I must tackle him before Julia meets Whetstone, in case I learn something vital that I can feed him.'

To say Gus looked downcast is the understatement of most years. 'But anything could happen if you tackle him alone, old son.'

'I'll warn him first that I've told a myriad people where I am going. I doubt if he'll risk anything whilst I'm actually with him.' I pulled a face. 'Afterwards, who knows?'

'You'll give me a tinkle to say you're all right, won't you?' Gus said, plaintively.

'Sure,' I grinned. 'But if the plumber still hasn't arrived, you'll hardly be on tap, will you?'

Yer actual tap landed just behind my left ankle as I rushed back across the patch to my Beetle.

Sandle's mobile home, for that's what it really turned out to be, sans wheels though it was, needed little finding. Just a call into the pub that Sandle mentioned when he originally called on me gave me all the directions I needed.

Directly the mobile home hove into sight, I stopped the Beetle, or, rather, slithered it to a standstill, for the snow, though now melting, was still thick enough to give trouble. Beside it, I noted, was parked a recent registration Fiesta. I wondered whether it was Sandle's or belonged to some visitor.

I got out of the car and ran down the track, hoping that speed might take whoever was home unawares. Once near the home, I bent down and loped like some Groucho Marx

188

in the hope that no one would spot me from the side windows. Certainly, I reached its side without any shouts or sound of movement from within. I pressed my ear to the peeling paintwork of the panelling and listened intently.

At first I couldn't hear or sense a dicky-bird. Then, shock, horror, the immobile monstrosity began rocking slightly and I withdrew my ear smartish before it was steel-smitten.

Hell, of all things I'd been prepared for, a rock-horror show was certainly not one of them. As the home continued to have a life of its own, I moved to beneath a window and raised my head inch by inch, until my eyes were just above frame level. I cursed as they met a broad expanse of brown curtaining, decorated (if you care to debase the word that way) with a gross sunflower pattern. On further examination, however, there was the slightest chink showing in the centre between the two pulled halves. I moved along until my head was in line with the chink, then, mega-cautiously, raised myself high enough to peer in.

Initially, I could see little, as the light level was so dim inside. But then, wham, suddenly what looked like a female leg shot up across the window, blocking out what little I could see. It was then I heard the gasps and groans.

'Shit,' I swore to myself. 'Of all the effing things to catch him doing.'

I must then have moved slightly back from my peeping Peter position, for my heel came down on the edge of what turned out to be an old hubcap; this then flicked over into a group of empty bottles that instantly started to domino down against each other with enough dings and dongs to waken the devil.

Within a split second, I heard a 'Fuckin' hell' resound from within the home, and before I could make myself scarcer, a face appeared through the curtains. A face I recognised. And the recognition was mutual. It was Linda Sandle.

There was no point in scarpering then. Rather the reverse. There was every point in staying. For now I could try the pulpit ploy on not just the one Sandle, but on a pair of them, so to speak.

It was Dennis who was first to the door. Just about clad, I was relieved to see, if only in a sweater and trousers. I noticed he hadn't had time to put on any socks, his white ankles peeking above his mock-lizard, slip-on shoes.

'What the hell are you doing here?' were his first angry words. But then he must have realised that such a tone was hardly the way to win friends and influence an amateur sleuth he wanted working on his side. 'Oh, I don't mean to be rude, Mr Marklin, but you see, you've caught me at a, well, awkward moment.'

'Awkward, Mr Sandle?' I queried. 'Why should making love to your wife be described as awkward?'

His eyes flicked back into the home. 'Oh well, you see, as I told you, Mrs Sandle and I are thinking of getting back together.'

'Oh, good. I'm so glad,' I smiled. 'A man needs a wife. A wife a husband. A boy a father.'

'Yes. I'm glad too,' he said self-consciously.

I picked him up. 'Yes and I bet Mrs Sandle is glad that the church has played such a big part in bringing you two back together again.'

He frowned. 'The church . . . ? Oh, if you mean Ted Fern and his do-gooding lot, they've had nothing to do with it. Hell, no. That would be the last – '

He stopped suddenly, as a bare arm prodded him on the shoulder.

'No, that's not quite what I meant, Mr Sandle. I'm referring to a few lessons learnt from the pulpit at Branksome Church in Bournemouth.'

His eyes flickered only the once.

'I don't know what you're talking about, Mr Marklin.'

'Yes, you do, Mr Sandle. I'm referring to the loot from your raid on the jeweller's shop. You didn't hide it in some house that has now been knocked down, but in what you thought was the safest haven in the world. A church. Branksome Church. Under the stairs leading to the pulpit.'

190

I heard Linda Sandle's shrill shout, 'Shut the door on him, damn you, Dennis.'

'Feeling the draft, Mrs Sandle?' I shouted.

But by then Sandle had come down the step and, obeying his wife's bidding, slammed the door behind him.

I immediately trotted out my 'Save Marklin' insurance scheme. 'I had better warn you that everyone knows where I've come this morning, Mr Sandle.'

I stepped back, as he moved towards me.

'Who's everyone?' he sneered. 'The bloody police?'

There was no answer to that, as he well knew. If I'd told the police, they would either have come with me or warned me off interfering.

He came right up close to me. Now I could see the lipstick smears on his stubble. Big deal.

'Just whose side are you on, Mr Marklin?'

At least I still rated a 'Mr'.

'No one's, Mr Sandle. I made that quite plain when you first came to me.'

He looked me up and down. 'People don't do nothing for nothing in this world. So what's your game?'

'This is no game. I just came here to tell you I know all about where you had that loot before you went inside.'

'You know nothing,' he snarled. 'Nothing.'

'Well, another nothing I know,' I persisted, 'is that one day you saw a little old lady messing about around the pulpit, after you'd found a necklace missing.'

I continued to watch his eyes. But this time, nary a single flicker. For a second he might have fooled me that I was barking up the wrong rotten tree. 'You followed her home to find out where she lived, then broke into her bungalow to try to find that missing piece of jewellery.'

I suddenly sensed another pair of eyes watching me. I looked behind him and met Linda Sandle's gaze. She was now dressed and standing at the door.

'Get rid of him, Dennis, for God's sake.'

He held up his square hand. 'Be quiet, Linda. I'll get rid of him right enough, once I've found out what he's really up to.' He looked back at me. 'It's fucking blackmail, isn't it? If you think I'll pay up, because of this bloody cock-and-bull story of yours, you've got another think coming, lover boy.'

Lover boy! I liked that, considering what I'd caught him at.

He went on, holding up a thick finger, 'You haven't got a shred of evidence for any of this shit of yours, have you?' He prodded me. 'Have you? Have you?'

Now, I only take jabs from doctors and then only when there's no alternative but lingering disease or death. I swept down the edge of my hand, as I'd seen in Bruce Lee movies and caught him on the knuckles. He didn't even blanch, sod it. I could have doubled up with the living agony that was now my hand.

'Watch it, Marklin. Don't try and get tough with me. I repeat, you haven't got a shred of evidence for any of this, have you?'

I couldn't deny it, so I parried with, 'I'm not interested in the jewellery, Sandle.' Two can play at omitting 'misters' 'But in who killed Fern.'

'Well, I didn't, you interfering sod. Even the police can't pin it on me, so what chance have you?'

I shrugged and glanced behind him. At his wife. She was by now looking rattled enough (Sorry. No sexual inference intended), I reckoned, to be Sandle's weak link. Anyway, it was worth a flyer.

'But they might be able to pin it on you, Mrs Sandle, mightn't they?'

The fear in her big blue eyes turned to panic. 'Dennis, for fuck's sake, do something.'

I just managed to dodge his fist as it swung towards my chin.

'Why do you look so scared, Mrs Sandle?' I shouted across at her. But in that instant she disappeared back into the mobile home, slamming the door behind her.

'Get out of here, Marklin, before I . . .'

I dodged another blow, only because Sandle's smooth-soled, lizardskins were having more trouble getting a grip on the snow than my Marks & Sparks' trainers.

192

'Before you what? Kill me?' This time his fist glanced my shoulder and I stumbled back. 'Or do you leave all the killing to your wife?'

He stopped in his snow tracks. 'Linda didn't even bloody know Fern, you bastard.' But his eyes were now less confident than his mouth and I could almost see his grey cells working. I didn't quit whilst I was ahead.

'How do you know, Sandle? You were inside a long time. I don't suppose your Linda has told you the half of what went on.'

That did it. He threw himself at me like a cornered tiger. No, that's far too noble a beast. But you get the picture. I think if it hadn't been so damned slippery, all my dodging around (or 'dancing like a butterfly', as Mohammed Ali used to term it) would have still meant a considerable period in intensive care. As it was, I was knocked back against what I took to be a post for a washing line, which promptly bent as I threw my arms around it to stop myself sprawling in the snow. Sandle also grabbed at it, or me, or both, but his forward momentum was too great, his trajectory too wide and he lost his footing, skidding on his stomach until his head doinged into an old oil drum.

I didn't hang around to watch the bump on his cranium grow, but pulled myself upright via the now curved and quivering post and started to run for my life back to the Beetle. Just as I neared it, however, I was struck an icy blow on the head and lumps of snow cascaded off my shoulders. I looked round. Over by a tree stood dear carrot-haired Trevor, just finishing moulding another snow missile to project at me. I grabbed for the door handle and just managed to get in and shut myself away, before the snowball arced over to splat across the bonnet...

12

As I drove into Bournemouth, ice still trickling down my neck, I tried to review my fraught time with the Sandles with a little objectivity. That is, after my heartbeats had stopped sounding like an artillery barrage from the Gulf War.

And as I brewed, my adrenalin count sagged considerably. For I realised that my flyer of virtually accusing Linda Sandle of Fern's murder would have panicked anybody, let alone the wife of the prime criminal suspect who had only just been released from his second guest-spot at the police station. I wondered if I could read as much into her look as I had originally.

As for Sandle's reaction to the thought of his wife ever having 'known' Fern (sexual inference here fully intended), let alone having murdered him, it was difficult to separate his mental reactions from his physical fury. All the same, however, I felt, somehow, that had he actually been the murderer, his behaviour might have been rather different. Oh, he would still have blown his top, no doubt, only it would have been instant and he probably wouldn't have bothered with any denial of his wife ever having known Fern. But the more I mused, the more I wasn't sure – even of that.

Thus, by the time I reached Dendron Park – my once yellow Beetle now slash-painted an ugly shade of brown by the slush on the roads – all the high I had momentarily experienced had more or less evaporated.

I left the car in the street, fearing that if I parked in the hotel forecourt, in which, anyway, I could see at least two police Rovers, Digby might well recognise the VW, dirt notwithstanding. Then, with my sheepskin coat collar turned up around my face, I went round the back and let myself in by some French windows. I received the odd questioning glance from the blue-rinses in armchairs, but managed to reach the staircase and then Julia's room without actually being stopped and questioned.

She was looking at her watch as she opened the door.

'Thank goodness you're here, Peter. It's five to one. I thought you might not be coming after all.'

'Sorry,' I smiled. 'I had rather a fistful of things to do. Hey–' I pointed to her devastatingly well-cut suit in dark blue, edged with white '–that should slay old Digby the instant he claps eyes on you.'

She pulled the slightest of faces. 'I wasn't quite sure, really, what to wear.'

'The choice is perfection,' I said, standing back and admiring her. I must say she looked as good as I'd ever seen her. 'Classily formal, yet hugs your slim figure enough to be utterly feminine.'

She looked surprised, as indeed I was, at my flowery outflowing.

'You should be a commentator at a fashion show,' she smiled, then licked her tongue around her lipstick to make sure it shone for her next guest.

'I wish I was right now,' I laughed, then hurried her over to a chair. 'Look, as I'm so late we'd better rehearse the stuff I'd like you to feed Whetstone right away.'

She sat down, crossed her elegant legs, then pointed at the large Victorian wardrobe that dominated the wall opposite the window.

'Hadn't you better try that for size first?'

'Sure there's time?'

'Yes, just about. As it happens, I rang down just before you came and Louise said they're running a bit late.'

I hurried over to the wardrobe and opened the ornate loop handle.

'I moved a few clothes out to make a bit more room,' Julia commented. 'They're under the bed.'

'Maybe that's where I should go,' I joked and saw her blush.

The inside of the wardrobe, which smelt of mothballs,

195

was certainly large enough for one medium-sized Whetstone witness, but its dark wood and solid construction were a bit claustrophobic. And that was without the numerous skirts, blouses and dresses still hanging from its rails.

I closed the door and came back to her.

'I'll survive,' I smiled and sat down on the edge of the bed opposite her. 'Before we start, I take it they'll ring to warn you they're sending old Whetstone up.'

'Don't worry, Peter,' she asserted confidently. 'I've made jolly certain of that at reception.'

I looked at her and something made me wink. To my surprise, she winked back.

'Now let's get down to it,' she urged.

I took a deep breath and began.

It was twenty-five-past one before the call came through.

'Good luck,' I smiled, as I moved over to my mahogany hide.

She crossed two slim fingers and held them up. 'Oh dear, now the time has actually come–' she began.

'You'll do famously,' I cut in. 'You know you will, Julia.'

Before she could talk herself out of any more confidence, I stepped in amongst her clothing and tried to shut the wardrobe door behind me. But to my alarm, I couldn't manage to make it latch, having completely ignored the simple fact that a wardrobe's sole purpose is to provide housing for clothes, not people. They do not have handles on the inside, surprise, surprise.

I popped my head out and stage-whispered, 'Can you give the door a push? Sorry.'

Julia quickly came over to me. 'You're not starting a cold, are you?' she grimaced.

'No, I hope not,' I grinned. 'If it's sneezes you're worried about, I'll put a finger under my nose.'

She slowly closed the door, looking at me the whole time she did so. She was obviously starting to worry that she had bitten off more than she could chew. I felt a bit of a rat for the situation I'd devised for her.

I suppose it was about three minutes later that Digby

arrived. I didn't actually hear the knock on the door, the mahogany acting as far too effective a sound baffle for my liking. Still, nobody wants startled clothes, now do they?

The sound of their voices seemed ominously remote. I leaned forward to keep my ear as close to the door as possible without actually putting my weight up against it. After all, if the catch were to give, my post-Christmas goose would be not only cooked but burnt to a cinder.

'Very sorry to hear about your indisposition, Mrs Trench,' Digby began. 'So very good of you to see me at all.'

Oh, the creep. Still, it fitted with my long-held estimation that Digby Whetstone was the kind of copper who still had that uncritical admiration for the upper class nowadays usually only seen in British crime movies of the forties, regurgitated on television – 'Now, Sir Travers, I really must apologise for one of my men mistaking you for a drunken driver the other night. I don't know what he can have been thinking of. Just because you were at the wheel when your Bentley careered off the road and ended up in the parlour of your cowman's cottage, killing him and his wife, their whippet, budgerigar and baby daughter stone-dead. Well, I can quite understand that after such a horrible sight, you'd want to reverse out again and come back here to Bowlow Hall and try to recover over a few drinks . . .'

Sorry. Back to Julia.

'Oh, that's all right, Inspector. Anything to help the force, you know.'

Even through my baffle boards I could detect that extra slice of superior charm Julia was serving up, as per instructions.

'Do sit down,' she went on.

There was a slight pause, whilst, no doubt, Digby obeyed her invitation, then he said, 'I hope not to be too long, Mrs Trench. I'm only too well aware that I am keeping you from your lunch.'

'Not to worry, Inspector. Whatever I've got has rather robbed me of any appetite, I'm afraid.'

I loved that bit. Not only did it support the reason for having the interview in her bedroom, but it meant that she

197

could now prolong the interrogation as long as Digby was willing to stay.

'All the same, I'll try to get through my questions as speedily as possible.'

'And I've then got a few questions for you, Inspector.'

'Oh really?'

'Yes, really. You see, I've been doing a little thinking about Mr Fern's death. And it's not very often I have a real live inspector of my own with whom to air a few thoughts.'

Oh, big, handsome Brownie points. I could just imagine Digby's freckled face trying to look modestly humble. And failing miserably, needless to say.

'I'd be only too happy to answer anything that's within my power, Mrs Trench. I might say, it's not often we in the Force have the chance to listen to really intelligent and considered comments from members of the public.'

Oh God. I tried not to vomit. In such a confined space, more for my own sake than anyone else's.

'Well, fire away, Inspector,' Julia replied, 'let's see how I might be able to help you first.'

Digby's questions proved to be fairly routine, much to my disappointment. Julia told me afterwards that most of them were more or less identical to the ones she and Clement had been asked at their first interrogation. As was prophesiable, they centred mainly on the two themes. One, what did she or any of the guests know of Fern, as a person, either at first- or second-hand. Two, what did anyone know of his movements on the last day he was seen alive. There was a very minor third line of enquiry – had Julia or any of the guests heard anything about any of Fern's friends, again either at first- or second-hand. It is at this point, perhaps, that it's worth picking up the story more or less verbatim again. for it's where Julia first started in on what we had rehearsed.

'Well, Inspector, it depends what you mean by "friends". Would you include, say, that man who used to look after his car. What was his name again . . . ?' (As if she didn't know!)

198

'Oh, Firestone. Anthony Firestone. That the fellow?'

'Yes, that's him.'

'You know something of him, Mrs Trench?'

'Maybe it's not important, Inspector, but . . . er . . . you see, it appears he's going out with one of the waitresses here, a Mavis Peach.'

Digby mumbled something I couldn't quite hear, because at that point I was concentrating on not sneezing. No, it was not a cold coming on. It was the scent of mothballs getting up my nose, quite literally. If I were a wardrobe designer I'd give them whacking great ventilators, if not for the convenience of the few sleuths like myself, then for the multitude of adulterers surprised in the act by unexpected husbands.

'Yes,' Julia resumed in reply to Digby, 'and from what I gather, this Tony Firestone might have some cause for not liking Mr Fern. You see, I have reason to believe the latter may well have made, well, a pass or two at Miss Peach.'

'Really? May I ask where you heard all this, Mrs Trench?'

'A little bird told me,' Julia replied, as planned. 'I really don't like to betray confidences, Inspector. Perhaps, for your answer, you should have a word with this Firestone. Who knows what you might learn, if you, say, leaned on him just a little. Is that the right word, Inspector? "Lean"? I hope I haven't made an utter fool of myself.'

My goodness, the lady was working well.

'I'll certainly follow it up, Mrs Trench. Thanks very much for the information. But while "lean" is a word sometimes applied to us police, it's not our practice, you know, to intimidate those we interview.'

One thing was for sure, though. Firestone *would* get leaned on now, my hope being that he'd get so scared he'd think twice about continuing his persecution of Mrs Robbins.

'Talking of interviews, Inspector, I hear that you have now released that other friend of Mr Fern's – a Mr Sandle.'

There was silence for a moment and then I heard Digby reply, 'Yes, we have. This morning.'

'He must be so very relieved to be cleared of all suspicion

199

at last. It must be terrible to know you are suspected of such a heinous crime as murder.'

I think Digby must have laughed. But all I detected was a crackly sound.

'I assure you, Mrs Trench, an old hand like Sandle is used to being suspected of all sorts of things.'

'But at least he's now cleared of a murder charge.'

'Don't misinterpret his release, Mrs Trench.'

Another silence. I took the opportunity to readjust carefully my position in the wardrobe, as my semi-huddled posture was causing cramp in both my neck and left knee. And screaming pain is really not too much up on sneezing, in those clandestine conditions.

'Tell me something, Inspector. As you may imagine, all the guests here – including, I admit, Clement and myself – are full of theories as to the whys and wherefores of Mr Fern's death. I have to say that the flavour of the present moment centres around some jewellery that I believe Mr Sandle served some time in prison for stealing. Now would that be one of your lines of enquiry still? Or have you learned something new and quite different that you are keeping under your hat, until you're ready to make your move?'

'We, naturally, are discovering new facts all the while, Mrs Trench. Like we now know from an examination of his shoes that Mr Fern was probably killed somewhere in the countryside around and not in the town of Wareham itself.'

'His burnt-out car was found in a country road, wasn't it?'

Bully for Julia for remembering. It was not a fact we had rehearsed.

'Yes, it was. We believe Mr Fern probably had an appointment with whoever murdered him and drove out to meet him in the countryside somewhere. Then his killer took his car and drove his body back into Wareham, dumped it in the graveyard and then drove out to an isolated lay-by and set fire to the vehicle. Then he might well have walked or even had an accomplice to give him a lift back to his own car. There are no signs that he was actually killed in that particular lay-by.'

Hmmm. So that was Digby's latest thinking, was it? Or, maybe, the only thinking he was as yet willing to divulge to even the more exalted of us mortals.

'Really,' I heard Julia say, reflectively. 'An appointment, you say. Well, having heard a little of Mr Fern's personal reputation, do you consider that his assignation could have been with a . . . woman? After all, it was rather on the late side to be gallivanting round the countryside to meet a man. Surely he would have arranged that sometime in daylight hours.'

'We're not ruling out anything at the moment, Mrs Trench.'

Good old tight-lipped Digby, sod him.

'A woman . . .' Julia was now in musing mode, so the words were hard for me to catch. 'Now, I wonder . . .'

'What are you wondering, Mrs Trench?'

'Do please call me Julia, Inspector. I have always felt the name Trench to be one of the most inhibiting of surnames. Maybe it's all the terrible fighting of the First World War that it conjures up.'

Another crackle/laugh. 'And I'm Digby. Not a name I particularly go for either, Mrs . . . er . . . Julia.'

'Well . . . Digby. What's passing through my mind is what role that Sandle's wife might have played in the whole affair.'

'Linda Sandle?'

'Oh, is that her name? Linda.'

If I'd had an Oscar, I'd have given it to her. After Digby had vamoosed, of course.

'Anyway, I'd heard he has a wife.'

'And why should this Mrs Sandle have played any role?'

'I'm not saying she has, Digby. And I dare say all I'm doing is letting my poor imagination get terribly overheated over nothing at all. But . . . er . . .'

'But, er, what, Mrs . . . Julia?'

'Well, I'm told this Mrs Sandle lives in a cottage on Mr Fern's father's farm. Is that right?'

'Yes, it is.'

'So . . . it could just be, couldn't it, that upon one of his visits to his father, the son might have encountered this Mrs Sandle. And considering his penchant for ladies . . . well . . . of a certain age, shall we say, he could just have struck up some kind of relationship.'

'I don't want to sound rude, but I think that's rather unlikely.'

'Why is that?'

'Firstly, it appears the younger Fern and his father hardly ever met after he left the farm, and Mrs Sandle has only been in the cottage for the last year or two. But secondly, and perhaps more importantly, the dead man's penchant, as you put it, for ladies older than himself, seems to have been motivated more by the money and worldly goods they possessed than by their characters or even physical . . . er . . . attractions, shall we say.'

'Oh. Well, perhaps you're right, Inspector. It's probably a silly idea. But then I'm not a professional like yourself, to see all the ins and outs and whys and wherefores of everything.'

'You couldn't be expected to know that Fern rarely visited his father–' Digby began, but suddenly Julia interrupted him, as if a brand-new thought had illuminated her mind.

'But Inspector, supposing . . . supposing . . . well, that Fern imagined there was money to be got from Mrs Sandle.'

'How so?'

'Blackmail.'

'Blackmail? What do you mean?'

'Well, I'm assuming that Fern knew that Sandle had been released from prison and had maybe heard, or assumed, that Sandle now had access to the stolen jewellery or to the money from its sale.'

'Go on.'

'Oh dear, am I not making myself clear?'

I liked that too. Ploy meets boy. I could just imagine Digby's servile, reassuring look.

She resumed. 'What I suppose I'm saying is that Fern might have threatened to tell Sandle of his relationship with his wife, unless she coughed up some of the proceeds from the sale of the jewellery. Bit far-fetched, I expect you think.'

'Not far-fetched, really. In our profession we discover far more bizarre and complex motivations and involvements than those you've described, I assure you. No, it's not its plausibility that concerns me. It's the fact that Mrs Sandle has been estranged from her husband for quite some time. Since comparatively early on in his sentence. I doubt if she would much care whether or not Fern told her husband about any such relationship. If it ever existed. Which I have to say, for the reasons I've outlined, Julia, I very much doubt.'

'But now he's out of prison, might they not now be getting back together?'

'Rest assured, I am keeping tabs on any developments that may help us nail Fern's murderer,' Digby parried.

'I'm sure you are, Inspector. I'd be the last person to try to teach you your job, believe me.'

Another crackly sound, which I took to be Digby clearing his throat. 'I wish all the public I have to deal with were like you, Julia.'

Oh, he was off again. Cringe. Cringe.

'But I'm afraid there are a few who seem to imagine that they know far better than any member of our Force, however experienced or expertly trained or qualified we may be.'

Dear, oh dear, I wonder who he could be thinking of.

I pressed my ear as near the door panel as possible to catch Julia's response. For I knew she could not have missed the dig.

There followed a longish pause before she responded, 'That wouldn't be a hint, would it, Inspector?'

Yet another crackly sound. 'Well, I wasn't really . . .' Digby began, but Julia would not let him finish.

'If it's my daughter and her television programme you are concerned about, then please let me assure you she has always had the highest respect for the law, ever since she was a child.'

'No, no, no, Julia, please. I wouldn't want you to think

we in the Force object in any way to the treatment we are
generally given by your daughter's crime-busting programme. It performs a very worthy local crimewatch function. No, no, it's not any member of your family–'

'Ah,' Julia interrupted. 'I can guess now who might be
getting under your skin, Inspector. Is it my daughter's . . .
er . . . boyfriend?'

I was amused by the hesitation as Julia groped for a word
to describe me. But full of admiration for her full-frontal
attempt to get Digby to expose himself in front of me, so
to speak.

'You mean Mr Marklin, I presume.'

'Yes. Peter.'

Lovely touch. I mentally blew a kiss.

Digby resumed. 'While it's true that Mr Marklin and I
have not always seen eye to eye in the past – especially over
the extent of the responsibilities of the private citizen in
crime detection and solution. But I assure you, Julia, Mr
Marklin's activities have always been much more a minor
irritation than a matter for any real concern. There are far
more weighty problems for our attention than the meddling
of the odd amateur who thinks, mistakenly, that he knows
best.'

God bless you and keep you, Digby Whetstone.

'I'm sure there are, Inspector . . . er, Digby. But I must
say it's all a bit curious, don't you think, that Mr Fern's
body was found actually on the grave of a relative of Peter's?
Now why would the murderer have wanted to do that?'

Well done, Julia. I thought she'd forgotten the last item
on our agenda.

'Pure coincidence, I think, Julia. At first, I must admit, I
thought there might have been some significance in the
choice of tomb, but now I doubt it.'

'But why cart the body of someone you've just killed to
such a conspicuous place, where it's bound to be found
quickly? That's what intrigues a lot of us here at Dendron
Park.'

'Graveyards are dark and empty places at night, you
know. Hence we have no witnesses to the disposal of the

body.' A pause and then he went on, 'And there's another thing. The murderer may have wanted the body found quickly to throw us off the real scent. For instance, as I have already mentioned, examination of the deceased's shoes have shown he was probably killed some good distance away from that church. You know something, Julia? You are all probably wondering why there was no attempt to conceal the body by burying it somewhere or dumping it in the sea or some lake, like the Blue Pool or whatever. Well, the really canny killer will know only too well that bodies have a nasty tendency to turn up in the end anyway, however clever their method of disposal. And its the very act and place of concealment that has, in so many cases, ultimately given the clue as to the murderer's identity. So you see, leaving a body in such a public place as a cemetery may not have been such a foolish act, after all.'

Gee. Now Digby was working well. I couldn't really fault his reasoning re my aunty's grave. And I was mighty relieved to hear he had given up trying to forge a link between me and the killing.

'Well, thank you, Digby. Once again you've shown up the yawning gap between the likes of us amateurs in Dendron Park and the truly professional.'

A little OTT, but I knew it was all to make me chuckle.

'Not at all. Well, if you've no more questions ... er ... Julia, I'd better let you have a spot of lunch at last, while I get round to the last few guests.'

Thank the Lord for that. The cramp in my neck and leg had returned some minutes before and had now spread to the other leg. I could not have survived my mahogany prison for much longer. As I heard Digby and Julia make their farewells, I made the mistake of not only stretching, but slightly altering my footing. As a result, I trod on the edge of what must have been a shoe. For a split second I lost my balance and reached out for something to hold on to – which, sod's law, happened to be a frock. Its wide neck slipped off one side of the hanger. This instantly uptilted enough for its hook to disengage from the rail. I tried to grab it as it fell, but in the dark missed it. The clatter as it hit the base of the wardrobe sounded, to me, like the start of the Third World War.

Over the commotion, I heard Digby's shout of, 'What on earth's that?'

Julia, bless her, instantly tried to cover with, 'It must be another of those silly hotel hangers. They're so old, the hooks keep slipping out of the wood. That'll be the third or fourth time since we've been here that Clement or I have been scared out of our wits by clothes tumbling to the floor of the wardrobe.'

I held my breath, full of admiration for Julia's quick thinking. (She told me afterwards, however, that she had already prepared such a story, were I to cause any noise.)

'Oh, I see,' said Digby, after a second. 'Maybe there's something to be said for those horrible wire hangers after all. At least they're all of a piece.'

A moment later, he was gone and Julia was letting me out of my prison.

'You still all of a piece?' she smiled.

I tried to stand up straight. 'I'll keep you posted,' I grinned back. 'But meanwhile, you were absolutely sensational, Julia. Really.'

She blushed. 'Was I? I really don't know. I can't tell you how nervous I felt all the time.'

I kissed her lightly on the cheek. 'It didn't show one whit. Know something? You really had Digby eating out of your hand. Move over Helen Mirren, Joan Collins et al.'

She went over to her chair, then looked back at me and said quietly, 'Peter, I . . . er . . . now realise what my daughter sees in you.'

'Oh Lord. Don't tell me,' I gulped.

'Yes,' she said. 'You make us feel so young.'

You could have knocked me down with a feather.

Julia insisted I stay for a bite of lunch with her and Clement. I must say, the latter seemed both amused and intrigued by our activities in the bedroom and was more relaxed in my presence than I can ever remember before. He actually managed to string a few sentences together longer than a quick burst of machine-gun fire and extended his attempts at laughter quite a way from his usual abrupt and unnerving bark.

I did not linger after lunch, as it was already nearly three and except for the Bessy Meade and Muriel Purkiss visit, I'd been out all the day. Not only did I need to open up shop, I also wanted a little time on my own to think quietly about what the day had brought. And to try to sort out a few simple grains from the mass of chaff.

However, no sooner had I parked the Beetle and let myself in the back door, than I heard the telephone ringing in the hall. I ran through, in case it was Arabella with some plum bit of news. But no. To my surprise, it was quite another lady on the end of the line.

'Is that you, Mr Marklin?'

It took me a second to place the accent.

'That's Mrs ... er ... Quaintance, isn't it?'

'Yes, that's right. I rang you about half an hour back, but couldn't get a reply.'

'Yes, I'm sorry. I was out.'

'Well, no matter now, Mr Marklin. I was just ringing to see how it was all going, like ... about Jacob ...'

'I'm still feeling my way, Mrs Quaintance, I'm afraid,' I sidestepped, not wishing to build up her hopes too high with undigested information or premature and reckless conclusions. 'Anyway, how's Mr Fern faring now? I do hope he's feeling a little better.'

'He's as well as can be expected, Mr Marklin. As well as anyone could possibly expect, with all the goings-on and that.'

I wondered whether one of the 'goings-on' might be what the dear little Trev had described as happening to Fern's cattle, but kept the thought to myself.

'I'm sure you must be a great help and solace to him, Mrs Quaintance.'

'Oh, I don't know about that. But what I do know is that the sooner that there Sandle woman moves out of the farm, the quicker poor Ted will recover.'

'I can imagine she must now be a constant reminder of

207

his son's death, with her husband being one of the police suspects.'

'Suspects?' she scoffed. 'It's wicked the way they've released him again, don't you think? I'm certain he must have had something to do with it all. Shifty-looking cove like that. Why I'm ringing you, in fact.'

'About Sandle?'

'Remember you said to me if I saw anything funny, I was to let you know, like?'

'Yes, I remember,' I lied. Not that I didn't recall the arrangement being made, but it had actually been at her request, not mine.

'See, ever since, I've kept an eye open for any funny goings-on. Down around the cottage, I mean.'

'Yes. Go on.'

'Well, that Sandle woman is up to something, all right. Wouldn't be surprised if she didn't suddenly up and do a midnight flit.'

'What makes you say that?'

'She had some old suitcases in one of the outhouses. And they've gone now. I did a bit of snooping, see. When she was out. And I looked in the downstairs windows too. There were clothes lying about and that, like she was about to pack, or something.'

The news did not surprise me. Dennis Sandle had probably put her on Red Alert for a quick disappearing act. With his apparent stack of readies, getting hold of false passports would be little problem. Then the world was their oyster. Provided, of course, they could elude any tails that Digby might have put on them. Acapulco, here they come. Or maybe even Rio de Janeiro by the jolly old sea-o. Shit. I tried to hide my feverish thoughts with, 'It could be, Mrs Quaintance, that she just wants to get away from all the suspicion that surrounds her husband. Can't be pleasant.'

'Don't you believe it, Mr Marklin. I'll wager it's that rotten murdering husband of hers she'll be going away with. And that will prove their guilt, all right, won't it, now? I wouldn't wonder if she didn't actually mastermind the whole affair herself, neither—'

208

She suddenly stopped.

'Come on, Mrs Quaintance,' I urged. 'Tell me what's going through your mind.'

I heard her take a deep breath.

'Well, it's like this, see. I reckon that Sandle must have had the crazy idea that poor Jacob had been responsible in some way for his being arrested years ago. After the robbery, I mean. Because I know they were acquainted then, see. Course Jacob had nothing to do with his arrest, I'm sure. But I wouldn't wonder if the suspicion didn't fester in that Sandle's mind, while he did his time. Nothing else to do but brood, now is there? So by the time he came out, he was just raring to get his revenge on him, see.' She took a breath. 'Maybe he didn't actually mean to kill him, mind. Just knock him about a bit to teach him a lesson. But when it came to it, well, he hit too hard, didn't he?'

I thought for a moment. 'Where does Mrs Sandle come into it, then? You talked about her "masterminding" it.'

She hesitated, then replied haltingly, 'Well ... see ... I don't reckon she likes the Fern family.'

I pricked up my ears. 'What makes you say that?'

Another pause, then, 'She's willing to take everything from Ted here, but never gives nothing back, she doesn't. Hardly pays any rent worth a mention, you know. And he's always giving that dreadful boy of hers things and that. She doesn't deserve any of it, she doesn't. Only out for number one, she is. I knew it when she first moved in. You can see it in her face.'

I couldn't much disagree with her snap verdict. More or less snapped with my own. But I was somewhat amazed at the vehemence of her loathing of Linda Sandle and pondered on its likely cause.

'But not repaying Mr Fern's kindness doesn't necessarily mean she doesn't like the Fern family, Mrs Quaintance. Anyway, there's a big difference between feeling dislike and masterminding a murder.'

Silence. Then, 'You sound like you're trying to defend her, Mr Marklin. I'd have thought a man of your–'

'I'm not defending anyone, Mrs Quaintance,' I cut in. 'Just trying to get things in a little perspective.'

'Men are all the same,' I heard her grumble semi-sotto voce. Which grumble more or less confirmed my suspicion as to the cause of her hatred for that Sandle woman.

'Anyway, Mrs Quaintance, thank you for letting me know about your suspicions that Mrs Sandle might be packing up to go. Is there anything else?'

A pause. Then, 'Yes, well there is, as a matter of fact.'

'Yes?'

'Well, I can't prove anything, mind. But that dreadful night, I was woken up by a noise. Now I can sleep through anything, as a rule, but somehow, I suppose, I knew the noise was on our – I mean, Mr Fern's – property.'

'What kind of noise?'

'As I sat up in bed and listened, I realised it was a car. And I'm sure it must have pulled in somewhere near the cottage.'

'What time would this be?'

'Oh, I didn't look. But it must have been in the early hours of the morning. Anyway, once awake, I couldn't seem to get back off, and some time later I heard the noise again.'

'The car leaving?'

'Must have been, I suppose.'

'Have you reported this to the police?'

'Well, no . . . no, I haven't. Because I've only just remembered it, really. Anyway, I can't actually prove the car was at the cottage, now can I? I didn't get up and dress and go and check. I reckon now, though, that it must have been Sandle. What would he have been doing that time of night down around the cottage, if he and that wife of his hadn't been up to no good?'

'I don't know, Mrs Quaintance. But again, thanks for the information. I recommend that you tell the police too. Even if you can't prove anything, it could well be helpful.'

I didn't get a reply, so I asked, 'Have you told Mr Fern about what you heard?'

'No . . . no, I haven't. Don't like to, see. He doesn't need any more reminders of what happened right now. Needs to be left in peace, he does.'

Drat. I wished she hadn't said that last bit.

'Yes, I guess he does, Mrs Quaintance. But all the same, he did say he wanted to be kept informed about any progress I might be making. When you rang, I was actually just thinking about ringing him.'

'But you said just now that you hadn't made any progress,' she protested. 'So why should you want to be bothering Mr Fern about nothing?'

'I had a question or two to ask, that's all.'

I could almost hear her thinking on't.

Then she remarked, 'May I ask about what?'

I could see she found my suggestion as welcome as a thunderstorm at harvest time, so I said, 'Oh well, never mind. I'll give him a call when I've got something more concrete to go on.'

And that was that, unfortunately. I'd run into the same barbed-wire entanglements she'd placed around Ted Fern which Gus had encountered on his first attempt to see him. I could see there was more to the round, ruddy-faced Mrs Quaintance than I'd first imagined.

I rang Arabella at the studios to update her on my day and get her thoughts. But her assistant informed me she had just gone into a script conference and was unlikely to be out for an hour to an hour and a half.

Not having my inamorata with whom to bounce ideas around, I rang Gus. As so often, he was an age in replying. His first words were hardly encouraging either.

'Know something? The perishing plumber still hasn't come. Bloody yard is a cross between a skating rink and Loch sodding Ness.' He sneezed. 'I've come in now, otherwise I'd have frozen stiff as a maiden aunt . . .'

Hell. He hardly sounded in the right mental state for any composed analytical thought. I dropped the idea of mental tennis, but did relate my time with Sandle, my wardrobe experiences and mentioned the housekeeper's vehement and ultimately obstructive phone call.

'Killed somewhere in the country, Digby said?' was his first comment. 'Well, that bloody narrows it down, doesn't it?'

I laughed.

'Still,' he went on, 'could have been just around Sandle's ruddy place, couldn't it? That's not exactly town, from what you've told me. After all, that car jack wasn't found far away from there, was it?'

'No. But then, it could have happened anywhere else. And if Sandle didn't do it, the jack was probably left in that scrapyard in an attempt to frame him.'

'Yer, well . . .'

And that's all I got from Gus, who suddenly announced he'd just spotted water starting to seep beneath his kitchen door, and with a 'See yer', put down the receiver.

I dragged myself through into the shop, but I already knew that sitting around waiting for deliveries of quick-frozen punters was hardly going to provide the mental food I needed for the rest of that afternoon. So, with a profound sigh on behalf of my, so far, patient bank manager, I left the shop closed, clambered into my winter gear, grabbed a torch and went out to the Beetle.

13

By then the main roads were clear. Although there was still slush in the gutters and the thin blanket of snow over the fields and hills made the late afternoon seem lighter than it actually was.

But once I'd turned off the road on to the track that led up to Ted Fern's farm, the going was far less easy. Even the Beetle, with most of its weight over the driven wheels, slipped and slid as it fought for traction up the slope to the cottage. By the look of the other tracks, mine wasn't the first vehicle to slither that way since the overnight snowfall; one of them, I supposed, must have been Sandle's Fiesta, when he'd come to pick up his Linda for their mobile-home love-in. To my relief, though, there was no sign of it or any other car outside the cottage when I reached it. Indeed, there was no sign of anything. Lights or life. The cottage, never exactly welcoming, in the darkness appeared downright spooky, if not forbidding.

I cursed. It had been the occupant, not the ruddy building, I had come to see. To confront her, whilst she was still rattled, so to speak, from my battle of words with her husband that morning, with my suspicions about her having known the murdered man. Beyond that, I hadn't really planned. All subsequent actions or accusations would have depended on the way she reacted. But now it looked as if I might have come too late, if Mrs Quaintance's guess about her packing up to scarper was well founded.

Wearily, I dragged myself out of the Beetle and, picking my way very carefully through the slush and ice by the light of my torch, made my way to the front door. Just for formality's sake, I did bang the knocker. But other than an eerie echo, no response did I get. After a due pause, I sidled across to what I knew to be the living-room window and shone my torch through the glass. By the time the beam had travelled as much around the room as physically possible from the window, I'd developed the distinct impression that Mrs Quaintance had been right in her assumption. The room was just too damned tidy. The kid's toys that I remembered in one corner had gone. So had the few ugly ornaments on the window-ledge. There was no sign of packing in progress, however. But there wouldn't be, of course, if Linda Sandle was well past that stage and had already upped and vamoosed.

Pulling my anorak hood up over my head – though the air temperature was not, I guess, actually below freezing any more, it was still low enough to separate brass monkeys from their often over-evident assets – I moved around to the side of the house, whose only window, to my chagrin, was on the upper floor.

The back of the house I more or less remembered from when I'd picked up the pedal car. An outhouse or two adjacent to the back door. Then, further over, a window which I had taken to be that of the kitchen. Mind you, I use the word loosely. It took the word 'unfitted' into whole new territory. Basically there was just a chipped white and brown sink on exposed legs. What looked like the kind of oil cooker you sometimes see in wartime movies on the box. A few battered bentwood chairs, two arranged each end of a stained and scratched table of diminutive dimensions. The third was lying on its side on the floor beside a cheap eau-de-Nil-painted (donkey's years ago, mind you) cabinet, with two panes of glass missing out of the four in the leaded lights of its door.

The only signs of recent or current occupation were a washing-up-liquid bottle on the window-ledge together with a grubby cloth, some crockery on the ledge of the cabinet and what looked like various packets of foodstuffs behind all that was left of the glass in the cabinet door. Again, I could see no personal nicknacks or toys or . . .

It was then that something shone back up the beam of the torch. I altered its angle and discovered where the reflection was coming from – some small shards of glass on the worn and torn lino. They were lying almost on a line

214

from the broken cabinet door above. I panned the torch further across and illuminated the toppled bentwood chair. All in all, it was looking as if Linda Sandle's leaving might not have been exactly peace and light.

I went round to the front and shone my torch over the path to the door. The snow had almost melted where it had been disturbed by footfalls. It was impossible to tell how many people had come in and out of the house that day. Certainly quite a few by the evidence of the clearance.

I returned to my Beetle and climbed inside to escape the bite of the keen wind that was whipping the top off the undisturbed snow and drifting it into the gulleys and hedge-rows. I sat for a moment behind the wheel, pondering my next stop. With all the signs pointing to Linda Sandle having flown the coop, I considered belting back to her husband's wheelless wonder in the hope of confronting her there, before they had a chance to Heathrow themselves to far-flung places. But the memory of my reception of the morning made me soon realise the chances of a one-to-one with the lucre-loving Linda were next to zero with Mr Subtle around.

I sighed and looked out of the windscreen as twisters of dry snow were whipped by the wind across the track ahead. I knew what was bugging me. And it wasn't just that I had seemingly arrived too late to catch anyone at the cottage. It was the sight of that overturned chair and the broken glass. Somehow, I didn't think that even someone as patently opportunistic as Linda Sandle would repay Ted Fern's kindnesses to her and her son by leaving his cottage with furniture awry and broken glass still littering the floor. In contrast, the living-room, though bare, had at least looked clean and tidy. It led me to wonder what state the rest of the rooms might be in, and for a second I was tempted to break in and see.

It was then that I realised my most sensible next step would be to go on up the track to see Ted Fern. Mrs Quaintance could hardly deny me entrance if I was on the very doorstep. I could then check on whether he had heard anything untoward on the night of the murder. Like the car that had woken his housekeeper, or whatever. What's more, he might be able to tell me for sure whether Linda Sandle had actually vamoosed. She might have come up to say goodbye, or have rung him. Or he or Mrs Quaintance might have actually seen her leave. Presumably picked up by her husband in his Fiesta.

Besides, there was one other little question I wanted to put to Ted Fern, although I knew it could be just the trigger to get me thrown off the farm. And that was whether he thought his son could have been seeing Linda Sandle on the side, so to speak.

I gritted my teeth, fired the starter and selected first. The rear wheels spun until they found enough grip to start off up the hill to Fern Farm.

All went fine until I'd crested the rise and was on the slope down to the farm itself. The Beetle, with its rearward weight distribution, treated the snow with contempt. All would have been hunky-dory on the downward stretch, had a rabbit not decided at that very moment to play a little game of headlight hypnosis and stop dead in my beams when halfway across the track.

Now, not being a bunny-hating son of the soil, directly I saw the red of his eyes, I did what most non-agrarians would do. I slammed on the anchors. I might even have got away with that, had I not been about to negotiate the last bend in the track before the final straight run down to the farmhouse. A bend where the snow had drifted most. The front wheels instantly locked. Although I swung the wheel to the left and took my foot off the brake pedal, the Beetle had developed a momentum of its own and slid inexorably forward. The welfare of the rabbit now seemed of secondary importance as I closed my eyes to brace myself for the Beetle's inevitable impact with the unkempt hedge ahead.

But, to my great surprise, there was no neck-snapping shudder or scream of tortured metal. Not even an explosion of windscreen or tinkle of headlamp glass. Just a shrill and uncomfortable cacophony of scraping sounds, as if Rottwei-

216

lers had somehow got Beetlemania, quickly accompanied by the protest of the fabric at being suddenly and mercilessly torn apart. The bough causing the latter must have missed my head by only a millimetre, as it scissored my poor old Volks's convertible top into two, quite unmatched halves.

When I dared to open my eyes, I found I was still moving forward. There was no sign of the hedge, as I had obviously passed clean through it. Well not exactly clean, but you know what I mean. What was worse, the headlights' beams were showing that the ground sloped sharply only some twenty or so yards ahead. I tried the brakes again. To my relief they didn't lock but instead started to slow the car. Over to the left I saw what I took to be a gap in the hedge and a gate. I swung the wheel over and the car obeyed. It was then that I looked up. And saw, instead of my roof, the blackness that was the sky. Two giant rents from just aft of the windscreen to just forward of the backrest of the rear seat. The fabric of my No Claims Bonus lay in tatters and I swore out loud. But I managed to bring the car to a stop a few feet from what turned out to be not a gate, but a gap in the overgrowth. One could hardly term it a hedge, so unkempt was it. Indeed, the whole small field that I had invaded was obviously not cultivated, due, I presumed, to the steep drop I had seen in my headlights.

I switched off, somewhat shakily, and got out of the car. To my consternation, my shoes sank deep into the snow which had obviously drifted towards the hedge. I realised at once that it would be tempting fate to try to circle the outside of the field in search of an opening back to the track, in case the Volks got stuck, or worse, locked its brakes and careered off the drop further down. Knowing it was hardly likely that I could get sufficient grip to go back up the field, let alone propel myself and car back through the hedge that we had penetrated, I got my torch from the front seat, took out the keys and slammed the door shut. There was nothing for it but to climb over the fence and trudge down to the farm on shanks's pony to get help.

I had just got my leg cocked to scale the fencing when the beam of my torch reflected back at me from something buried deep in the wild tangle of scrub and brambles which constituted a great part of the hedge.

I de-cocked my leg and played the torch across the dark and forbidding mass of overgrowth. Again I saw that reflection. Curious now, I picked up a slat of wood which had obviously once formed the bottom rail of the fence and started to beat back the brambles and dead vegetation so that I could see better into the interior of the nightmare tangle.

Gradually a curved shape materialised. At first I took it to be some ancient agricultural implement or part of an old tractor, but the more I uncovered, the more I realised the curve was the roof line of a derelict car. My torch beam was being reflected off its miraculously still intact rear window.

Curiosity now sated, I disappointedly threw down the piece of wood and started once again to scale the fence. It was only when I was over and, with my anorak hood up over my head, starting to walk cautiously down the slippery track, that my hedge find took on any significance. It was then I realised that the shape of the car was, indeed, familiar. Dinky had made a wonderful model of it, just after the war, in its '40' series. Morris Oxford 409, to be precise. I had two mint specimens currently in my shop. No great shakes of a discovery on its own, sure. But put together with what Digby Whetstone had found in the Wareham car dump, then . . .

It was whilst I was trying to digest this very connection that a shout suddenly shattered the stillness and I almost jumped out of my frozen skin.

'Hold it right there.'

I stopped dead in my tracks and then heard muffled footfalls behind me. I slowly peered around. At that moment, the moon broke through the clouds. Just enough for me to see a brand-new glint. And this time not off glass. But, shit, gun barrels. Two of them. And big bloody bore, to boot.

'Turn around. Slowly.'

I swallowed, but then realised that the voice was familiar.

'That you, Mr Fern?'

'What of it?'

I pulled the anorak hood down off my head as I turned.

'It's me. Peter Marklin,' I said loudly; remembering his deafness. 'I was just coming to see you.'

The barrels quivered slightly, then, thank God, slowly lowered.

'Oh, it's you, is it? I didn't recognise you, with your head covered.'

He came forward and now I could see his face, albeit dimly, under his regulation-type farmer's tweed cap. There was no smile of recognition, let alone of welcome. Mind you, I might have startled him almost as much as he had me.

'What you doing in my field then? I saw you climbing over, back there.'

I pointed towards the fencing. 'I was in my car coming down and I braked for a rabbit and lost control.'

He came right up to me, his shotgun, thankfully, at the dangle from his left arm.

'You did what?' he frowned.

I knew a true man of the soil wouldn't reckon a Brer Rabbit saving caper, especially if said caper punched a great hole in one of his briar patch field boundaries.

'I tried to avoid . . . this rabbit,' I repeated, this time avoiding his eyes, 'and my brakes locked and I'm afraid my car skidded through into your field. It's still there. My car, I mean. I was coming on down to see if you could give me a push, or something . . . to wherever the gate is . . .'

He looked across to the field, then back at me.

'You'd better be coming back down to the house. No point in us freezing to death out here talking about it, is there?'

The merest hint of a smile played across his tight mouth.

'No, no, there isn't, I suppose,' I agreed and he saw me shiver.

Ted Fern was his taciturn self all the way back down to the farm. And I was hardly in the mood for chat for chat's

219

sake, after my trail-blazing experience in my now scratched, dented and rentaroofed Beetle. I certainly had no intention of embarking on my intended line of questioning in the dark and frigid chill of the slippery slope that was his track.

It was not until we were in the kitchen, where he parked his twelve-bore up against the wall and took my coat, that he even asked what the original purpose of my visit to his farm had been.

'I wanted to have a word with Mrs Sandle,' I replied truthfully.

He looked at me and cupped his ear. I repeated my statement, only louder.

'And why would you be wanting to do that, Mr Marklin?'

I took my courage in both hands, remembering to keep the volume up. 'I have a feeling that she may have known your son, Mr Fern.'

He looked me up and down, almost as if I had suddenly become a complete stranger to him, then beckoned with his hand.

'You had better come into the parlour and explain yourself,' he said quietly.

I followed him through into the room where I had first met him. It looked even more funereal now than I remembered it. He offered me the same seat as before. Opposite the well-hung bull on the wall.

'Now what's all this you've got into your head about my poor Jacob?'

He hadn't really framed it as a question. More a negative answer. But, as in *Mastermind*, I'd started, so I had to finish.

'I have no real facts as yet to support my theory, Mr Fern, I have to admit. But I still think it's possible your son might have known Mrs Sandle—'

'Never,' he interrupted gruffly. 'My son know a woman like that—' He stopped suddenly and shuffled in his chair. Then went on, 'I mean, no, it's just not possible, I tell you straight. Anyway, why should my son have had anything to do with . . . Mrs Sandle? I told you before, he hardly ever came up here to the farm to see me, let alone anyone else.'

I had to plough on. 'You've never spotted him or his car at the cottage, then?'

'No. Never. Of course not.'

'What about your housekeeper, Mrs Quaintance? Has she ever mentioned–?'

He cut me off. 'No, never.'

'Perhaps I could ask her before I leave. Just in case.'

'She's not here,' he said quickly. 'She's gone to her sister's over in Dorchester. Staying the night.'

That explained why I had seen no sign of her when I'd arrived.

I changed tack.

'When I called at your cottage, Mrs Sandle was out. I took the liberty of looking in a downstairs window and it appears as if she may have actually moved out. Would you know anything about that?'

He looked down at his strong, work-worn hands.

'She's gone. This afternoon.'

'And her boy, Trevor?'

'Sandle came over and took him earlier. So she could pack up in peace.'

'And then he came back for her?'

'Must have, mustn't he?'

'You didn't actually see them go, then?'

'No. I've got better things to do than hang around waiting for a bastard like Sandle.'

I thought for a moment. 'But you do know she's gone?'

He took the point. 'She came up and saw me.'

'To say goodbye?'

He nodded, then suddenly said loudly, 'Look, Mr Marklin, I didn't invite you in to be bombarded with questions about . . . that . . . lot.'

It wasn't difficult to see that the word 'lot' stood in for quite a few of the racier words in the English dictionary. Or that Fern was incensed at the whole thought of Linda Sandle's sudden leaving, and, what was worse, for whom and with whom she had left. No doubt Fern now regarded his whole do-good mission on her and her son's behalf to have been an abject failure and her abrupt departure as no

221

proper recompense for his obvious generosity towards them both.

Then, narrowing his eyes, Fern went on: 'Anyway, Mr Marklin, what on earth made you make any connection between my son and . . . that woman?'

I took a deep breath. 'It's just possible, Mr Fern, that your son met his death up here on your farm. The police say they now think he was killed somewhere in the country and not in a town. And your housekeeper has told me that she was awoken by the sound of a car that night and she thinks it may have been down the track, somewhere near the cottage.'

He glowered at me. 'You don't want to take any notice of Madge Quaintance. Her hearing's sometimes even odder than mine. She mistook a cow for a car horn only last week and told me I'd got visitors, when all it were was . . .'

He stopped in mid-sentence.

I mentally finished it for him. 'A cow in distress.' Like staggering about with BSE disease.

'So you heard and saw nothing that night, Mr Fern?'

'Nothing. Why should I have? There was nothing ruddy going on. You don't want to give no time to my house-keeper's fancies. She never liked . . .'

Again he stopped. I pencilled in, 'Mrs Linda Sandle.'

'So you don't reckon your son could have been killed up here?' I asked, in the softest tone commensurate with Fern actually hearing me.

'No, I don't.'

I sat forward in my chair, mainly to prevent a broken spring corkscrewing up my evening, so to speak. But also to add urgency to my next question.

'Tell me, Mr Fern, did you ever once own a Morris Oxford? Late forties, early fifties model?'

Again his eyes narrowed. 'What makes you think I might have, Mr Marklin?'

'Well, just a while back, when I was clambering over your fence to come down here to ask for your help, something glinted in the beam of my torch. I discovered it came from the rear window of an old car, completely overgrown and

222

buried in the bushes. A Morris Oxford. Bearing in mind that the police believe the murder weapon to have been a jack from that kind of model, well, it just does contribute to the theory that your son might have met his death around here.'

Fern suddenly rose from his chair, obviously finding the possibility of his son having been murdered so near home deeply disturbing. And no real wonder. But his next question did surprise me. I wasn't too enamoured of its tone, either.

'How well do you know old cars, Mr Marklin? Are you some kind of vintage expert or something?'

'No, I wouldn't say that. But being an old-toy buff has helped me identify old vehicles on quite a few occasions.'

Fern came round to the back of my chair.

'Well, it's failed you this time, all right. That car in the field is an old Standard Vanguard I used to own. Not a Morris. Used it for years to tow stuff around the farm when it got too old for the road.'

He inclined his head around the side of my chair. Now I know what Long John Silver must have undergone with his sodding parrot on his shoulder. Most disconcerting.

'Had the same engine, see, as a Ferguson tractor I used to own. Made by the same firm, they were.'

Sounded plausible. I didn't really doubt that, at some time, Fern had actually owned a Standard Vanguard. But I was still pretty sure the shape in the undergrowth was that of Dinky's 40g Morris Oxford and not their 40e Vanguard, in spatted or unspatted versions.

'Well, I . . . er . . . the light wasn't too good, I must admit,' I parried.

Fern came out from behind my chair, went over to the fireplace and picked up a poker to prod the coals in the grate into a little more life.

'So, have you got any more questions to ask me, Mr Marklin?' He stood up, still holding the poker, and looked at me. 'Because if you haven't, let me ask you one.'

'Go ahead,' I invited.

He wagged the poker at me. 'Why the bloody hell are

223

you wasting my time up here when it's plain as a pikestaff who you and the police should be after? And that's that criminal Sandle. He caused my son's death and why that Inspector Whateverhisnameis doesn't ruddy arrest him before he flees the country, I can't imagine.'

I stood up. I felt a trifle vulnerable seated, staring at a circling poker tip.

'What makes you so sure it's Sandle now, Mr Fern? Did his wife let anything slip to you, perhaps, when she came over to say goodbye?'

Getting no reply, I went on. 'To kill someone, you have got to have a motive. So what have you worked out as being Sandle's?'

To my relief, he slowly lowered the poker. 'Well . . . he could have been . . . trying to get his own back at me, like.' His tone lacked conviction.

I frowned. 'I don't quite understand.'

'And I thought you were supposed to be a bit of a detective. Can't you see? I took his wife in, didn't I? Gave her a nice home. Saw that the boy didn't want for anything . . .' His tone now started to change from purely explanatory to something very different and I listened with mounting curiosity. 'Even gave him my Jacob's old pedal car that I had stored in the attic all these years . . . Hardly charged her no rent, would have let her stay for nothing, if need be . . . long as it kept her away from that jailbird of a husband of hers.'

Fern slowly subsided back into his chair and let the poker slide from his fingers to clatter down on to the brass fender. His eyes, thank the Lord, were now off me and stared into the once again faltering flames of the fire.

He went on, his voice not much above a whisper. 'For months it all seemed as if it was working and that she'd almost forgotten her past life with that dreadful, sinful man and I began to hope . . . to hope that . . .' He took a deep breath. 'But no, not many days after they let Sandle out, I could see the change in her. At first, I tried to say to myself that it was just me imagining things and that Linda was not a Sandle any more, but the born-again woman I so wanted her to be–'

He stopped abruptly, then pulled himself up straight in his chair. When he spoke again, his tone was back to the standard gruff formality. 'But never you mind about all that, Mr Marklin. What I mean to say is that I reckon Sandle resented – no, worse – hated the changes I'd tried to make in his wife. And in her outlook on this good life. No doubt, he reckoned – rightly – that I had been doing everything in my power to stop her going back . . . to the likes of him.'

'And you think he killed your son as some kind of punishment or even warning?' I queried. 'But surely, murder is a bit extreme–'

'Nothing's extreme with a man like Sandle, Mr Marklin,' Fern all but shouted. 'And when the Devil drives . . .' He sank back in his chair and closed his eyes, as if the thought of the Devil had somehow seared his mind.

I didn't say anything for a moment. Then I asked in a voice only just loud enough for Fern to hear, 'Did you try to stop Linda Sandle from leaving this afternoon, Mr Fern?'

He did not respond. Or open his eyes.

I pressed on. 'Did you have an argument with her down at the cottage? In the kitchen?'

Again, nothing.

'And the cabinet window got broken and a stool overturned?'

I saw his closed eyelids twitch. His fingers tighten on the arm of his chair, the brown knuckles bleaching white.

'But she still went, didn't she, Mr Fern? Went and left you. And all you stand for. Did you then have to watch as Sandle came over to pick her up or did you have to get her a taxi? You would hardly have taken her over to him yourself in your car, would you?'

The eyelids twitched once more, but that was all.

'And talking of cars, Mr Fern, that was no Vanguard I saw in those bushes. That was, without any question, a Morris Oxford. And the jack that killed your son came from such a car. What are you trying to do, Mr Fern?'

I went over to his chair. 'Whatever you may have wanted

225

her to be in your mind, Linda Sandle is not anyone you should be trying to protect. She's just a money-grubbing, self-seeker from way back, out for the main chance, wher-ever it presents itself, whoever may be offering it. She took you for a ride. Your cottage and all your care and consideration she just absorbed and took for granted, whilst all the time she was–'

Fern's hand suddenly reached out and grabbed my wrist.

'That's quite enough, Mr Marklin,' he exploded, his eyes now as fierce as his grip. 'You don't know what you're talking about. Linda wasn't anything like that. Not the real Linda.' I noted his use of her Christian name.

He stood up out of his chair, but still held on to my wrist. Now, lowering his voice, he went on, 'It was only when the Devil came back to tempt her in the form of that criminal she had once married when she was young and knew no better, that . . .'

He stopped and I could feel both his tension and his passion transmitting itself up my arm.

'That what, Mr Fern? What exactly did your Linda do when Sandle was released?'

Receiving no reply, I continued. 'She saw that main chance, didn't she? The chance of at last getting her hands on all the money her husband would now be collecting for the stolen jewellery. Only there was a snag. I reckon she was none too keen on having to take the thief and the proceeds from the loot as a job lot. Separate, I reckon, is how Linda probably saw the deal. After all, years have passed since she has lived with Sandle and, if it's any comfort to you, I doubt if she has any fires in her heart stoked for him any more. No, I suspect she planned to pretend to go back to Sandle, just to keep tabs on what he was doing with the money and where he kept it stashed. At the opportune moment, she would vamoose with it, prefer-ably without him. But even then, not necessarily alone, Mr Fern. With someone of her own choice.'

I suddenly flicked my arm up and managed to wrench it free from his grip. I quickly moved back to behind my chair, for I was well aware my next flier of a theory might cause Mount Fern to erupt all over me.

'Someone much younger ... more refined ... better looking ... a far more fitting partner for what she would now be. A lady with lots of lovely money. There was just one person who she either already knew or had heard of and could easily get to know, Mr Fern. A person, what's more, who she was aware had more than a liking for older ladies with substantial private means.'

I hated every minute of this, but I had to go on. At least now I no longer had to look into Fern's Rudolf Hess-style stare, for he had reverted to looking blankly at the dying embers of the fire.

'And that was your son Jacob.'

I waited, but he didn't seem to have heard me. I raised my voice a few decibels and went on. 'Oh, it was probably Linda who did the seducing, not your son. Or maybe it was purely the money that won him round. Either way, my guess is that she thought she would get him to agree to run away with her. Somewhere far from Sandle, where he wouldn't be able to afford to go hunting for her. South America, perhaps. Like Rio de Janeiro.'

Sod it. Still no reaction. But I kept a wary eye on the poker on the hearth, just in case. What could I do but now bring my theory to some conclusion?

'But something must have gone wrong. I don't know quite what. Either your son wanted out at the last minute and they had a row. Or he'd decided he could have the best of both worlds. By staying with what he'd already got – Louise Robbins and her Dendron Park Hotel – and then blackmailing Linda by threatening to tell Sandle of her plans and their affair if she didn't dub up for his silence.

'Your son's decision, whatever it was, could have made Linda blow her top. Probably, as he was going out to his Fiesta after telling her everything was off, she picked up the first thing she found lying around in the bushes or garden – which happened to be your old Morris's jack – and struck him down. What happened after that, I'm not quite sure. Perhaps she telephoned Sandle and told him

227

some cock-and-bull story about your son making unwelcome advances to her or whatever, and asked him to come over and help her dispose of his . . .'

I couldn't go on. Ted Fern had suffered far too much torture recently, without my turning any more knives in his wounds. I took a deep breath, but it didn't really help. I still felt a bastard for flinging such a load of manure around his son's name and, no doubt, blessed memory.

'I'm sorry, Mr Fern . . .' I mumbled, albeit loudly, 'but I want you to see what kind of person I think Linda Sandle to be. I do hope I might be wrong, but I really don't think so. And I take your silence to mean that, maybe, you think I haven't got it all up the creek.'

I grasped the door handle, preparatory to leaving. I could hardly have asked him to help me extricate my rentaroof after all that, though I knew it would mean a frigid trudge to the nearest phone box to call Gus or, perhaps more advisedly, the nearest garage with a tow truck.

'When I've gone, I think you ought to ring the police, Mr Fern. You owe it to your son. And you owe nothing at all to this Linda Sandle. Quite the opposite. She may have robbed you of the greatest single gift anyone–'

Ted Fern suddenly erupted from his chair and seemed to stand ten feet tall and almost as wide, blanking out the fireplace.

I thought for a second he was about to throw himself at me, or at least reach for the nearest handy weapon, which happened to be the poker, but his voice, when it emerged, was almost the exact opposite of his fearsome stance and appearance, being low and moderate in tone.

'Mr Marklin, I . . . er . . . can't let you leave without giving you some help with your car.'

I waved my hand. 'No, please, I can manage.'

He moved towards me. 'After all the time and trouble you've spent over my . . . problems, I really must insist you let me do my little bit on your behalf.'

I felt between the . . . whatever and the deep blue sea.

'But it's cold and dark and, well, I may leave moving the car until the morning, anyway.'

By now he was beside me at the door. Until that close proximity, I had not realised quite how big a man he was.

'Let us both have a go at moving it. If we fail, I'll ... er ... drop you back to your place in my car.'

I couldn't very well disagree without causing further offence. So I nodded my agreement. He leant across me, opened the door and ushered me into the corridor. When we reached the kitchen, he went to the coat rack by the door and handed me my anorak and scarf.

'Won't you need a coat, too?' I suggested.

'No, Mr Marklin. I've been out in worse weather than this without one.' He flexed his arms. 'We farmers find too much clothing only restricts our movements. Makes even simple jobs take twice the time.'

There's a good bit of old country logic and codswallop for you, I thought to myself. Only bruited abroad, of course, by those farmers who actually survive severe winters. But I let it ride and opened the kitchen door to let myself out.

I was right out by the gate to the cattleyard before I looked behind me. What I then saw in the pale moonlight made any meteorological or hypothermic considerations zap down to bloody zero.

14

I had not seen Fern pick up the shotgun. But then I hadn't been looking. I instantly stopped and turned to face him.

'Not after the rabbit that caused me to go through into your field, are you?' I gulped, hoping my jocular tone might lighten his dead-serious and dead-set expression. 'Wasn't his fault, honest.'

Abject failure. All I got was a 'Don't go up the track, Mr Marklin. You and I are taking a little detour, I'm afraid. Over the fields.'

He was afraid. That was a laugh. Well, not really. Quite the reverse. I sidled over and hung on to the rails of the cattleyard. A useless manoeuvre in reality. But I needed something solid right then to cling on to.

'Mr Fern,' I said, as firmly as I could muster. 'I need to get back to my car. I realise that all this must have been a great shock, so why don't you go back inside and . . . ugh–'

A prod in the ribs from two fat barrels cut off my plea for sanity before it had really got going.

'Hurry up, Mr Marklin. Over to the right, you'll find a gate. Open it and–'

This time, I cut in. 'Look, Mr Fern. This is madness.' I then saw, to my horror, from the look in his eyes, that my last words might well have been an accurate clinical description. 'What on earth do you think you're doing? Protecting Linda Sandle, is that it? Protecting the very person who could have been responsible for your son's death?'

He didn't respond. But his gun did. With a second prod to my ribs.

I had no option but to let go of the rail and stumble forward towards the gate, which I could now just about discern about ten yards or so ahead to my right.

'Why are you doing this, Mr Fern?' I shouted back to

230

him. 'Is it for that son of hers, Trevor? Because if she's implicated and goes to jail, he won't have a mother?'

It was a wild try, but it was the only possible reason I could imagine for Fern's present alarming and laundry-making behaviour. After all, he might have always blamed his own son's transgressions on the fact that he had been deprived of a mother for most of his life.

'Get on, Mr Marklin, and shut up.'

I got on, but I didn't obey the second bit.

'Look, what the blazes do you think you're trying to achieve? You've done nothing in this whole affair to blame yourself for. It's not your fault if Linda Sandle hasn't lived up to your high expectations.'

I turned around as I reached the gate, hoping to see a smidgen of softening or, even, sense in his expression. But shit. There were neither. And he came right on up to me, until the barrels pressed into my anorak once more.

'Over you go, Mr Marklin,' he ordered.

I looked behind me. The snow-covered field rose quite steeply and then lost itself in the darkness. What was very clear were the many recent tractor tracks that curved up from the gate to disappear somewhere off to the right.

'Where are you taking me?' I asked, trying unsuccessfully to look him in the eye.

'You came up here, you say, to see Mrs Sandle, didn't you? Well, I'm taking you to her,' he responded, still avoiding my eye-line.

'She's still here . . . ?' I began, then the words froze in my mouth.

Suddenly I saw again the broken glass and the overturned stool in the cottage kitchen. A further prod from the twelve-bore brought me back to the equally horrific reality of the present.

'I said climb over, Mr Marklin. Now get on with it.'

I looked around me, I suppose for help. God knows why. The US cavalry have never even been to Dorset, as far as I know. Hearing no thunder of hooves, I reluctantly climbed over the gate and landed in the mud and slush that the tractor had made. I instantly thought of running for it, but

231

knew that before I could reach cover or disappear into the night, a thousand little pellets would have made my back into a colander.

My brain raced as I watched Fern heave his big frame over the gate with remarkable agility for his age, especially as he had to keep his gun pointed across at yours truly. I came to the rapid conclusion that I must have got his present motives all wrong. He wasn't trying to protect Linda Sandle at all. How could he be, if she was . . . (gulp) . . . dead and he'd killed her when, presumably, he had found out that she had been responsible for the death of his son. No, he was now, I guessed, trying to protect himself. Against, I presumed, my probing around any further into his son's murder, or now . . .

As he jumped down and made an alas but momentary gesture of the gun to the right, I tried to busy myself a little with the thought that just maybe Linda Sandle was still alive. Perhaps Fern had locked her up in some barn or other over the hill. Or better still, that she had decided that a life with her jailbird husband wouldn't be any great shakes after all, and she had got Fern to hide her away somewhere on the farm.

As I trudged on ahead up the rise, the snow coming up over my shoes where it had drifted in the wind, I decided to come out with a full-frontal.

'If I'm just going to see Mrs Sandle, why do I need to do it at gunpoint?'

Getting no reaction, I stopped and turned to face him. Now the barrels pointed directly at my tummy button. I knew I risked getting more tummy buttons than either of us had had hot dinners, but I just had to ask.

'Do I take it from your silence, Mr Fern, that Mrs Sandle might also have taken this little trip at gunpoint?'

Again nothing. I pointed down at the many tractor tracks in the snow, parallel with which we had been plodding.

'Or was she, by then, past caring how she came?'

He tilted the twelve-bore so that it was directed up my nostrils.

'You've killed her, haven't you, Mr Fern? You took the

law into your own hands and meted out your own punishment.'

''Tweren't mine,' he at last responded. 'Were God's.'

Hell, Marklin MD had been spot on with his madness
diagnosis.

'I think God might have preferred you to let the normal
processes of British law take their course,' I said, as quietly
as his hearing could manage. I was expecting another prod,
but, thank the same God, I didn't get one. I went on, whilst
I still could, in the only vein to which I thought he might
respond. 'Anyway, I'm quite certain He wouldn't want you
to kill again, Mr Fern. This time it would have nothing to
do with the punishment of a sinner but with the protection
of yourself, your own skin. In addition to God's own holy
verdict, the British courts of law might well regard a second
killing—'

He suddenly laughed out loud and the sound echoed
eerily across the hill.

'Second . . .' he repeated and snorted, rather than
laughed again. 'Oh, you know nothing . . .'

Shit. Suddenly a light bulb exploded in my head and I
shut my eyes to try to absorb the horrifying revelation. That
it was Ted Fern himself who had killed his son.

But why, why, why? Because his son had begun an affair
with the woman the old man obviously doted on and had
tried to convert to a sober and saintly way of life? Hell, that
might well have caused a serious or permanent rift between
the two, but murder most foul? Now, had it been a man
like Sandle who had once again corrupted her . . . ?

In another blinding, light-bulb flash, I now, at long last,
saw it all.

Oh God, I'd been so obtuse, ignoring such obvious clues,
because I, like so many, could not ever bring myself to
suspect any father of having deliberately killed his son.

'Look at me, Ted Fern,' I said as firmly as my now shot
nerves would allow.

His eyes flickered and he slightly lowered the gun. To
the region of my heart now. Big deal.

233

'You're right. I did know next to nothing a second ago. But not any more. And I'll prove it to you right now.'

More flickers. But no interruption or further prod of the gun, thank the Lord. The longer I could keep talking, the more chance there was that ... Oh, I didn't really know, but wearing out one's voice box was infinitely preferable to wearing a wooden one six foot under.

'It was dark and cold that night. I reckon you'd been keeping an eye on events at the cottage ever since you began suspecting that Linda Sandle might be about to leave and go back to her husband. You had probably seen his Fiesta outside the place before. When you saw a Fiesta there again, why, you naturally assumed it must be his. You waited somewhere outside, until the man you assumed to be Sandle eventually left the cottage. He was muffled up to the eyebrows against the cold. So you couldn't see his face or figure clearly. People in winter clothes are often almost impossible to identify quickly. You hunted around for a weapon and came across that jack from your old Morris, and ...'

I broke off and made a useless sort of gesture with my hand.

Fern's eyes slowly lifted until they at last met mine. But still he said nothing. I kept talking, as if my life depended on it. As it only too obviously did.

'We all should have guessed the truth right from the start. Just by where you left your son's body. In the hallowed ground of a church. There you knew he was bound to be discovered quickly and have a chance of a proper Christian burial. But we tried to see other, more devious motives in the choice of a graveyard. None of us made the connection of the same model of car being used then by your son and by Sandle. If only we had. Then only one life—'

Suddenly Fern cut in for the first time. His voice, though low and totally bereft of any emotion, startled me. I took a step back and almost lost my footing in the snow.

'I knew my son's car, you see ... the Porsche he had built ... I didn't know ... Oh God, I didn't know it had broken down and he'd hired a car like Sandle's ...'

I held out a hand. I could see it shaking. But I had to make an overture of some kind.

'Mr Fern, why don't you come back to your house with me now and we'll talk some more and maybe, then . . . ?'

'It's too late, Mr Marklin.' To my horror, his eyes reverted to the manic stare and his voice took on the note of some demented evangelist.

'I know now that the Lord must have willed the death of my son. To punish him for his transgression against the laws of the good book. And He chose me, his father, to be the executioner, to show me the path I must follow with all sinners against His laws. Fornicators, adulterers, criminals, the faithless, transgressors of every kind . . .'

Hell, he had gone into that faraway land where I knew I could never reach him. A land whose laws would sanction any horror he cared to commit. Nay, sanctify and bless his every action. But I couldn't just give up. Now I wasn't relying on my persuasive tongue to save me. Just the ticking of the ruddy clock.

'I'm no real sinner,' I tried, but he laughed in my face.

'No sinner, Mr Marklin? By your own confession you live with a woman who is not your wife. And from what I hear, not so much a woman, neither, as a young girl. There are years between you. Why, you could almost be her father. No sinner, indeed. You are as wicked as the rest of this terrible world.' He gestured with the shotgun. 'Now turn around and follow those tracks. Don't stop until you come to the pit.'

'Pit?' I swallowed.

Then I got the prod I'd been expecting and saw his finger increase pressure on the trigger. I turned and started to plod in the line of the tracks. I could hear his heavy footfalls behind me.

'Yes, pit, Mr Marklin. But don't worry, you won't be alone.'

Oh great. What a relief.

'Linda Sandle is already there, isn't she, Mr Fern?' I shouted back to him.

'The Devil had taken possession of her again, Mr Marklin. She was going back to Sandle. I had to stop her. But she's not alone either.'

Hell's bells! Just how many exactly had Fern killed? I hadn't counted on more than two. Now rising to three, if there was not some miracle, divine or otherwise.

He went on. 'There are the corpses of others who have caught the mental sickness which now seems to infect the whole of our sad, sad world. They will be fitting companions to you both.'

'Sickness,' I muttered to myself and then the penny dropped.

Ten Fern was about to inter me in a pit that he had obviously prepared for the cattle which Linda Sandle's son, Trev, had described. The ones with the so-called mad cow disease, BSE. I shivered uncontrollably at the realisation that in a few minutes, I would be the filling in a giant meat sandwich, deep underground.

It was not long before we crested the rise, and there below, I could see the unmistakable silhouette of the tractor, the shovel of its digger projecting upwards at an angle, as if saluting its recent achievement – the dark rectangular scar in the snow which extended deep in front of it.

As I stumbled down the slope, I slipped and fell heavily on to my back, slithering in the snow and slush.

'Not yet, Mr Marklin, not yet,' was Fern's grim reaction. 'There's still a bit further to go.'

As I gathered myself up from the ground, I looked up at him and shouted, 'Fern, you're mad. You'll never get away with this. The police will be crawling all over your farm directly they find Linda Sandle is missing, let alone me as well.'

He looked at me, a contemptuous turn to his mouth. 'Do you think I or my Maker care what they do? And even if they do eventually find your bodies, it will be too late. God's divine justice will already have been done.'

Bang went the last argument my numbed brain could concoct. Fern obviously did not now care a damn whether his crimes were discovered or not.

Another gesture with the gun had me propelled further towards the dark and dreadful excavation in the snow. Now I could see the tangled carcases of his dead cattle, legs intertwined and sticking upwards at crazy angles. There seemed to be at least two animals already in the pit. With two stacked at the side next to a long ridge of excavated earth. All was clearly in readiness for the last of the dramatis personae of this tragedy – me.

I wondered whether he planned my death to be quick and neat. Well, as neat, that is, as the splatter of a shotgun can ever make a killing. Or whether a swing of its butt would knock me unconscious into the pit and the cattle, earth and tractor would take care of the rest.

'Go to the very edge,' he shouted to me.

Instead, I stopped abruptly. Not to disobey him, but because my eyes had just made the sickening discovery that between the two carcases of the cattle already in the pit, there was a limb twisting upwards, as if trying to grasp the very heavens. For a split second I thought it to be still alive and moving. But it was only a trick of the moon's dim light, playing across the scarlet-tipped fingers.

'Oh my God.' I put my hands up over my eyes.

I felt Fern come up beside me. 'Now, I see, when it's far, far too late, you call upon His name.'

And those were the very last words I can remember, before I heard something rushing through the air, and then . . . the proverbial and sweet Miss F. Adams.

I can't, to this day, quite work out what I remembered next. I guess it must have been the pain. At first, I recall, I couldn't quite sense which actual part of me was screaming out its agony. Wasn't too surprising. As I slowly, very slowly, became aware of where I was and what was happening to me, I naturally tried to lift myself up or, at least, move the odd limb. But nothing, plug nothing, seemed to function. Correction. I could just move my head slightly to the right. To the left, my cheek hit up against something stiff and dark that was too close to my eyes to get a focus on.

As the seconds of my returning consciousness ticked by,

237

the pain from wherever became so searing that I couldn't suppress a scream. I hardly heard it over the cacophony going on around me. Suddenly lights flashed across my surroundings and I shut my eyes tight against the glare. But not before I had seen, to my horror, why I couldn't move a muscle worth a damn. I was pinned down by the bloated carcase of one of Fern's mad cattle. And the something that was stiff and hard against my left cheek was its deep-frozen rear end. (I've never ordered a rump steak since.)

By this time my brain was just about starting to cope with a little analysis of what the hell was going on. And more vitally, what the ditto I might be able to do about it. The cacophony was clearly Fern in his tractor, no doubt starting to push the wide ridge of earth that I had seen earlier back into the pit. That also explained the intermittent sweep of lights. Crazy bastard, he had to be able to see what he was doing to sinners like me and the late Linda Sandle.

From the sound of things, he had elected to start filling in at the end furthest from me. But a fat lot of good that was going to do me, if I could move no more than my throbbing head. (Yes, by then I'd identified one source of pain.) It would just mean I'd have a mite more time to contemplate my own impending death by suffocation. Though I doubt that had been amongst Fern's cold calculations. After all, he had probably assumed his shotgun swipe to my head would keep me under until I was truly under – six feet or more.

I summoned up all the strength that pain had left me and made one more attempt to activate anything below my neck. This time I did manage to raise my right shoulder a smidgen or so upwards. But the effort half killed me, magnifying the intense pain, whose other source I could now just about guess. It was one of my legs. The left one, as far as I could tell. The agony spelt only one thing. It was broken. No doubt when the carcase had toppled down on to it.

Hell. That was all I needed. Now I knew that even if I could manage to get out from under the carcase before I was smothered by Fern's tractor, I'd be a limping lump of a target for his twelve-bore. But I couldn't just lie back in

238

the pit and think of England until I was munching my last meal – of Dorset's good earth.

I took as deep a breath as the weight on my chest would allow and started to try to manipulate my shoulder some more. My mind had now cleared sufficiently for me to have worked out that the beast on top of me was lying at a slight angle. Which explained why I could move the shoulder at all. Logic dictated that, ergo, I should be able to move the arm presumably still attached to that shoulder. The initial problems were, one, I couldn't, and two, where the hell was it, anyway?

I closed my eyes again as the lights returned fleetingly, the tractor sounding ominously near. At last I got the grey cells to work sufficiently to tell me that my arm must be doubled back under me. If I could only work my shoulder high enough off the damp bottom of the pit, I might just about be able to extricate it.

I concentrated every whit of my strength on doing just that. But every time I raised myself an inch or two I obviously fretted the nerves of my broken leg, and it gave me hell. I know I must have screamed out half a dozen times before, at last, I managed to half wriggle, half drag my right arm from under me.

Like the crass idiot I am, I felt a huge sense of relief at having at least freed even as little as an eighth of Peter Marklin Esquire. Once I'd got it clear, I was tempted to raise it aloft and wave it like mad. Two things stopped me. The minor one was what bloody good would it do to let Fern know I was once more in the land of the conscious. The major one, I could hardly manage such a manoeuvre anyway, as the whole arm was now as numb as a politician's conscience, and was progressively with every second beset with an attack of pins and needles that felt like daggers and swords.

A moment later, I suddenly heard the tractor stop and go into what I took to be reverse. Hell. Fern was obviously changing his position. And that could only mean in one direction. Nearer me. Like, maybe his earth-mover was even now setting its sights on a line that would cover me in the next few forward drives. Shit, why the blazes had I been in such a hurry to come up to the cottage and Fern's farm? If I had only been patient and waited for Gus's ruddy plumber, then he'd have been with me. Gus, I mean. And I doubted even Fern would have taken on two of us, let alone his old childhood mate from way back, Gus Tribble.

I struggled frantically to pull my body out from under the literally dead weight of the balloon-like carcase by pushing my right arm forward against the soil. But, newly dug, the earth just slithered away under my braced palm and I could get no purchase at all. Even if I had succeeded, I doubted I could have survived the stinging pain long enough to have completed the action. Feeling dizzy now from both the hurt and my exertion, I collapsed back and the left side of my head struck the cadaver's rump. My cranium now knew what a punchbag feels like after a workout by Mike Tyson.

Whilst I fought to get both my breath back and my mind in some kind of focus, I heard the dreaded grate of gears and then the throb and knock of the tractor's diesel seemed to make the very earth vibrate as it edged directly towards me. A few seconds later and I felt the first particles of soil bounce off the animal's body and on to my face.

The noise of the engine and the falling soil became so deafening that at first I did not hear the other sound. But just as I was about to close my eyes and thank whoever for giving me a taste of an Arabella heaven before I was snuffed out like a candle, I saw the lights flash across the side of the cow's body. They couldn't have come from the tractor, as the illumination was on my side. Jesus, there must be someone else in the field.

Still the earth kept coming. Now no longer in dribs and drabs, but in a regular fall. I screamed out at the top of my voice, whilst I still had a mouth that was unbunged. I raised my right arm as high as I could muster and waved it around in mad circles in the hope that the lights might pick up the movement.

It was then that I heard the sound of the tractor change,

as Fern slipped it out of gear. There was a clanking, which I took to be the digger protesting at such a sudden stop. The earth kept falling on to and around my face for quite a few more seconds. Then silence. A bloody wonderful, magnificent silence I gulped into my lungs and filled my soul with – up to its bloody brimmy brim-brim.

I hardly felt the pain now as I strained to listen for voices, which, thank the Lord, were not long in coming.

'Mr Fern. Looking for. A Mr Peter Marklin. Found his car. Down the track . . .'

I relaxed my neck muscles and turned my head to kiss the first thing (the only thing, in fact) that met my lips. The ice-cold earth of Purbeck that had been about to smother me. For the machine-gun delivery was unmistakable. It was that of my common-law father-in-law, Clement, In-the-Nick-of-Time, Trench.

I shouted my head off.

'I'm here. In the pit.' Waving my only free limb, I added, 'I'm under a cow.'

I heard Julia's voice. 'Peter, what do you mean . . . ?'

But her voice was drowned by the sound of the tractor starting up once more, grating its gears and, thank God, reversing away. Then another bout of grating and it was off, presumably back down the slope.

A second later, I saw the considerable silhouette of Clement Trench against the sky. The instant he spotted my frantic waving, he clambered down into the pit and leaned across the carcase that was using me as a pillow.

'Hey, old boy. What on earth–'

'Ted Fern,' I cut in. 'The man on the tractor. Tried to kill me.'

Clement looked behind him, then back at me.

'He's getting away.'

'Don't go after him,' I said instantly, detecting Clement's drift. 'He's got a gun and he's killed twice already.'

By this time I could see Julia's silhouette at the side of the pit.

'You're not . . . hurt or anything, Peter?' she asked hesitantly.

'I'm not peppered with lead shot, no Julia. But I've got
a heavy attack of mad cow disease at the moment. Think it
might have broken my leg.'

'My God, old man,' Clement muttered. 'We'd better go.
Get some help. Get this thing off you.'

'Right. Thanks,' I winced, then forced a smile. 'By the
way, what the devil brought you two up here?'

He reached across and actually took hold of my hand.
This was a Clement I had never witnessed before.

'Thank Julia for that. Her idea. Tell you later, when–'

He was interrupted by the sound of a car horn.

'It's the police,' Julia shouted across to us. 'I can see their
blue light flashing down on the track.'

I rested my head back against the soil. So dear Digby
had taken some note of Julia's Oscar-winning bedroom act,
with its sharp pointers to the occupant of the Fern farm
cottage. A little late maybe, but at least he might now be in
time to apprehend her killer before he . . . Before he what?
Escaped? No, I knew that wasn't Ted Fern's style. To run
away. He'd be far more likely to batten himself down in the
farmhouse and stand prepared for a long siege. (Accurate
forecast. That's just what he did. Lasted all night.)

Meanwhile Clement had let go of my hand and was
scrabbling away at the carcase, trying to raise it a little. But
the rocking motion only sent greater stabs of pain up from
my leg. I gasped.

'Making things worse?' He bit his lip. 'Wish I had a
winch. In my Range Rover. Have you out. In no time.'

This time, I touched his hand.

'Thanks Clement. You and Julia saved my life, you know.'

Even in the darkness, I could sense his embarrassment.

'Arabella. Never have forgiven us. Anything happened to
you.' He cleared his throat and looked up as another car
horn echoed from the direction of the track.

This one was no wind-tone job of a police Rover, but a
tinny beeb I'd heard and winced at only too often. So the
cursed plumber had obviously been and gone and released

242

Gus to go charging around the countryside to catch up with me.

I smiled to myself. I seemed to be attracting quite a crowd, lying under a bloody cow. I wondered whether some cattle might be an answer to the shortage of visitors to my shop.

I didn't see much of the rest of the drama. Though I could not help hearing some of it. Police sirens piercing the night as the marksmen arrived with their night-sight rifles. The echo of the loud-hailer ultimata to Fern to come out of his farmhouse and surrender. But hats off to Digby. He did get a police Range Rover to me fairly smartish. And an ambulance, whose crew fussed around me as burly bobbies attached chains from their vehicle's winch around the recumbent carcase.

The next ten minutes or so I prefer to forget. I still grit my teeth whenever the memory comes back. The removal of the animal seemed to take for ever whilst the police and ambulancemen argued about how best to draw it off me without causing further injury. In the end, they settled for a gentle application of the winch combined with sheer muscle power from all the boys in both shades of blue in order to raise the dead weight a smidgen as it was dragged clear. Even with all their care, the pain became excruciating. And what was worse, once I was free to move my torso a little, I discovered I couldn't, not without making my ribcage feel as though it was being savaged by a Rottweiler.

Suffice it to say, though, that they did eventually get me on a stretcher and into the ambulance. I was whisked off to hospital, the siren no doubt putting the fear of God into every Dorset motorist. And guess who I had at my side, looking much more like death than yours truly felt. He kept repeating over and over, 'Bloody hell . . . I'm sorry, old mate . . . so effing sorry.'

So I kept repeating. 'There's nothing to be sorry about, Gus. I got myself into this whole thing, not you.'

He wasn't having any. 'But Ted was my friend. I really wanted you to help him, see.'

I tentatively extended a hand out from the stretcher. 'Gus. Shut up. You weren't to know what Fern had become. Or that he had killed his son in mistake for Sandle.'

Gus sniffed, then plugged his ears with his great fingers as the siren wailed once more.

When it had desisted, he muttered, 'That Madge Quaintance must have guessed something right from the start, I reckon. She should have ruddy told us right away, instead of leaving things till tonight.'

If I'd been able to move, I'd have sat bolt upright at this point.

'Gus, what on earth are you talking about? Her "leaving things until tonight"?'

He blinked. 'Got something to tell you, haven't I.'

'Have you?' I sighed.

'Yeah. Didn't come round to the farm alone tonight, see. Had that housekeeper of his with me.'

'What . . . ?' I began, so he told me. The plumber had gone and he had just finished swabbing up when Madge Quaintance had suddenly appeared on his still damp doorstep, saying she was looking for yours truly.

Apparently, she had been at her sister's over in Dorchester, as Fern had told me. But the idea and timing of that visit had been entirely Fern's. Seems he had more or less forced her into going right then, and the housekeeper, once she'd got to her sister's place, had become increasingly concerned about Fern's motives for wanting her out of the way. In the end, she had guessed that it must have something to do with Linda Sandle. She confessed to Gus how she had known for ages that Fern had become obsessed with 'that woman and her salvation'. Now she was worried that her employer might have been planning some kind of showdown or other that evening with either Linda, who seemed to her to be about to vamoose, or with her husband. Or maybe even both. Mrs Quaintance told Gus she just couldn't sit around at her sister's any longer while Ted Fern could be getting himself into a situation that might go badly out of control.

So, she had got her sister's husband to drive her over to

my Toy Emporium to get my advice. Finding me out, she had gone on down to Gus's place, having got his address at our local boozer. (Where else?)

My brain and body were feeling so shell-shocked, I had to ask Gus to repeat odd bits of the story, but in the end I got sufficient of the gist to say, 'So you came on up to Fern's place with her, to do a bit of Ercool Parroting of your own, eh? Not to see if your poor old mate was still alive and kicking, then?'

I shouldn't have said it. Gus's face, already ashen, took on a mortified-by-guilt aspect that outdid anything seen at the Old Bailey.

'No, honest, old love. I was worried sick about you. Should never have let you—'

I encored an extended arm. 'Only joking,' I cut in, then winced as my ribs protested at even this slight movement. 'Trying to keep my mind off . . .'

I stopped suddenly, relaxed back and closed my eyes. But, instead of the darkness eliminating any visions, it magnified them. I saw the stiff, scarlet-tipped image of Linda Sandle's arm, as it reached up to claw at the sky. I twitched my head over to one side and couldn't stop myself crying out. But the siren had started up again and Gus, thank the Lord, did not seem to have heard.

I swallowed hard and tried like mad to think of Arabella. Before I could conjure up her vision and make it picture-perfect, I felt the ambulance gently braking to a stop. A moment later and I was offloaded into the squeaky-clean corridors of Bournemouth General.

15

'Must say. Wife and I. Never forget. This holiday.'

I need hardly tell you who was rat-tatting that little thought. We were in the beamed cosiness of the Jug and Hare. (Yes, we did, at last, get to it. Digby and his wife must have stayed home that night.) And we'd just repaired from the dining area to have our coffee in the little room that looked out on to the garden.

It was four days exactly after my near-burial. Clement and Julia's last night, before they ranged and roved back to their Shropshire. And it was Arabella and I who were throwing the dinner, so to speak. The very least we could do to express our gratitude for her parents' US cavalry rescue of their so common-law son-in-law.

'I don't think I'll forget your holiday, either,' I laughed, then instantly winced. I saw Arabella's hand go to my plastered leg.

'You all right?' she asked anxiously.

I couldn't help laughing again. Though in the last four days I had tried to avoid anything that would tickle my broken ribs, strapped up as I was from waist to armpit like a half-finished Tutankhamun.

'Sure,' I reassured. 'Only hurts when I–'

Shouldn't have said that. Set Arabella off, then Julia. Even old Clement smiled. Hell, again I failed miserably to keep a straight face-cum-torso. If this went on much longer, I could see myself having to join the Masochists' Society.

At that point, thank God, the waitress arrived with our drinks, so we all sobered up. Well, not literally, but you know what I mean. When she'd given her little bow and gone, I held up my brandy glass.

'To Julia and Clement,' I toasted. 'Without whom I wouldn't be sitting here plastered tonight.'

Clement waved his hand. 'All Julia. Don't thank me.'

I had better explain. That dreaded day, my common-law in-laws had decided to have a cream tea in Corfe, and then, for a change from Dendron Park, to have their dinner in Swanage. Having toured around the latter, however, they had not found anywhere that took their fancy, their original choice having turned out to be closed during the winter months. So they decided to return to Dendron Park after all. On their way back, Julia had suggested she'd rather like to take a look at Fern's farm and Linda Sandle's cottage, as they seemed to be not far off their route. Once there, they had noticed the hole I had made in the hedge and had seen in their headlamps the yellow of my Beetle in the field.

As Clement explained to me in hospital, 'Got your bug now. Julia. Don't you know. Fancies herself. Some kind of. Miss Marple. Wardrobe did it. Bet my bottom dollar.'

He was on a dead cert, I would think. Julia had talked about almost nothing else over the last days except the Fern affair. I guessed that even when she was back on their estate on the Shropshire Mynd, she'd still be what you might call a closet detective.

Julia raised her own glass. 'And to you, Peter and Arabella. It's dreadful to say it, I know, but I can't ever remember having had such a stimulating vacation.' Then she looked directly at me. 'But much more than that, it's given Clement and myself a chance to really get to know you, Peter.'

'Drink to that,' Clement nodded and proffered his glass to clink on mine.

'Never mind,' I said, to cut the schmaltz, 'I'm still staying with your daughter.'

Then I did feel Arabella's hand. Now somewhat above the plaster cast. I glanced at her. Still her fingers continued their walkabout under the small table.

I cleared my throat and tried to divert my mind from . . . you know what . . . by saying, 'Wonder when they'll catch up with Sandle.'

'Not until. Runs out of money. Wouldn't wonder,' Clement opined. And I guessed he was right.

From what Digby had told us, he reckoned that Sandle may have actually come over to the farm some time that night. To pick up his wife. Hearing or seeing all the brouhaha around the place – cars, tractors, flashing lights and all – he turned on his heel and raced back to his mobile home and his son. Then they both just vanished. His Fiesta was discovered the next day. In Wiltshire. In the car park at Swindon station. But of the man himself and his son, there was still no trace, although Sandle's picture had been broadcast on local and network TV.

Trouble was, the obvious scale of Sandle's loot money was quite enough to buy him and his son a safe haven, false passports and a passage to just about anywhere in the world. Though I somehow doubted he'd be rolling down to Rio by the sea-o, as per Jacob Fern's apparent plan for the lucre-loving Linda and himself.

'What do you think will happen to Ted Fern now?' Julia asked with a heavy sigh.

'If his lawyer's got any sense,' Arabella replied, at last removing her errant hand, 'he'll recommend a plea of insanity. Madge Quaintance, that housekeeper of his, called on Peter at the shop this morning. Ostensibly to see how he was. But really to apologise for having risked his life by not voicing her suspicions long before.'

Julia frowned. 'What do you mean, exactly?'

I answered for Arabella. 'Well, she confessed to me that she had known Ted Fern had gone out that night, late. And hadn't been indoors all the time as he'd claimed to everyone, including the police.'

'Why on earth didn't she speak up then?' Julia instantly reacted, before immediately trying to answer her own question. 'She must have been in love with him, I suppose, all those years. But even so, when it's a question of murder–'

'It wasn't a question of murder, in her mind,' I cut in. 'She made a big point of that this morning. You see, she was absolutely certain that Fern would never have killed his own son, whatever the circumstances or state of their relationship. So she didn't think her keeping silent about his being out that night was the key to the finding of the murderer.'

'So where did she think he had gone?' Julia queried, putting down her glass.

'She didn't really know. She even wondered if he had just gone into the cattleyard, to take a look at the cows. Seems he had known for some time that his herd was infected with BSE but was unwilling to admit it, even to her, let alone to the authorities. He'd claimed God would never have chosen to send down such a plague on him and his herd, and all that stuff . . .'

'Hell,' I heard Clement murmur.

I nodded and went on. 'She told me Fern's religious mania really developed after the death of his wife, Jacob's mother. Of cancer. She'd been almost a carbon copy of Linda Sandle, it would seem. A good-time girl, whom Fern tried, pretty unsuccessfully, to convert to the straight and narrow. When she died young, he regarded it as God's punishment for her infidelities and so on . . .'

'Seems none of the farmworkers were safe from her,' Arabella high-eyebrowed to her mother. Julia coloured and found refuge in her glass.

'That plea. Insanity. Should stick,' Clement fired off.

'Maybe,' I sighed. 'His planting of that old Morris jack in the car dump next to Sandle's place, though, may sound too deliberate to be bona fide crazy . . .'

I suddenly stopped and pointed an accusing finger at my common-law mother-in-law.

'Julia, it's all your fault. Here we are celebrating on your and Clement's last night with us in Dorset and what do we talk about? Death and madness, murder and mayhem and things that go bump in the night.'

'Must be crazy too,' Clement commented drily. Then quickly added, as he saw Julia's instant look of disapproval. 'Mean all of us. Not just you, my dear. Understand.'

Julia laughed and reached out for her husband's hand. 'There's just one last thing,' she persisted. 'And then I promise I'll get off the ghastly subject for good,' She looked across at me. 'Bessy Meade asks particularly for us to give you her love, Peter. And her thanks, too. She says to tell you she and Louise Robbins have had a long, long chat and that the fake Porsche thing is back from that mechanic in the garage and is now up for sale. Apparently it was Louise's money that bought and converted it in the first place.'

'Digby must have really scared Firestone off, I guess, as per our closet calculations,' I commented. 'Little does our dear Inspector realise what a manipulated man he was that day.'

Clement coughed. 'Should have heard him. After the ambulance. Taken you off. Claimed. Always suspected Fern. Course he hadn't. But there.'

I grinned across at Arabella. 'Should have heard him when he came to the hospital to see me next morning. Blew his top about my meddling in a case he said he'd more or less already got sewn up. And that I'd better watch it in future. There were no guarantees he'd be around to save me again from the inevitable consequences of my own fatuous actions, tra-la-la-la.'

Arabella's hand again went walkabout. 'But he's right about you watching it in future, my darling. This time it came just too damned close to having a second grave bearing the Marklin name in that churchyard.'

I picked up my glass and raised it.

'To dear old Aunty. She and her Christian cemetery held the real clue to this whole sad affair all the time. We just didn't see it, that's all.'

'To dear old Aunty,' Arabella echoed and clinked. 'May she rest in peace now.' Then she added with a grimace, 'But without any relatives to keep her company there for yonks and yonks and treble yonks . . .'

Now it's spring again and the sun is cracking the Purbeck hedges. I can at last look back at the Fern case with a degree of objectivity. Now, of course, I see only too clearly all the clues we missed, and all the blind alleys up which Gus and I therefore blundered. But it's not a question of pride. My regret is not that we were crass enough to have made all these omissions and mistakes per se, but that if we'd had our wits more about us, we should, for instance, have made a connection right at the start between Fern

250

having the name of my Toy Emporium in his diary and Linda Sandle's selling of the pedal car. It's only too obvious in hindsight that she must have asked him if he could find out who, in the area, might be interested in paying the best price for it. And bingo. His enquiries obviously turned up my name and shop.

Having made a link between the murdered man and Sandle's wife that early, Gus, I or Arabella, or any one of us, might just have sussed out the rest in time to save the latter's life. That's the real regret. And it's a jumbo-sized one, which will bug me, I'm sure, until the grim reaper does finally arrive for me sickle in hand, and points a gnarled old finger towards St Mary's churchyard and that deadsit of my aunty's, where the whole grim saga started.

As to the rest? I'm glad to say that the Dendron Park Hotel seems to be thriving anew under a born-again (no religious connotation) Louise Robbins. Bessy Meade reports that the owner is at this very moment employing a professional interior designer to come up with plans to reshape and give new style to the whole place. Bessy has actually met him. He's recently widowed, apparently, and she – Bessy that is – has high hopes that something a little more than a good professional relationship may develop between him and Louise Robbins. We shall see.

We'll also have to wait to find out whether a reported sighting of Sandle and his son in Portugal's Algarve will come to anything. The previous report of their being seen in Amsterdam proved a bum steer, so . . .

Physically I'm fit as a fiddle now. But Arabella still claims that I twitch the steering wheel every time I pass a field full of cows. And talking of driving, my Beetle now looks better than any fiddle has ever done. After all, what violin has ever sported spanking new yellow paint and a white (yes, white, not black this time. Aren't I flash?) soft top that actually does keep out the rain?

As for the other car that more or less started it all . . . Well, after everything, I just couldn't bring myself to pedal it to anyone. So I donated it to the children's ward of the hospital that mended me. At least there it will provide the innocent fun and excitement that those disabled Welsh miners who made it all those years ago really intended.